NO ESCAPE

"I could have killed you at any moment since you entered this room. The gun in your cape is irrelevant—so are your combat skills. Don't speak of what I can and cannot do."

The Proctor recovered quickly, and smiled. "I am well aware that you have acquired certain . . . disciplines, Tyrees. But I am not one of your acolytes. My brains are not misted over by a . . . self-induced religious fervor. The finest human physique has certain limitations, and the slightest aggressive motion on your part would result in . . . eeaahhh!"

On the backs of his eyeballs, the Proctor registered the attack—but only after it was over. In one splinter of time Tyrees was still hunched on his elbows in the chair; in the next the heel of one hand was under the Proctor's jaw and jamming his head back painfully. The other hand gripped his throat as if it were a stalk of corn about to be ripped away and thrown into a basket.

"You see? You see what an easy thing it is to die?"

ROBERT O'RIORDAN

CADRE LUCIFER

ACE SCIENCE FICTION BOOKS
NEW YORK

This book is an Ace Science Fiction
original edition, and has never been
previously published.

CADRE LUCIFER

An Ace Science Fiction Book/published by arrangement with
the author

PRINTING HISTORY
Ace Science Fiction edition/May 1987

ISBN: 0-441-09019-2

Ace Science Fiction Books are published by The Berkley Publishing Group,
200 Madison Avenue, New York, New York 10016.
PRINTED IN THE UNITED STATES OF AMERICA

This one is for the PURPLE MOUSE and the FAT CAT. Both cute and consummate pests, they are ultimately irresistible.

CHAPTER ONE

Pol Tyrees was exhausted. He was a dry husk animated only by the desperate blue of his eyes. They were directed at the tilted screen that dominated every Regnum vessel's bridge. The screen was a window on the Void, an alien infinity that always threatened but was never understood.

"Pol . . ." A hand reached out and gently shook him.

The man in the command chair did not respond. Whatever gave him life was strung out through his eyes, through the screen, and beyond. The hand belonged to a diminutive old man with a wispy beard and an expression of infinite compassion on his face. He shook the shoulder again.

"Pol . . . Pol-Nesol-Rast."

Lines of strain formed on Pol's face, and his lips pulled back, stretched taut as if by gravity across white teeth. There was a slight shudder, a tremor like that felt by an orbiting station when a space vessel docks, and the husk came to life. His eyes fell away from the screen and two hands rose to palm his forehead.

"You must rest, Pol."

"Wha . . ."

"You have . . . depleted your energies. To go further is to . . . destroy their source."

"I . . . I can't stop, Meta-sol." His face took on some color as he rubbed it, but the voice was raspy and his hands quivered under pulsing veins. "We're still

1

not safe . . . I'm still not good enough to . . . The pathways . . .''

"Yes, Pol of the hidden stars—the pathways." The old man's voice took on a note of sadness, the sightless eyes wavered. "The pathways you see in the Void may guide us to safety. But who will guide after you are . . . consumed by your own sight?"

"I'm alright, Meta-sol."

"You are not," said the old man with affronted dignity. Like all Tercians, he took the spoken word at face value: one spoke the truth or one lied; one did not dissemble or disguise out of courtesy.

Pol stopped his rubbing and smiled with rueful affection at his mentor. "Well . . . yes, I am getting pretty weak, but you must understand. I can still make out charted pathways, *galactic* pathways that spray out this far. That means Regnum vessels can get to us. They were able to get to Tercet that way."

The mention of his home—a world Meta-sol never expected to see again—tightened the muscles of his face, pulling shot-white eyebrows together. "They cannot . . . move their machines in the Greater Void?"

"Not unless they can follow a charted pathway out. They cannot get reliable readings to run on the intergalactic pathways . . . as I can. That is our advantage, Meta-sol— our only advantage. I'm not good enough at plotting them yet."

Pol thought of the angry message he had left for the Chairman of the Regnum when they were running for their lives: ". . . we can ring and stalk your puny galaxy with the impunity of a hawk at a beached and bellowed whale." Now, dizzy with fatigue and disoriented by a mind that kept dragging its anchor, he had to resist an impulse to laugh at his own temerity. Most of the week since their escape he had spent in the command chair: he'd progressed from an ability to simply *detect* the pathways, to a hit-and-miss stabbing in his attempts to align *Reacher* on them by feeding coordinates to the navigator. It was like playing hopscotch on a spider web. He would look through the screen and see/smell/feel the ghostly patterns forming in the Void, a weave of beautiful lightened filament that slashed meaning into the insidious black. This alone was a satisfying experience; it was an illusion, but it granted him the power all Seers sought: to summon up a portrait of the face behind the dark mask that laughed at all things living— and therefore dying. He could look upon its design, chart its pathways, and believe for a time that choices were there. Then he had to throw a stone into his own glass; he had to translate what he saw/smelt/felt into uncompromising numbers, numbers that the technic could feed into the NAVCOM to position the ship and alter her gravity status so the pathways would accept her incursion—so that the barrier of light speed could be skirted, a law of physics denied by one higher. It was a cruel intrusion of reality, of hard fact upon metaphoric gossamer. Nine times out of ten, when he pushed out the numbers, *Reacher* made a sloughing, whalish turn in normal space instead of the intended, delicate twirl that would send her dancing on the filaments beyond time and space to a place light-years away and deeper into the Void.

"Can you see them, Meta-sol?"

"The pathways?"

Though he had been blind a century since the Purging—a voluntary ritual undertaken at puberty—Meta-sol saw no incongruity in the question. "With *my* eyes I do not. But I see them through yours. Your powers of sight continue to grow, Pol-Nesol-Rast. At the Gathering they . . . made me afraid. My fears also continue to grow." It was at the Gathering of Seers on Tercet that Pol was given his new name: son of Meta-sol, out of the darkness, it said—and that said it all. The guidance of his adopted father had enabled him to explode through the iron-ribbed walls of what he was fashioned to be—the freakishly talented Cadre officer—into what he was destined to be—a free man holding grim reign on blood-raw energies that no one had ever known before.

Around Pol the light flicks and hums of the bridge, and the staring eyes of too-long frightened space-crew technics joined with his body in a quiet, choral scream for sleep. His will, sharp and muscle ruthless from a lifetime of use, voiced the question whose answer he already knew.

"Why are you afraid, Meta-sol?"

The old man removed his hand from Pol's shoulder to join the other atop a gnarled wooden cane, his Seer's badge of office. Eyes that were blind but spark-lit fell from the screen to Pol's face, then to the deck at their feet.

"I am afraid of the depth of your powers, my Pol, and where they will lead. I fear . . . not what you are, but what you might . . . become."

They were speaking in voices so low that if others were to take their parts, they would see lips moving but hear only murmurs, little more than shaped exhalations. Pol nodded slowly. There was a time—a lifetime—when his only reason for breathing was to avoid disappointing another man, Petr Tyrees, his grandfather. It almost cost him an identity of his own. Ironically, it was Meta-sol who saved him, and now he instinctively fought down the impulse to fear his disapproval as well. He loved the old man—but he would never again allow another human being to alter his chosen course. *He* would choose. He would pay the exacted costs or collect the accounts receivable.

"Meta-sol. Would you wish me to deny what I am? Would you have me stagnate as I did before you helped me? A Regnum Security puppet—their prize Cadre One? Would you have me striving to maintain the political system that ordered Tercet—your home and your world—blasted into oblivion?"

These were the harshest words, the most assertive words, he had ever spoken to Meta-sol. He knew that his fatigue was partly responsible, and he was about to reach out to pull them back, but Meta-sol was already responding. His voice was even lower, as if each word carried a burden too heavy for its small puff of sound.

"No, Pol-Nesol-Rast, I would have you do none of those things." He turned slowly and walked falteringly from the bridge like a blind, old man. He was over 130 standard, but he was also a Tercian Seer, and Pol had never before seen him move so hesitantly.

"Meta-sol . . ." His soft call was answered only by the tap of the Tercian's cane as it sought the doorway. As Meta-sol disappeared, Pol realized with some shame how totally immersed he had become with the pathways. His

Tercian friend had never used that cane for finding his
way—not on his home world. It had to be the alien
environment—radically alien to Meta-sol—of *Reacher* and
space, that so disoriented him. And Pol had not noticed.
Perhaps it was stress as well. A man so finely controlled. . . . But there had been no complaints, no. . . .

I do need sleep, thought Pol. He let his head fall to the
back of the command chair and stared once more at the
screen. A megalomanical murderer controled the civilized
galaxy. A man who could order the obliteration of a
populated planet was certainly capable of ordering the
death of the Cadre Proctor, his grandfather, with all the
concern of indolent afterthought. At this moment Regnum's self-appointed deity would be calling upon every
resource he commanded to find and destroy *Reacher*. If I
can improve upon my shaky mastery of the pathways, he
thought, we have a chance of escape, perhaps even of
revenge. Perhaps if I get to the Chairman, the Regnum
will some day record me as a hero. But Meta-sol . . .

His thoughts were interrupted by the explosive arrival
of Hans Bolla. He came wheezing onto the bridge in
uncharacteristic haste, eyes blazing and cheeks puffing in
and out.

"All right, Pol, that's it. You are now off duty." Like a
sack of gelatin, his pear-shaped body continued to undu-
late when he came to a stop.

"Meta-sol sent you?"

"Yes. Now get out of that chair, Tyrees. I am well
acquainted with the tenacity in your blood, but it didn't
stop me when your grandfather carried it around, and it
won't now." Pol rolled his head to the side to stare at
Bolla's florid face, and smiled thinly.

"I believe you. You were the only one I ever knew who
wasn't afraid of him. Why was that, Hans?"

"We will talk history another time. Shall I have you
carried to a bed? Sedated, perhaps?"

Excepting his voice, everything about Bolla was comic.
Hangdog jowls swung from the pendulum of a bulbous
nose when he spoke. The lines of his shoulders made
smooth, lazy parabolas downwards and away from each
other until they reached a level somewhat above his knees,

then they bent hastily to rejoin. The clownish appearance and affable manner masked a layer of steel that stunned people when they ran up against it—as Pol did now.

"Huh! Well, I guess we never did establish who was running the show, did we?"

Bolla rocked back on his heels and locked his fingers—a considerable feat—across his paunch. "You've been giving the orders—ever since I hit Tercet, as a matter of fact," said Bolla with a cherubic smile. "I had no problem with that, my boy. You were the Cadre One—you were trained for command. And your Seers, well, they follow *you.*"

"You said, *had* no problem."

"That is correct. Meta-sol tells me you are near collapse." Bolla's eyes narrowed with seriousness. "I should have stopped you sooner, but I wasn't sure. We are all damned souls if you don't stay in one piece, Pol. You've been driving yourself hard, but maybe for the wrong reasons."

Pol felt anger breaking through his fatigue. He had spent too much of his life jerking to someone else's strings and never seeing the puppeteer; the determination to remain his own man in future bordered on paranoia. "Assuming you had the wherewithal to stop me," he said in a voice unfamiliar to his old guardian, "pray tell me what is wrong with my reasoning."

Bolla's jaw dropped in surprise. "You've just confirmed Meta-sol's fears. You are not yourself, Pol. . . . Yes, I have the wherewithal. Look around you."

In spite of himself, Pol did just that. He had been on many bridges, and physically this one was no different. Technics hunched over their controls; muted buzzes, clicks, hums created the fettered tension that always played its part in the atmosphere.

"I see nothing that might threaten my authority, Hans. On the contrary, *I* sit in the command chair."

Bolla nodded, still wide-eyed with alarm. "The fact that we are having this dispute at all bothers me, Pol; your notion that tested and loyal friends would vie with you for power bothers me; it also bothers me that you're so far gone you don't know that the crew follows my orders, not yours."

In a flood as numbing as an injected drug, an appalling despondency spread through Pol with Bolla's words. He was utterly spent, his systems defiantly shutting down, slipping free of a will that had no interest in denying the truth. He was starving, but revolted by the thought of food; sleep driven, but unable to close his eyes. His mind was drained of all but one screaming thought—FOOL! He could barely find the strength to reach out and clasp Bolla's hand; yet another shock to a man who knew well that Pol was not given to such gestures.

"Hans," he croaked, "I . . . Sorry."

A soft ping from the SCANCOM console charged the bridge. A technic hit two keys before swiveling to the command chair.

"Contact, sir! Intercepting vector." He swiveled back to his screen. "Single vessel. Its speed . . . Must be Regnum Battlefleet."

The SCANCOM technic turned frightened eyes to the command chair. He saw Tyrees galvanize, pushing himself ramrod straight before collapsing into a boneless heap at the foot of the chair.

CHAPTER TWO

"All right, Captain. It's your show now."

Bolla was glaring at a harried-looking man with prim and pinched features in the sterile white uniform of a Regnum Transport captain. He pursed his lips, a habit that pulled the vertical planes of his face even closer together and made him look like a cartoonist's stickman. He conveyed the impression of one attempting to suppress a toothache.

"Mr. Bolla, I am a *Transport* captain. I've never had anything to do with the military—and our pursuer is from the *Battlefleet!*"

"Captain Mariet, neither you nor I have a choice. Outrun that—that war machine—or destroy it. Fail, and we all join the ridiculously scattered molecules of that black stuff out there." Bolla gestured with his neckless head toward the screen.

"But we do have another choice. We can surrender!" Mariet was visibly agitated. For emphasis, he had thumped an arm of the command chair, then pulled his thin hand back as if it had been jolted with electricity.

Bolla watched him closely. "No, I covered that rather poetically under molecular dispersion. They won't want prisoners, Captain."

"We don't know that for certain."

"Ah, but we do. Didn't Councilman Leeth and I show you the evidence? Conspiracy. A galaxy-wide hoax to

8

whip the public into a mindless fear of boogie-man aliens. Outright murder, including that of a Cadre Proctor. Good God man, you were *with* us when we came to warn Tyrees and the Tercians! That madman considers *Reacher*'s human cargo a greater threat to him than the Trade Wars.''

"*That* I don't understand.''

"You've only to understand the Chairman. *He* understands the Trade War barons—power grabbers on a smaller scale, but like him. Concepts like the Pax Regnum are meaningful only if they can be used.'' Bolla had assumed his calm, compelling lecturer's voice like a comfortable coat, but small beads of perspiration had formed on his pate, and his eyes never left the captain. "But Tyrees and his Seers truly frighten him. He knows they can do things other men cannot; he knows Pol has more reason to hate him than any man alive, and Pol is even more threatening than the Seers because *nobody* knows what he can do—not even himself.''

Bolla paused as if in thought, running a hand absently under his baggy blouse. "Did you know that the Chairman and the Cadre Proctor—Pol's grandfather—watched him, manipulated him like a queen bee in a glass beehive? From the time he was a child. He didn't know until Tercet, but he was a living experiment. They programmed him, fashioned him out of putty for service in the Cadre because even early on he surprised them with what he could do. I knew Petr Tyrees well, Captain, and I can guess what happened. He loved his grandson, but he loved the Cadre more—his 'duty' I suppose, as the man responsible for the security of a galactic empire.'' Bolla sighed. "But under Meta-sol's training on Tercet, Pol's little talents grew into something neither of the watchers could understand. All of a sudden their pet Cadre One, their prize robot, was outstripping his program; furthermore, he *knew* about his programmers and was cutting the strings. Petr died before he could finish his objections to the Chairman's plan to atomize Tercet.''

The SCANCOM's soft ping interrupted Bolla's lecture. Its technic turned, somewhat startled by the empty command chair and the physical incongruity of the two leaning intently toward each other over it. He spoke to the chair.

"Uh, revised intercept time . . . sir. I think they've increased their gravity well to maximum now that they're off the galactic pathway. Intercept time . . . twelve point two hours." When neither man responded, the technic swiveled back to this console.

This time Mariet slapped both hands on the chair arm before jerking them away. "How could you possibly know all this, Mr. Bolla?"

Bolla sighed again. One hand still rubbed the oblong of his belly under his blouse. "As a Special Commissioner I had access—no, I *controlled*—a machine intelligence octopus called Anavex." He smiled. "I never did finish developing it as a probability predictor, but that beast could tie into any security program ever devised—and that included the Chairman's own system. He had all of his conversations automatically recorded. I had the privilege—after the fact—of hearing the order that murdered Petr Tyrees. The tapes that convinced you to join us came from the same source . . . but I stray from the point. Just know this: the Chairman wants us dead, and he won't be misled by moral principles." Bolla's tutorial voice was still calm and confident, but tiny purple veins had begun to surface under his eyes and along his nose. He said with the hesitance of innocence, "I suppose you could . . . just conceivably, win a gamble on the Chairman's gratitude by turning us over to him."

Mariet's mouth dropped open. In such a needle face, it formed a narrow set of parentheses bracketing only two teeth. Nevertheless, he managed to convey a sense of affronted dignity. "Mr. Bolla, I joined you because I was shocked that the First Citizen could be such a . . . such a criminal, a travesty of everything the Regnum was meant to preserve. And even if I feel no particular loyalty to you or your 'Seers,' I remain committed to Councilman Leeth. As Minister of Transport and Communications he was my superior. I followed his orders and still do. Your suggestion that I would betray him is repulsive to me, sir—him *or* his friends." In spite of the sincerity that dripped from his words, Mariet looked downwards with his last phrase, blinking fearfully at the seat of the command chair.

"Fine. I accept that, Captain. But where does it leave us?"

"Well, Councilman Leeth is not here."

"And?"

"He saved Tercet, did he not? By locking our information into the communications net and threatening to release it? That maneuver also bought our escape, did it not? Leeth left us to muster political support to oust the Chairman. Who knows what he has been able to accomplish. That Battlefleet vessel may even be friendly!"

"A friendly war machine," snorted Bolla in disgust. "Forget it, Captain."

"But you must accept the possibility!"

"No."

"This is not a fighting vessel, Mr. Bolla! We're a—a toy compared to that thing!" Mariet pointed a rigid finger at the tiny, pulsing nub of light on the screen. "We have one laser cannon, *one laser cannon* designed for defense against tin-can mavericks who don't have a planet to call home! And me! You want me—a milk-run civil servant captain—to cross swords with a juggernaut. I'm no Tyrees, no hero, no Quixote . . . no fool!"

Mariet had the physique and demeanor of one who postured almost out of habit, for effect. Bolla had, quite deliberately, been scraping away at the hand-rubbed veneer the stickman had spent a lifetime polishing. As the sacs under his chin went moist and itchy, he wondered with the part of himself that was always detached, what he would find underneath.

"Leeth is dead."

"What? What!"

"He and the whole crew of the other ship."

"No . . ."

"Yes. Our little ploy, our bluff about the communications lock, was called. The Chairman probably pulled in the experts, and their verdict was accurate: little opportunity, less time. I was to receive daily graviton signals. I got two. Two. That means that in something less than three days from the run from Tercet, Leeth's ship was blown to hell."

"But . . . why didn't you tell me!"

"It would have served no purpose."

"You mean you weren't sure of me without Leeth!"

Bolla shrugged. Under the blouse his hand closed on the butt of a small and powerful gun. "Nor am I sure of you now—even though it's as I said: you really have no choice."

Now the captain was truly angry. He closed his fingers into a bony fist and shook it at Bolla. Oddly, he nodded his head up and down at the same time.

"So! Yes, indeed. Yes. And now instead of being a very minor cog in the machinery of a corrupt Chairman, I am supposed to be a . . . a what? An easily manipulated flunky for an old, academic theorist turned rebel? You and Leeth made it sound like you had a . . . *cause*, and a chance to make things *right*."

"We did."

"Ha! You are a tub of mediocrity—like me. Maybe Leeth—"

"We are running out of time, Captain. Will you help us or not?"

Mariet tried to purse his lips, but they kept collapsing back on him. The hidden gun butt was oiled with Bolla's sweat.

"Tyrees . . ."

"Can't help us. Sedated. Damn near dead, according to Meta-sol."

Mariet's nod became a shake of the head. The change in plane marked a change in his emotions. He looked like a hungry man sorting through rotten fruit.

"But . . . this has become absurd! Just like Tyrees. He . . . he took the command chair as if it belonged to him, and had the rest of you panting around here like . . . like grade three space crew! We go pell-mell into intergalactic space, just begging for oblivion, and I'm supposed to bother my vacant mind only with *Reacher*'s functional status. Now this, this demigod, this defrocked Cadre One, folds under the first crisis, and you hand me back the chair so I can fry in it!"

In spite of the gravity of the situation, Mariet felt rather proud of his speech. He turned his back to Bolla, hands on hips, and threw his head back—the gesture a demand for

justice from above. Bolla's complexion purpled. He pulled
the gun from his waistband, but kept it under his blouse.

"You know nothing of Tyrees, Captain. If you did, I
wouldn't have to listen to this. Nothing I could tell you
would make you understand. So, for the last time," he
said in a quiet murmur, "will you help us or not?"

Mariet's back stiffened as if his spine had felt the presence of the gun. He was still facing away from Bolla, so
the rotund, amiable professor, sweat now darkening his
clothing in large patches, was able to remove his weapon
and arm it. The captain's neck swiveled slowly. The bridge
crew was never to turn from their consoles except to
address their commanding officer. Some of their backs
were as stiff as Mariet's, whose gaze stopped short of
Bolla in its arc and fell to the command chair. Abruptly he
took one long stride and dropped into it.

"SCANCOM!"

"Yes, sir?"

"Intercept time?"

"Twelve point . . . one five hours, sir."

"Range time?"

"Uh, sorry sir, I—"

"Firing range, man! You are part of a *fighting* vessel
now, SCANCOM—best remember that." A strange smile
gashed the sparse rectangle of Mariet's face. "Battlefleet's
missiles can be effective up to a parsec."

"Right, sir . . . uh, eleven point nine, sir."

Bolla stood there blinking, a comic Buddha mystified by
the vagaries of the creatures he was meant to teach, as
Mariet blissfully took control of *Reacher*. Bolla did not ask
the captain his plans; instead, with lugubrious unsteadi-
ness, he plodded from the bridge.

He stood a long time in the corridor in front of the
elevator doors, unable or unwilling to palm the touch pad.
He stared incredulously at the weapon, still sweat-sticky in
his hand. What am I doing here? he asked himself. Could I
have really used this thing? What are *any* of us doing here?
Martyrdom is egotistical madness, especially when it's a
sacrifice in a vacuum—literally, in this case—where no
one can learn from it, if only to share in its dubious glory.
Tyrees . . . he has the stuff of sainthood, perhaps, but I

don't seem to. He also has the stuff tragedies are made of
—he's bigger than the rest of us, and sadder, somehow.
Me, I'm made for what I was before I got caught up in this
mess. A man who can approach ecstasy in the eating of a
splendid meal; a man who will admit no equal in his
knowledge of the collective behavior of his kind—but the
individual human being is a mystery to me. I don't understand him, and I don't think I want to. So what am I doing
here? he asked himself again as he leaned against a wall
and mopped his haggard face with the end of a loose
sleeve. I made the noble decision to resist the madness of a
self-styled demigod after having spent a scholarly lifetime
denying the possibility that *any* single man in a galactic
society could have a significant effect on its destiny. And I
still believe it! I'm more deluded than the Chairman. . . .

But then there's Tyrees—*he's* only one man . . . or is
he? Bolla smiled wryly at the memory of Anavex refusing
to accept Tyrees as a human variable. Anavex was his
brainchild—a probability program that quickly rendered its
own hardware at the university inadequate. So with the
help of his old friend, Petr Tyrees—Pol's grandfather and
the Regnum's Cadre Proctor—he gained access to the big
stuff: the computer facilities and the data of the Regnum's
security institution. He was made a commissioner. Anavex
brought to the surface what politicians were instinctively
aware of for years: the thousand-year-old galactic empire—
the Regnum—was falling apart; the Pax Regnum was moribund. The Hub, its star-packed core, was breeding rebels
of the ancient ilk who were hacking out baronies measured
in light-years. Their weapons and their tactics were those
of economics, but their victories were just as ghastly in
terms of blood-suffering as the sword-wielding hordes of
old. Anavex predicted it all, long before the Trade Wars or
its boardroom generals were accepted as reality. When it
became apparent that his "probabilities" had been accurate, Bolla was suddenly the Chairman's oracle—and the
Chairman was suddenly a prophet, so he took on to himself the appropriate prerogatives.

In the middle of it all, when the Cadre Proctor told
Bolla what had been happening on Tercet, Bolla tried to
input Pol Tyrees as a variable factor into Anavex. The

entire program crashed. He would always remember
Anavex's last words, flashing like a dying galaxy on the
black screen as it whirred and purred its protests before
falling into limbo: ERRORERRORERROR TYREES UN-
ACCEPTABLE HUMAN VARIABLE.

Pol Tyrees, and his Seers, could not be assimilated into
the massive psychosocio probability program because it
refused to accept them as humans. They simply did not
function within its defined parameters. Which was precisely why the Chairman feared them, thought Bolla. Why
do *I* not?

He sighed and pushed himself away from the wall. He
was bone tired, and the longer he stayed awake, the more
he was inclined to unleash his doubts. But some things
remained undoubted: that the Chairman had the potential
of becoming a slouching monster, a long chapter of horror
smearing the pages of human history; that Tyrees could be
. . . could be what?

Bolla worked his shoulders and arms like a tamed and
overfed gorilla, trying to ease tension-locked muscles. Behind his eyes he saw an image that had been painted there
almost forty years ago: Pol and his grandfather. The boy
staring up at the tall man in the dramatic black uniform as
a worshiper would gaze at a carved image of his deity, full
of awe and longing and pride and a painful desire to
please—or perhaps not to displease. Pol was then the
buzzing skinful of ganglia that all boys are made of—but
much, much more, and only Petr Tyrees had a dim suspi-
cion that this was so. He put his grandson on a training
regimen, designed for service in the Cadre, which would
have warped an ordinary child permanently. . . .

Bolla snorted at the folly of his own musings. Ordinary?
Warped? There was nothing to measure Pol with. He
stabbed furiously at the plate until the elevator doors slid
open. During the smooth lift upwards, while staring at the
blinking indicator lights, his very scientific mind was suddenly shot with a very unscientific revelation that surprised
and strangely pleased him. Whatever he was, Tyrees was
the cleaving edge that sliced a clean, new direction: unknown, dangerous, perhaps even catastrophic—but it was
new. If his brainchild Anavex proved anything, it was that

mankind was ignominiously yoked to a cyclic path that led him on to higher and higher planes of despair. The modes of his movement became more sophisticated—donkey to starship—but the impulse was the same. Predictable. Or Anavex would have been useless. Predictable *and* self-destructive. But obviously Tyrees was a break in that cycle. The violent systemic resistance to his very existence was itself evidence of that. So, right or wrong, it would be exciting to be a part of whatever happened. In an explosion of awareness that verged on pain, Bolla realized that his years of oracular prediction, the drugged swinging over the abyss from which arose the stinking gasses of man's rhythmic failures, had made him into a dour and dismal cynic. He had become a pampered and petted oracle of doom.

As the doors slid open, he also realized that his belated epiphany would sour into yet one more cosmic irony in a few hours if *Reacher* found herself staring into the blaze of a laser cannon. With renewed vigor he trundled quickly down the corridor.

After turning the corner into the sick bay, he came upon a scene that stopped him dead in his tracks. It was like stepping unawares into another dimension, another universe where white magic struggled with black, where wizardry vied for something even more valuable than life. In the clinical surroundings of *Reacher*'s medical facility, sterile and uncompromising, three shawled and bearded Tercian Seers knelt in a semicircle around the head of a surgical bed. On it was stretched the body of Pol Tyrees. A sheet left him naked from the waist up. The musculature was so perfect, the skin so translucently pale, that his form seemed the master work of a devout sculptor who had finally found the illusive marble that would answer to the shape, rendered by his worshiping hands, of the dying god that shone in his mind.

Head bowed, arms outstretched, Meta-sol's two hands lay atop one another on Pol's forehead. The other two Seers, in similar poses, each had hands resting on one of Meta-sol's shoulders. That alone was enough to widen Bolla's eyes and drop his jaw; but it was the light that flung a soft witches' spell at his heart. Around the still figures, the air was burning—a red glow that pulsed with the rhythm of a man's breathing, becoming fainter, a ghost's breath, an arm's length away. Heat touched him lightly, withdrew, touched him again. Bolla didn't know what he was about to say, but he started to speak before something clamped on his lungs so forcefully that not even a gasp escaped. For the first time in his life he wanted to kneel and pray.

He stood there for a long time, like a small boy spell-bound by the craft of a master illusionist, but only the pulsing light hinted at the possibility of life in the scene. Finally, without conscious will—though he was having difficulty breathing—he backed slowly out of the sick bay and into the corridor. He stumbled down it a few feet before his knees started to wobble, then he leaned against a wall, slid down it and landed with a soft plop on the deck. His ankle hurt because it hadn't straightened out in time.

Okay, okay, he said to himself. So you think you've seen a bloody miracle. He steadied his breathing and said aloud, "Ridiculous." Deciding he was overtired because his body was malfunctioning, he refused even to think about it. He would rest for a while. He would close his eyes and rest for a while, that's all. Soon he would recover and take care of things. Getting old, you know.

It seemed that he had just finished that thought when a familiar voice broke through. How irritating.

"Dr. Bolla . . . Hans. Are you all right?"

Pol Tyrees was bending over him, looking as composed and indestructible as ever. But how . . . ?

"Are you all *right*?"

"Yes! Yes, of course, I'm . . . I was just waiting." Pushing off Pol's arm, Bolla struggled to his feet. "You . . . *you're* not all right, though. What are you doing out of bed?"

Pol stood back, giving Bolla enough room to rouse himself as he shambled and ducked and pawed like an irritated bear after hibernation.

"I'm okay now, Doctor. Meta-sol and a couple of Seers . . . uh, helped me."

"You were sedated! You keeled over on the bridge!"

Pol smiled in the way those who knew him—as well as he could be known—recognized as a closed door.

"Just fatigue. I'm fine now. Let the Tercians rest awhile, will you? I'd better get back to the bridge." Without inviting a response, he left a thoroughly confused professor of psychological sociology scratching his head like an overgrown baboon.

Bolla at first started after the figure gliding swiftly down the corridor, but the memory of the pulsing light stopped him. He turned and trotted like a drunkard back to the sick bay.

The three Seers all lay on surgical beds. Obviously they had been lifted and placed there, because their positions were as uniform and formal as bodies arranged by a mortician. Bolla assumed, quite calmly, that they were indeed dead. An insane image jumped on to a backdrop of his mind: Pol Tyrees, with tubular tentacles suction-sealed to the bodies of the Seers and a smile of rapacious satiation on his face, siphoning off their life juices. He shook his head angrily and almost stumbled to Meta-sol's bed. That white, wispy, translucent beard fell from chin to chest, but there was no stir even in those delicate strands. Bolla rolled his eyes upwards, and the part of him that remained a distant watcher wondered why heaven—even in extragalactic darkness where gravity was a moot question—should be in any particular direction, let alone one opposite the feet. Then the faintest whisper came.

"Doctor . . . Bolla . . ."

He looked down, but at first there was nothing to see. He stooped lower over Meta-sol, until his cheek almost touched the lips. There was a light feather of coolness brushing his sweat-damp skin.

"Meta-sol . . ." He had to wait a while before the whisper came again.

"We . . . are . . . well. We . . . rest."

"But . . . what's wrong with you? Are you dying?" A stronger puff of breath hit his cheek. It might have been a snort.

"We are *all* . . . dying. Go. Help Pol-Nesol-Rast."

CHAPTER THREE

When Bolla had finally struggled his way back to the bridge, his breath was coming in short gasps. To his surprise, Pol was in the command chair, with Mariet attentively by his side. On the screen was the blip of light, considerably brighter now, that was the Regnum Battlefleet vessel. Both *Reacher* and her pursuer were on CFM—conventional flight mode—since they were not on pathways, but the latter had a higher cruise maximum and was gaining at an alarming rate. The fact that the chase was taking place farther into intergalactic space than any ship had ever deliberately gone before, was testimony of the Chairman's determination to destroy them. The value of a Battlefleet vessel and crew was incalculable.

Bolla waited until his breathing steadied. "Uh, excuse me, gentlemen."

Mariet's head jerked from the screen like that of a swivel-necked child's toy. He hadn't noticed Bolla's arrival, and was strung with tension. Tyrees didn't take his eyes from the screen, and answered as though he had been waiting for a question.

"Of course, Doctor. You are quite recovered?"

Bolla came to the chair, noticing in Pol a calm vitality he hadn't seen since long before Tercet. "How long have we got now?"

"Less than four hours," said Mariet. His chin went up,

as if proud of the honor of counting out the last minutes of his life.

Pol simply stared at the screen for a time. Then he shot an oddly defiant look at Bolla—and a single statement. "Well, Doctor, we are out of options. With your permission, Captain?"

Mariet nodded with the solemnity of a king to his hangman.

Pol returned his eyes to the screen. "NAVCOM."

"Yessir?"

"Clear the screen."

"Sir."

The large, framed rectangle over their heads went slate black. From either side of the command chair the bone-thin captain and the humpty-dumpty professor stared at each other in shocked amazement, as if to say, "Look at us. Suitable in appearance for the comic stage, perhaps, but not this, not *this*!"

As they watched, Tyrees's body, with the natural ease of a snake slackening its death grip, let slip the tension in his muscles. Blood seemed to withdraw from his skin, leaving it even more pale. Then, softly bursting with light, the screen came alive again. This was the scene they had watched for several days before Tyrees's collapse: a multi-colored but indistinct wash of gently curving lines that changed subtly when whispers from the command chair fed coordinates into NAVCOM's voice-activated computer; six bridge crew, insides gnawing with fear and silent attention; two absurdly dissimilar observers numbed by unfamiliar thoughts. Dominating it all was a body, a whisper, an unblinking pair of terrible blue eyes.

But there was something different this time, something added. Bolla could feel it, and he knew Mariet could, too, though the captain would not want to acknowledge it—a dry, crackling buzz in the air, as if its chemistry had been charged with a new diffusive substance. It tingled the skin, flared the nostrils. The buzz could even be heard—but not by the ears. Bolla was suddenly, and very deeply, frightened. He looked once again at the captain and saw the pinched face struggling to keep its composure.

Without warning, slashes of light—blue/green/yellow/

red—flared through the bridge like sword strokes. There were startled cries as hands flew up to shield eyes already burning from a glare that transformed the bridge into a holofilm set under desert light. Some actually hit the floor. The screen was a furnace door sprung open, pouring forth the deadly brilliance of which stars are made. The eyes of the body in the command chair did not falter, but from its lips came a low moan.

As suddenly as it came, the light died. Swear words of shock and confusion came from the crew. Bolla could see only the afterimages of colored silhouettes plastered on the backs of his eyeballs. After blinking away rushing tears, he could make out Mariet's elongated feet and the pedestal of the command chair; then they began to swoop in a dizzy arc up and away from him. He didn't know he was falling, because his sense of balance was riven and his stomach was pushing its contents ignominiously upwards, forcing the air out of his lungs. He retched painfully. That detached part of himself wondered when he would begin to choke on his own vomit. As his ears began to ring with sounds only the demented were meant to hear, he felt a horrible pang in his groin. In a miasma of pain and nausea, his hands became claws, and they raked with instinctive terror at the source.

Then a miracle happened.

A wash of balm, cool and calming, soothing, soporific, came like a mother's hand. Fluids of the womb lapped over, around, through. Peace that only his unconscious remembered, wrapped him in tender folds. He smiled. He dreamed. He dreamed for an infinity or two before the voice.

"Don't be afraid. I'm sorry. It's over now. I . . . I didn't know . . . the Seers . . . ."

Bolla didn't open his eyes—they were already open—but he could use them now. He could see the top of Mariet's head two feet away; the man was struggling to lift it from between Bolla's still gently throbbing thighs. Two arms descended, went under the captain's knees and shoulders, and lifted him like a child into the command chair. When they returned, Bolla feebly waved them off. The rest of Pol Tyrees came into view as he went down on one knee. Was it an hour or a day ago that he had looked up into those mesmerizing blue eyes from the same position? Had he reached that point in senility where the child became the father of the man?

"What happened, Pol?"

"It's okay, Doctor. I think I've made a breakthrough. I can see the pathways with real clarity now." A strange look, one that might have been on the face of the first hypnotist when his first subject went under, had crept into those bland features. "It was wonderful, like . . . the Seers must have given me. . . . It just took me by surprise, and I lost control. I'm sorry." He helped Bolla to a sitting position. "Rest while I see to the others."

As Pol went about the business of propping up and reassuring a thoroughly dazed and disoriented bridge crew, Bolla pulled himself to a standing position beside the command chair. His legs wobbled, but rather pleasantly. He was an infant standing in his crib, hanging onto its rail.

"You're smiling," said Mariet.

"Huh?"

"You're riding a flaming nova into oblivion, and you're smiling." Bolla gazed idiotically at Mariet, a feather-filled doll sitting loose and gangly, ankles and wrists and neck askew, as if their joints were waiting to be connected.

"Well . . . yes. Exactly, my friend. I'm riding a nova. And so are you. Interesting isn't it?"

Tyrees was back suddenly. He always moves like that, thought Bolla. Like falling water. Fluid, quick, of a piece. Energy under great pressure, released carefully. Graceful explosions. Sculpted power. A nova. Leashed.

"Captain, it's going to be close. I'm sure of my coordinates now, but the nearest usable pathway is at least two hours' run. Do we *have* two hours?"

Mariet hesitated only for a moment. "We can probably beat the ship there, but not her cannon. Give me your readings and I'll get a precise figure."

Mariet took the readings to NAVCOM as Pol resumed his pose in the command chair. Bolla was beginning to feel himself once more, which meant that he was once again driven by his life-long harridan—an irritating, never appeased shrew. He thought of the impulse as many men who have that special kind of woman that could be cursed, but never deserted: to him it was the desire— no, the *need* to know. Curiosity was far too mild a term for it.

Tyrees sat, cocooned in that peculiar calm that always had the reverse effect on those around him, waiting for the captain's information. Bolla slapped a hand on the chair's arm and spun it through the quarter arc that brought Tyrees abruptly in front of him.

"Pol, tell me what's going on."

"Tell you *what*, Doctor?"

Bolla also disliked being treated like a child—or worse, a credulous fool. "Look! You can't expect . . ." He paused to collect himself. "You can't expect blind obedience here. No, hear me out," he said when Tyrees started to respond. "Listen to the old professor of psychology for a change. Okay?

"There are about forty crewmen on *Reacher*. Every one of them, every *one* of them, Pol is being plagued by questions and fears he's never had to deal with before. Your Seers aren't exceptions, and neither am I. So . . ."

Bolla let go of the armrests, put his fists on hips that might have been there twenty years ago, and stared down at Tyrees with the look he reserved for bright but stubborn graduate students. "You will grant at least one of your bemused cargo—who may well have only an hour or two to go on breathing—the privilege of knowing what is going on in that head of yours."

By this time Tyrees was smiling somewhat ruefully. "I take your point, Doctor. I guess I was taking a lot for granted. Old Cadre habits die hard." Bolla watched the smile die as the younger man thought about things that had been cast out to float in his past like messages in a bottle. "But it's not easy to explain . . . even to myself. I think . . . I think Meta-sol and the Seers did a lot more than restore my strength. Now I seem to have . . . a more powerful battery." He snorted at his own metaphor, as if to denigrate it, but Bolla knew that Tyrees's growing powers both frightened and mystified their possessor, though the fear was largely unconscious. He had spent a lifetime being different from others, and still resented that fate.

"And therefore your . . . perception of the pathways is enhanced?"

"That puts it mildly. This time when I reached out through the scanners, it was like . . . like being *pulled* out there! Before, the pathways were just fuzzy filaments of light; now they're clear, strong, colorful, and burning with . . . with energy, I suppose. . . ."

Tyrees's eyes at this moment were burning, too. His facial features were so unremarkable as to be nondescript; even his body, though trim, was deceptively average looking. It had always been the dense blue eyes that were noticed. Now Bolla watched them burn with a kind of passion he could not identify—sainthood? Awe? What?

"I sort of . . . left the door open too wide, and it overwhelmed me, came back on me. That's what hit the rest of you. When I recovered, I dampened everything, and it all fell together. The pathways vary in nature with their colors. Intensity lessens with distance. There was one pathway—an almost straight spear of red—that seemed to go on through the galaxies . . . forever."

"That's not possible," said Bolla, thinking that he was beginning to understand what Meta-sol feared about Pol-Nesol-Rast, his spiritual son, though he had never taken Bolla into his full confidence.

"No," said Tyrees. "It's not, is it?"

Before Bolla had a chance to dig deeper, Mariet came flapping back, face paler than ever.

"Two hours. Two hours and a few seconds. It's as I said: we can beat the ship to the pathway, but not its laser cannon."

"Can we hope for a miss?" asked Bolla.

Mariet only smirked at his ignorance, but Tyrees answered calmly as his gaze returned to the screen. "There is no such thing as a miss, Doctor. Is there any way we can boost power, Captain?"

"This is not a sophisticated vessel, sir. We are now cruising at maximum speed toward the readings you gave me. I've already done all that can be done, and that's damn little. Unless your coordinates are out."

"The coordinates are accurate."

"Well," said Bolla, making a gesture of resignation

...long enough for the screen to go fuzzy, then he

...see Bolla? A trial. A public trial. And the crew
...—''

...en to me,'' said Tyrees in a voice that cut through
...ain's words like a blunt axe. ''Until there's an
...nt otherwise, you will obey my orders. You will
...gain attempt to resume command on impulse.''

...et swallowed a quick rejoinder because he had
...the look in Tyrees's eyes—cold, utterly unequivo-
...ked and deadly blue stones.

...ry well. I—I should not have interrupted. But we
...eassess.'' The skin on the captain's face was stretched
...heap upholstery over his narrow skull. His tongue
...d at dry lips. ''Doctor Bolla was overreacting. We *do*
...hoices here, and . . . and we have no right to fling
...the lives of the crew.''

...of a sudden, and accompanied by such a powerful
...of vertigo that he was embarrassed, Bolla was visited
...e most abject of wishes—not to die. Oh, please my
...r, not to die. He dared not speak.

...Jo, we don't have that right,'' said Tyrees, ''but
...dor thinks she does. Her intention is to destroy us—all
...—''

...But,'' sputtered Mariet, ''you heard the Cadre One.
...''

...heard him. He was lying.''
...What? How could you know?''

...lla had succeeded in pressing down, if not away, the
...whose cold hands had closed around his heart. He
...d upon the distraught captain with more empathy
...and said, ''He knows, Captain, he knows.''

...Don't patronize me by repeating ridiculous statements,
...e. He couldn't possibly—''

...e was the Cadre's best milker, Captain—an interro-
... He reads a body like you read words. Unconscious
...cal movement, voice inflection, and more, I'm sure.''
...glanced at Tyrees, who seemed to be following the
...rsation with only part of his mind. ''I'm also sure
...ore a question of natural talent than training. His
...ather thought so.''

with his stubby arms, ''then all we can do is keep running, and hope they don't fire as soon as they come into range, right?'' He smiled benignly at Mariet. ''And when would that be, Captain?''

''Can't be calculated precisely. Certainly less than an hour, perhaps as little as forty-five minutes.''

The three men fell dumb for a time, watching the blip on the screen that might have been a light cursor indicating the beat of a heart. The crew, young and not so young, trained to maintain silence while on duty on the bridge, simmered in the juices of their own thoughts. Even for those who had spent most of their lives in the artificial womb of a spacecraft, the very palpable sense of threat seemed unreal because the evidence of it was so innocuous. In spite of the glamor of their craft, it typically inspired boredom more than anything else. In fact, after a time the carefully controlled existence lulled, brought about a sense of security that ordinary life with the earth of a planet under their feet did not. Now their womb was awash with something deadly, and the taste of acid was in their mouths. The calm, alien voice from the command chair only made it sharper.

''TELCOM''
''Sir?''
''Prepare to transmit. Battlefleet frequency.''
''Yes, sir. Mode?''
''Visual.''

Mariet frowned. He was still having difficulty listening to a stranger command his crew, no matter how impressive that stranger was. His question was one word: ''Why?''

Tyrees spoke not to him, but to the blip of light above. ''Because it can't hurt . . . and if they respond—on visual—I might learn something that could help.''

Mariet's frown deepened, but a corner of Bolla's mouth pulled up, and he nodded. A tiny bleep came from the TELCOM station.

''Beamed and ready to transmit, sir.''

''Transmit . . . Battlefleet vessel. Battlefleet vessel. This is transport vessel *Reacher*. Do you receive?''

They waited, knowing that their radio burst would take a few seconds to reach their pursuer. Tyrees's eyes penetrated the screen. "Come back on visual," he muttered. Suddenly the screen buzzed with static. Then a picture of two men jumped into sharp focus. Tyrees had to push away the sense that he was watching a single drama for the second time—the same scene but with different actors. The first figure he had expected, resplendent in the white-and-gold uniform of a Regnum Battlefleet commander; the second, he had not. Deep black cape—shimmering black. The waxy face and still hands were all that was revealed of the man beneath.

Cadre One.

I am looking at myself, thought Tyrees. As I was. Did others fear me as I fear him now?

Just before boarding *Reacher* on Tercet, he had torn such a cape from his shoulders, throwing it angrily away from him. There had been a soft *swoosh* before it hit the red dust.

"*Reacher*, this is *Condor*, Regnum Battlefleet," said the figure in white. "I am Commander Flaan. To whom do I speak?"

Tyrees paused long enough for Bolla to entertain a new thought: he *still* doesn't know who he is. The clinical behaviorist, the part of him that was never far from the surface, was instantly on the alert. The man was a miracle, an evolutionary phenomenon, but there was clay in him yet, for he still struggled against the puppeteers in his past. Bolla saw Tyrees's chin lift a fraction.

"I am Pol-Nesol-Rast, Seer. *Reacher* is no longer a Regnum vessel. Why do you pursue us?"

Again and as always, there was another delay in voice transmission, but the visual remained constant. They now saw the motionless portrait of the two men as they were as they waited for *Reacher*'s reply. When it arrived, they watched *Condor*'s commander look to his dark companion. It was no surprise that he was really in charge. There were only a few dozen people in the galaxy from whom Cadre Ones took orders, and a battlefleet commander was not one of them. It was the Cadre One who spoke.

"You are Pol Tyrees. A traitor to the Regnum and the brotherhood of the Cadre. Your assumption of primitive religious trappings is just another obscenity." The delivery

was in a monotone, but there wa ing that articulated the words. Ju thought the message burst was continued.

"I have never heard of a case Cadre One. Personally, it would gi watch you and your nest of shamen sun. However . . ." The man twitch to one side, lips curling with disgus "My assignment Directive is expli voluntarily, you will be placed under Regnum for public trial." The numb toward the screen, now smiling softly or attempt escape—as you are doing wish."

After the pause became long enough of a burst, Mariet treated Bolla to a h nothing. Tyrees seemed unaffected, tho riveted to the screen. His next words we as if he were engaged in a mildly intere after dinner.

"*Public* trial is it? The Chairman generous—and self-destructive, considerin reveal. What of the rest of us?"

"The Tercians are to be detained for quest assume that is he standing beside you—is also rested, though the charge may not be treason crew will be allowed to go free—after being dec of course."

This announcement caused *Reacher*'s steal sidelong glances at one another. Ma col by speaking directly to TELCOM.

"TELCOM. Interrupt transmission."

The technic swung around to look beca not come from the command chair. Tyree have heard, but Bolla, who had come markable man as his personal project, no of his lips before he spoke.

"*Condor*, we require time for a cor . . . TELCOM. Interrupt transmission.

himsel
pounce
"Y
will n
the c
agree
neve
M
cau
cal.

mu
lik
fli
ha
a

Mariet was now totally confused. His voice had a note of pleading in it. "Is this true?" he asked Tyrees. "We have less than thirty minutes if—"

"I can usually tell when a man is lying. It's a question of matching unconscious signs with conscious ones. Lies have to be deliberate—conscious and artificial when compared to a natural state. Some men are more difficult than others."

"Show me."

"We don't have time for games, Captain. I need your cooperation. . . ."

"You can have my cooperation *forever* if what you say is true, because that'll only be a few bloody minutes!" Mariet was now jangling like an elongated doll dangled on the end of a string. Tyrees took a careful look at him and sighed.

"All right. Quickly, then. Make a series of statements about yourself. Mix in some lies."

"Well, uh . . ."

"Get on with it! Short and factual."

"Yes, yes. My . . . my mother's name is Seekh."

"True," said Tyrees without hesitation.

"My father died a year ago."

"True."

"The . . . the color of my son's hair is red."

"False—a lie."

Mariet paled, but plunged on, stuttering out his trite assertions as if they were a list of his virtues on Judgment Day. "G-Gelda was my dog's name."

"True."

"She . . . she died when I was eight."

"False."

"I loathe wine!"

"A lie."

"I love peas!"

"Lie."

"I paid a bribe for my captaincy!"

"That is true."

"I . . . I . . . oh, my God," wailed Mariet, covering his face with his hands.

Bolla put a hand on one thin shoulder. "That's enough, Captain. Get a hold on yourself."

Mariet nodded behind his hands. "I'm . . . I'm okay. I'll follow your orders, Mr. Tyrees. You are a better captain for *Reacher*, anyway."

"I'll need your technical expertise, Captain."

Mariet shrugged the comment away, thinking about the time remaining as he stared at the blackness of the screen. Tyrees looked, too, for a time before speaking. "TELCOM."

"Sir?"

"Reopen transmission. Vocal only."

"Yes, sir . . . ready, sir."

"*Condor. Condor*, this is *Reacher*. We accept your terms. We are reducing speed. Please acknowledge."

Bolla's several chins jiggled with amazement. Mariet could only look on stupidly. In a few seconds *Condor* responded.

"Message acknowledged. We will transmit boarding instructions shortly. *Condor* ends."

"End transmission," ordered Tyrees. "NAVCOM, reduce to docking speed."

"So," said Bolla. "You surprise me once again. You can't be giving up?"

"Desperate, yes. Giving up, no."

"I thought you said they would blast us, surrender or no."

"Well, there's no point in throwing away a few million credits of starship, is there? Since they have the option. They might even want to bring us back for a more tidy disposal after extracting information. I'm sure they'd like to get their hands on Meta-sol and the Seers."

"So? What's the point in prolonging the agony then?"

Tyrees smiled. "We're going to take *Condor*."

CHAPTER FOUR

A light-year beyond the flat plane of the spiral galaxy called the Milky Way, two starships lay as if suspended between the silk and satin curtains of a dream scene. From one perspective the dreamer would see, softly glittering, a pair of fragile sculptures, cream white and vulnerable against the ominous black satin of infinity; from another he would see them as incongruous forefigures in a spectacular display of silken starlight. In either case they seemed abandoned, like delicate toys, too frail for this place of alien immensities.

The two were joined by a short umbilical, the term rendered more appropriate by *Reacher*'s smaller, less imposing size and shape. She was designed for movement only, her innocence a part of that design. Indeed, she was now *Condor*'s foundling.

Most of *Reacher*'s crew was confined in the maintenance wardroom off *Condor*'s cargo bay. Except for Meta-sol, the Tercians were incarcerated in the only facility aboard meant for that purpose, perhaps because they represented the largest unknown factor to the captors. The remaining four—Tyrees, Meta-sol, Bolla, and Mariet—awaited the pleasure of the Cadre One in the officer's wardroom near the bridge. All were subdued. Bolla considered it his function—he was the psychologist—to puncture the bubble of glum depression.

"I'm too old for this, you know."

No one responded. Meta-sol sat, a sallow image of himself, eyes closed. Mariet's head rocked slightly atop his stalky neck, his body draped over a lounge, a hanger of slack gristle under the uniform. Tyrees, looking more alone than any, stared fiercely at the bulkhead.

"Yes, far too old. And out of my element, of course," chuckled Bolla as he reached out to touch Meta-sol on a knee. "Perhaps even more than you, my friend."

The Tercian did not acknowledge the words, did not even open his eyes.

"He's still resting," said Tyrees. "He's not interested in polite conversation just now."

"Perhaps *you* are, then. What do we do now? You had some magic in mind before they scooped us up like pretty little goldfish, didn't you?"

Bolla was startled to see Tyrees's eyes flare with blue anger, though there was none in the voice. "I have no magic to offer."

"A plan, then. You were thinking of *something* surely— otherwise we should have kept running until they blasted us out of the sky . . . sorry, out of the space."

"No, no plan. Just an intention."

"Oh. I see. Lovely."

"I'm not a witch doctor, *Doctor*. Neither are the Seers. As for embracing your own destruction, you've always had that choice. It's up to you to exercise it when you wish."

Blotches rose on Bolla's cheeks. He took a step backward, as if under a sudden blow, asking himself what trigger he had pulled. He recovered quickly, chastising himself, both for feeling hurt and for not knowing well enough the only man he considered worth knowing well. Tyrees had turned his back on him and was speaking to Mariet.

"Captain, are you familiar with this vessel?"

"What?"

"Can you run *Condor*?"

"Well, yes, I suppose I could. After some tinkering, especially with her armaments. But how do you—"

"Good." Tyrees rose abruptly. "We'll try to turn them around first. Captain, you were able to see—"

The wardroom door hummed open and the Cadre One stepped inside. He waved back an armed crewman as it slid closed.

"Sit down, Bolla, Tyrees. The rest of you stay exactly where you are."

They obeyed. Meta-sol's eyes opened—his only reaction. The man in black stood there for a moment, studying each in turn. Like all Cadre, he was clean-cut and hard of line. Like all Ones, he exuded confidence.

"You're not a very impressive lot, are you—for fearsome rebels. But I won't make the mistake of underestimating you. I am not armed. You *might* be able to overpower me with an ex-Cadre's help, but then the door simply wouldn't open. So, let's establish the ground rules for the passage home."

He took three strides forward and slipped into the chair farthest from the group. He was a handsome man in his prime—closely cropped but rich auburn hair flecked with gray at the temples; clear brown eyes that never wavered; strong features dominated by a jaw that was a little too strong, as if it had been copied from the statue of a fictional hero. He was tall—Mariet's height, but twice as massive—and no one had ever seen a suggestion of fat on a Cadre security officer above the rank of Four. His own rank shone dully in the black piping of the stiff collar, though he was not wearing the cape.

Tyrees realized that he had been looking at the uniform rather than the man, and wondered if others had regarded him that way when he was Cadre. He had no regrets about renouncing that life, but still felt a twinge of nostalgia for its very real sense of brotherhood and commitment. Perhaps, he thought, some of that commitment had begun to slip. The thousand-year-old Pax Regnum was now a joke because of the Trade Wars, though the general public had only a vague awareness of it. A Cadre One would probably know about Bolla's work; would certainly know about the political corruption festering among the Regnum's leaders, who were desperately, illegally, gathering more power to themselves, ironically hastening the destruction of the system they believed they were protecting. Perhaps this man was ripe. . . .

"Young man, do you know that you will die soon?"

The curiously soft, yet penetrating voice of Meta-sol threw the single sentence into the silence like a dagger. The Cadre One had been about to resume speaking, but now his mouth was frozen open. Meta-sol was bent forward in his chair, leaning on the gnarled cane and staring intensely with his blind eyes. He waited politely for a response, but none came.

"When one is granted the . . . privilege of knowing, one should prepare."

A look of pure anguish spread like a horrible disease over the Cadre One's face. It lasted but a moment, the wash of a wave; the next was rage. He screamed something and exploded out of his chair. With a wide, furious sweep, he drove the cane from under Meta-sol's hands. Before it smashed into the bulkhead, the same hand was swinging viciously back, this time in a fist, aimed at the dead eyes. There was a crack of bone and a howl of pain—but the howl came from the Cadre One. His wrist had struck the hard ridge on the back of Tyrees's forearm, a few centimeters from the Tercian's face.

Eyes wild and breathing heavily, the man in black fell back, surprised but still riding on rage. In the short pause that followed, he seemed to identify in Tyrees a more worthy target for his killing anger, for he spun away the chair behind him and went into a low crouch, one forearm rigid and on the horizontal just below his eyes, the other a vertical piston below it. It was a standard Cadre combat position designed for attack. Tyrees had only reacted to protect Meta-sol, and was mentally unprepared. He threw up a guard to take a blow to his throat that was only feinted, rendering himself vulnerable to the real one. In a beautiful, fluid motion flowing out of what appeared to be a heel-of-palm strike to the neck with his right hand, the One's whole body spun, pulling his left foot with whiplash force through a wide, three-hundred-degree arc. When the heel impacted on the side of Tyrees's knee, he folded down like wheat under a scythe. Pain shot through his leg and up the highways of his body.

But pain to Pol Tyrees was a chemical trigger. Somewhere in his brain synapses fired—and reality changed.

Outside motion was slowed down, colors jumped a notch in brightness. His senses, suddenly starved, sucked in data voraciously. Quite consciously, he turned off pain centers. He rose to his feet at leisure and watched his opponent wade through cement toward him.

The man had already been forced to readjust his attack, surprised to find Tyrees so quickly on his feet again. Still fueled by white-hot rage, he used his shoulder as the fulcrum for a swinging strike from below. It was targeted for a kidney and came in straight, palm up and mid-knuckles foremost, because single-plane blows were the hardest to defend. But the target disappeared from view. It vanished like an image switched off a screen, and his fist was riding in an upward groove.

It rode so high that his body was following it; it rode so high that his feet had somehow left the floor. Up. For a long time, it seemed, up. Then there was a hand under his chin, and ever so gently, it seemed, it tipped him around until he could see his feet wagging at the ceiling. He only had time to close his eyes before he hit the plasteel floor.

When he opened them again, he was looking through a gauze of pain and nausea, and he was sitting in a chair. Anger was gone. Will was gone. Even purpose was gone.

"Why did you attack Meta-sol?"

"Leave me alone," he murmured.

"Tell me why."

"Ask *him*. He knows."

"Then you *are* dying."

"Yes . . . I was the only one who knew. I'm sorry, I just couldn't . . . I had no right. But how did he—"

"He's a Seer. What's wrong with you?"

"Tumor—in my brain. Found it too late. Inoperable. I have a couple of months, I guess." He put one hand to his forehead as if he could feel it there. "Why should you care?"

"Perhaps I don't, but Meta-sol does." Behind him the Tercian nodded.

"Life is the only sanctity; death the only curse," he said.

Tyrees smiled. "There may be other curses. What is your name?"

"Radis."

The Cadre One was almost fully recovered now. He pulled himself forward and rose gingerly to his feet. He looked at the strange group before him with eyes less confident, but there was no compromise in his words.

"I apologize for my . . . outburst. But nothing has changed. I will—"

"You will treat our deaths as less significant than yours, obviously," said Tyrees.

"What?"

"Your Directive. Destroy us if we resist or run, bring us back to Regnum for a slower death if we surrender. Correct?"

Radis hesitated. Something churned in his stomach. He looked at Meta-sol sitting as he was before, calmly leaning on his cane. "Yes . . . those are my orders."

"A tumor is more appealing."

"Deus misereatur," whispered Bolla.

Radis was discomfited, but refused to be swayed, knowing they were playing upon him. "My duty is to defend the Regnum. You are traitors."

"Is he a traitor?" Tyrees pointed at Meta-sol. "Tercet isn't even a member planet!"

Radis's mouth quivered. "*You* are," he hissed.

"Yes, I am. Correct me if I am wrong: your orders prohibit interrogation." Tyrees paused long enough to know. "Ask yourself why."

Radis said nothing, but he was beginning to look at Tyrees as he would a demon—and he was afraid. He asked himself why he should be afraid of anything now, *anything*. Nevertheless, this man could reach inside you. . . .

"I ask only one thing of you. Let us show you some holofilm recordings."

"My orders expressly forbid the gathering of *any* kind of evidence, including verbal."

"A Cadre One working blind," said Tyrees scornfully. "How are you to know if you are doing your 'duty' for the Regnum, or dirty work for corrupt politicos?" In spite of the bitterness of the words, they were flinted with conviction. Radis had to listen to them.

"I was part of the Brotherhood most of my life. Do you

think I threw it away on a whim? Look at these men. A Regnum commissioner—you must know of his work; a Transport captain with everything to lose; a Tercian who had never seen a starship three years ago. Why are they here?"

His powerful jaw rigid as a hammer claw, Radis shook his head and started to turn away. The voice stopped him.

"Listen to me! Are you afraid of the truth? You shouldn't be afraid of anything now." Hearing his own thoughts echoed disturbed Radis further. He almost covered his ears like a child. "Did you know that Councilman Leeth, the Regnum minister, was blown to hell along with a whole spacecrew?"

"Enough!" blurted Radis. "No, I didn't know . . . assuming you're telling the truth. But I did know he had disappeared." He let out a long sigh. "Show me your evidence."

Tyrees showed no sign of victory or relief. He simply pointed at the wardroom's single console. "Just patch us into *Reacher*."

His decision made, Radis moved without hesitation to the console chair. "I can't do it directly." He hit a key. "TELCOM." A voice issued from a speaker in the chair's wing.

"TELCOM here."

"Security Officer Radis in the wardroom. Is the captain on the bridge?"

"No, sir. He's still seeing to the other prisoners."

"Patch me into *Reacher*'s main computer."

"Yessir. Uh, I'll need the interface code, sir."

Mariet reached over Radis's shoulder and tapped in a five character string.

"Thank you, sir. Half a minute." Radis settled in to wait for a few seconds, then suddenly leaned forward again. "TELCOM. One more thing."

"Yes, sir?"

"When the patch is made, cut yourself *out*. That goes for the captain, should he return to the bridge. Understand?"

"Yessir."

Radis leaned back again, put his boulder jaw in one palm, and stared glumly at the small screen. Bolla had worked closely with the rigorously trained Cadre personality for years and always found it fascinating. Now he looked at the number One slumped in the chair—his potential executioner—and felt only pity. He shuffled forward.

"Officer Radis, I can do this more efficiently, I think."

Radis nodded and moved to give Bolla the console. Before he had settled his bulk into the chair, TELCOM signaled that the patch was operative. Then the observers were witness to something rare enough to make them forget the burlesque physique of Dr. Hans Bolla. Computers were a constant variable in all their lives, so they had seen it before, but that only made their recognition—and appreciation—more immediate. Bolla was a virtuoso. He was sitting at an unfamiliar board, but like a pianist before any fine instrument, it didn't matter. His fingers caressed rather than struck the touch pads, and he played them with no less speed, offering a running commentary as he went.

"I can call on over five hundred k-bytes of data related to the Chairman's machinations—holofilm, audio only, and some transcripts. Most of it I siphoned from the Chairman's automatic surveillance system, and the rest came from the Cadre Proctor himself.

"You won't want to see it all, so I'll hop around. This one is one of our earliest, but it's just audio . . . there."

Out of the speaker came the voice of the Chairman and some sort of media advisor. They were discussing strategies to excite the public as close to panic as they could manage without losing control. Make them believe in the Alien. Make them afraid. Make them ignore the failings of the Regnum and its leadership and unite in the effort to seek out and destroy the extragalactican. Direct it at the simpleminded. Make nothing official, nothing subject to careful scrutiny. Put suggestions into their popular songs, their prayers, their commercials, their jokes. Express directly only our concern, nothing else. Let them play with it. Let them laugh about it. Let them wonder inside, and be afraid. That will give us the rope we need to deal with the upstarts in the Hub.

Before it was over, Radis was shifting uncomfortably in

the chair he had dragged near Bolla's, but he was unconvinced.

"It does fit," he admitted. "There was a whole section of Cadre—Alien Security—on it for years. Still is as far as I know, but they got more publicity than results. 'Ghost Chaser Section' we called it. Ran all over the place checking out Holtz Effect readings. Never met anyone in the section that I considered a good officer."

Tyrees smiled to himself. He had once been in that section. It had taken him to Tercet and Meta-sol.

"But as much as I dislike it, this is just political shit—rotten, putrescent, historical political shit. Always there. Besides, the recording can't authenticate the speakers by itself."

"No indeed," said Bolla, warming to his task. "Consider it an hors d'oeuvre." He resumed his finger dance on the keys. Sometimes there was an unconscious flourish in his fingers. "Here you can *see* the Chairman."

On the screen Radis saw the Chairman's bullish figure behind a massive desk. "Sit," he said. Another figure came into the picture. He was tall, silver-haired, sternly cut.

"That man used to be your Cadre Proctor, Radis. Listen carefully," said Tyrees.

Radis noted a strange, forced cast to those words, as if each had been released from a vice. It took him only a few seconds of watching the screen to realize that the tall man with the Chairman was Tyrees's grandfather. He cursed softly.

As the scene unfolded itself before him, he had to remind himself that it was not part of a commercial holofilm. The conflict was intense, and the stakes were high. The Chairman's fist came down on the desk, and he came around it like a panther circling for the kill.

"Stop right there! Your judgment is blurred, Proctor, contaminated by a sense of guilt. I see things quite differently. What your grandson has become is not a 'breakthrough,' it is a *threat*. That band of . . . of *Seers* is a threat. You are responsible for the security of the Regnum: have you not considered what would happen if that primitive tribe of mind tinkerers was unleashed in the middle of a civil war? There would be no such thing as security! The Trade barons would stop at nothing to gain their services or learn their insidious little tricks.''

Radis cursed again, less softly. He was cursing the Chairman, all those watching with him, and all man's blood-spilling folly. He was cursing the curse that had been laid on him. He would be dead soon. What difference did it all make, anyway?

The Chairman was now wagging a finger at the Cadre Proctor, at the children's hero, as if he were a hero's child.

''Just before you walked through that door, I was informed that your grandson's life implant stopped sending— now, don't get excited! Obviously, the timing is too much of a coincidence. He's not dead, he's interfered with the implant *himself*. Pol Tyrees is not 'more than human,' Proctor, he is *alien*—and dangerous.''

There was a long pause at this point, so long that a message appeared on the screen verifying that the silence was legitimate. The Chairman was rubbing the heavy black hair on the back of one wrist absently as he stood over his antagonist and studied him with great care. The Cadre Proctor sat like one overcome with fatigue; perhaps also with the despair of having foreseen what was to come. His eyes were leaden, his tongue slow.

''Chairman. Those are the words of paranoia. If you are suggesting . . . The Council will never permit . . .''

''The Council will do as I say! I've demonstrated that to you often enough in the past, Petr. Accept the inevitable: in less than two months that festering little ball, Tercet, will be reduced to a cinder. Its location is ideal because no one will ever know.''

''Chairman!'' The Proctor was pushing out of his chair.

''And if you don't know where your duty lies . . . remain seated! . . . Thank you. You should know better, Petr. One more second and you would have been a dead man. There are elements of my security system even you don't know.''

The Proctor fell back. Added to his crumpled look of defeat was one of surprise, perhaps because such failure was new to him. His eyes, a less startling blue than his grandson's, slid from the Chairman's face to the floor as he spoke.

"Strange, you've never called me Petr before, have you? I wonder how far *I* have gone—from grandfather to Cadre officer—oh, Pol, forgive me."

The Chairman snorted. "In spite of all that steel, you do have a maudlin streak, don't you, Petr? You're getting too old. How far have you gone? I'll answer that one. When you accepted this post, you took it as a bribe for your silence on the Holtz Effect. No! Let me finish. Never mind the rationalizations about Regnum unity. You took the bribe. I offered it when there were other ways, more certain ways, to keep you quiet, but not because I have your latent soft spots. You've been a good Proctor, Petr, one of the best. Without you, the Trade Wars might have reduced the Regnum to a farce by now."

The Chairman's tone had become more conciliatory. Now he put a hand on the Proctor's bowed shoulders. "Listen, my friend. The office of Proctor of the Security Cadre was vacant, as I told you, because of the death of its previous holder, right? Well, he died because his opposition to me at the Council table was becoming a nuisance. You see, Petr, the Proctor's personal safety isn't the only reason for keeping his identity a CEO classification: it's a very powerful office, and secrecy makes things so much simpler, if he should become expendable. You are becoming expendable, too. There is no bribe this time, Petr, just a choice. . . ."

The screen went blank. Then words appeared: RECORDING TERMINATED. CHAIRMAN'S CODE WORD SPOKEN.

Bolla nodded grimly and hit the escape key. "He was a hard man, but he was my friend. Two days before that . . . episode, he had me begin gathering data on the Chairman. Any doubts about authenticity, Officer Radis? I realize this sort of thing can be faked."

Radis shook his head sullenly.

"Well, nobody could glue all of this stuff together, in any case. Now, would you like to see—"

"No. That's enough. Turn the thing off, please."

"Convinced, Radis?" asked Tyrees. "You just watched the Chairman of the Council of the Regnum about to murder the Cadre Proctor, and order planetary genocide."

"I know what I watched, damn it!"

"Are you still determined to carry out that man's orders and call it 'duty'?"

"Just what do you expect me to do?" spat out Radis angrily. He spun out of his chair and slapped a gaming piece off a table. Before it crashed into a wall, he was firing a less rhetorical question at Tyrees.

"Tercet. What happened there?"

"We blackmailed him. With that information." Tyrees jerked his head at the console. "It bought us enough time to get off-planet. Leeth didn't get very far, however."

"No, damn it! *You.* What happened to *you*?"

Tyrees hesitated. "I became a Seer," he said.

"And what the hell is that?"

Bolla watched Tyrees hesitate again, took note of the desperate brightness of Radis's eyes.

"Tell him, Pol. Tell him what you can."

"About the 'magic,' Doctor?"

"Please."

"All right," sighed Tyrees. "I'll try. Radis, I've always had, well . . . certain acuities. Until Tercet, you could put most of it down to an abnormally high level of sense perception. I could also control certain autonomic body functions consciously—heartbeat, for example. This is what first caused my . . . the Cadre Proctor and the Chairman, to take an interest in me. On Tercet I met this man,"—he looked with affection at Meta-sol—"and I guess you could say he trained me, helped develop what was already there. The Seers have dedicated themselves for a thousand years to increasing their knowledge of the mind and body. That's about it."

Tyrees seemed content with this explanation. Radis was not.

"That all sounds rather innocuous." He pointed at Meta-sol, who had again disappeared inside himself, though this time his eyes were open. "But he *knew* about me. How could he know?"

"He can . . . tell things, some things, about the human brain, through its electrical activity. Just as he 'sees' objects, largely through heat differential."

Radis looked hard and long at both of them. He was still

agitated, feeling the pressure of postponed decisions and of the void that presses upon every man, always—except with him it pressed closer. He could feel its coldness.

"You're like him? You can do the same things?"

"Some of them, yes. But we're different somehow. We're still . . . learning about each other."

"Different how? Why is the Chairman so afraid of you?"

Tyrees's brow furrowed in thought. He ignored the second question. "How? That's hard to say. I don't really—"

"Yes," said Meta-sol, almost in a whisper, still unmoving, his eyes caught by nothing anyone in the room could see. "There is a difference. Pol-Nesol-Rast has . . . greater power. Strength that is unknown among us. He lacks . . . direction."

Radis paced to a bulkhead, then back again. "My back-up data mentioned the graviton pathways. It's true then. You can read them. That's how you got out here so fast, right?"

Tyrees nodded. "More or less."

"*Intergalactic* pathways."

"Yes."

"Then how were we able to overtake you?"

"I'm improving too slowly. By the time I was sure of the next plotting, it was too late. You were on our backs."

Tyrees moved slowly to the wall, where he picked up the gaming piece, studied it like a chunk of ancient pottery, and held it out to Radis.

"Your move."

Radis, too, studied it carefully for a moment. Then he reached out and took it from Tyrees's hand. He shrugged.

"I'm with you. What the hell—you can have me for the rest of my life." He flipped the piece over his shoulder and smiled, eyebrows arching high in irony.

Tyrees shook his hand very solemnly, as did the rest. Radis actually seemed rather jaunty, even cavalier now, about a decision that turned his former life inside out. But the others knew that this training and experience were of incalculable value. He made such a striking, virile figure standing there with hands on hips, shaking his head in musing wonder at his own state of affairs, that his medical condition seemed unforgivable.

"You know what the next step has to be," said Tyrees.

"Of course. Take *Condor*. What else can there be? I hope you'll be able to tell me *how*, however. I command the mission, not the starship."

Bolla gestured at the console. "If we showed the commander our data . . ."

"No way. Not this man. He's strictly military. He follows orders. Period. He won't follow mine if I denounce those of the Chairman himself."

"There's also the little matter of the crew to consider," said Mariet.

"Well," said Radis, thinking out loud. "We do have numbers— and surprise. If I set up certain conditions, then spring you all at once—"

He was cut off by the characteristic *brup* of a speaker being opened. It was not the one belonging to the consol, but that of the wardroom at large.

"This is commander Flaan."

With the possible exception of Meta-sol, every man in the room felt an icy hand fondle his bowels.

"*Reacher* prisoners, Officer Radis, for the last several minutes I have been listening to you on the intercom. Your plot to assume control of *Condor* by force has been recorded. Officer Radis—consider yourself under arrest and confined to the wardroom. You will be handed over with the others to the proper authorities when we reach Regnum."

CHAPTER FIVE

The prisoners in *Condor*'s wardroom stared in stunned disbelief at the intercom speaker on the ceiling. Like archetypal figures deeply buried in their mythologies, they looked up, horrified and outraged by the maleficent power of their gods.

Mariet groaned and pounded a skinny fist into his palm. Bolla puffed out his cheeks and forced a hiss of air through this teeth. Radis was the first to react purposefully. He strode to the consol and jabbed a key.

"Commander, I wish to speak to you privately, please."

Before he finished speaking, Flaan's image formed on the screen, anger set fiercely on his face. "Your 'request' is denied, Officer Radis. The wardroom will remain sealed and guarded. I will not discuss—"

"Fool!" screamed Radis. "You incompetent *ass*! I had these traitors in the palm of my hand! Get that fucking door open . . . now!"

The commander's face blanched to raw whey. Anger melted into surprise, then indecision. "You ordered TELCOM to—"

"Of course I did! For *their* benefit."

"I . . . you have been too compromised. I can't—"

He was interrupted by a cry from Radis. On his own screen all Flaan saw was a forearm come crashing into the side of Radis's face. He had been able to turn just enough to take part of the blow on his nose. The gout of blood impacting on the consol lens told Flaan of its force. He stared numbly through the smear at the overturned chair. There was still a great deal of noise coming from the speaker.

The gaming table shattered under the weight of the two hurtling bodies. Both hit and rolled, but Tyrees was faster, and Radis was only on the rise as a foot tore up the side of his neck. He fell back, fighting for balance, but Tyrees was on him like an enraged animal throwing blows from every direction, with every limb. For each strike Radis blocked, he took two others. Even Bolla and Mariet winced at the violence and speed of the attack. The blows were cuts and slashes, edges of bone and boot, those of a skilled but maniacal sadist lusting for blood and bruise—the badges of suffering—rather than victory. Radis was still on his feet, but blood-soaked and swooning when the door hissed open.

"Stop or you're a dead man!"

Commander Flaan stood behind three armed crewmen. Two of the laser rifles were aimed at Tyrees, the third covered the others. Tyrees's next strike was stillborn, a hand raised over its opposite shoulder, about to be pulled by the leading elbow down and across in a slashing chop. Its sleeve was red with Radis's blood. Radis's arms were still flinching, jerking in anticipation of blows from unpredictable directions. Finally he lowered his hands, blinked at the blood in his eyes, and crumpled to the floor.

"Back," said the commander. "Stand back. I'd just as soon kill you now."

Tyrees was breathing heavily, and there was a mad flare in his eyes that took a while to die. For a moment it seemed he might leap at the rifles. Instead he spat at the body splayed at his feet, and backed away.

Nothing else was said. The crewmen dragged Radis out and the door hummed closed behind them. Bolla went to the head and returned with a damp cloth. He tossed it to Tyrees.

"Wipe yourself off. Some of that blood might be yours."

Already Tyrees seemed to have returned to his habitual calm. He took the cloth and began to wipe at his hands.

"That was educational," said Mariet, though the flippancy in his voice was absent from his expression. "A little . . . messy, perhaps."

Tyrees ignored him.

Bolla sat with a tired grunt, his low-slung body suddenly too much of a burden. "You surprise me again," he said to Tyrees. "The anger . . . well, we all share that. But . . . that was a, a *slaughter*, Pol, and it will change nothing."

"A slaughter, Doctor? Good."

"He deserved it," said Mariet, nose jumping higher.

Tyrees threw down the cloth. "I have to wash up." He took Bolla by one wrist and pulled him to his feet, leading him like a docile hippo to the head. "Captain, how do you work this thing?" Mariet frowned his puzzlement, but followed quietly.

When the door closed behind them, Bolla spoke before Tyrees could. "I'll be damned. I think I know."

Tyrees smiled. "Going by your reaction, it was convincing enough."

"I was convinced all right. How do you know Radis was just putting on an act with the commander? Never mind. I hope he knows *you* were acting. Some acting."

Mariet only shook his head in wonder.

"He knows," said Tyrees. "Cadre don't fight like that. And his defense was only token."

"Are you sure you didn't overdo it?"

"It couldn't be overdone. I hope Flaan is impressed by Radis's appearance, because there's nothing else wrong with him."

"Oh, no," said Bolla sarcastically. "Just a few liters of blood, a few cuts, contusions, welts, and bruises. You must be able to—"

"Drop it now," said Tyrees. "We've been in here too long already." He opened the door and led them out.

Through it all, Meta-sol had sat, still leaning on his cane, just as he sat now. Tyrees walked over to him and put a hand on his shoulder.

"Are you all right, Meta-sol?"

The old man nodded slowly.

"I don't know about the rest of you, but I can use some sleep," said Tyrees. Then he raised his voice to a shout.

"Maybe later our charming hosts will remember to feed us."

They went about the business of arranging the furniture into something suitable for sleep, and dimmed the ward-room to near darkness. All of them needed rest badly; nevertheless, no one slept immediately. Each stared into the gloom, taking measure of his life after his own fashion, pitting it against a foreshortened—or terrifying—future. Mariet found his imagination hardest to deal with, and shifted restlessly on his lounge. Bolla could take some refuge in his natural stoicism. He wondered what was going through Tyrees's mind, but dismissed the impulse to talk to him. The man had grown increasingly remote since Tercet, and he had *always* been aloof. Too much on his plate, perhaps. And Meta-sol—what of him? On his own world he was one of a few unique men who were—unlike the Chairman—not only obeyed, but venerated, even wor-shiped. Now he sat in the darkness in an alien place, largely ignored, perhaps considering himself useless, per-haps thinking he would never be with his people again, even should he be allowed to live out his old age.

Bolla spoke softly at the bent shape in the chair. "Meta-sol? Are you awake?"

He was rewarded by a very gentle chuckle. "Doctor. You make too much of a . . . distinction between sleep and wakefulness. There are many . . . layers, and no walls between them."

"I see. Which layer were you in, then?"

"Not in the one you call sleep. I rarely have need of that."

"Meta-sol, you're as bad as your protégé over there. Both of you are allergic to straight answers."

"That is an expression I am not familiar with, Doctor, but I can . . . taste its sense. The problem may be that there *are* no 'straight answers.' However, I was in the layer that allows rest without . . . inhibiting contemplation."

"And that is simply a matter of choice?"

"Yes. As are most things of significance. There are but two . . . exceptions." His words were sighs of sound in the morbid light.

"Which are?"

"Birth and . . ."

"And death, of course," added Bolla.

"Of course."

"I would like you to explain for me exactly why you made one of your choices."

"I will if I can, Doctor."

"Why did you choose to be here, to follow Pol-Nesol-Rast?"

Bolla could just make out the shadowy sphere of Meta-sol's head turning toward him, could just make out the shadowy voice that finally, grudgingly, came from it.

"Because he is my savior."

"What?"

The head turned away again, almost disappearing in the darkness. Bolla closed his eyes, but did not sleep.

CHAPTER SIX

The four prisoners were awake and about, taking turns going to the head, Mariet and Bolla grumbling about their empty stomachs, before the wardroom door slid open again.

"I trust you slept well?"

Radis stood there, grinning, arms folded. He was wearing his cape, thus rendering his aspect, with its magnificent jaw and uplifted brow, even more heroic—but his altered face would never appear on any statue. It boasted a half-dozen angry colors, cuts that had not yet closed, swellings and knobs that were almost comic. He looked at their stunned expressions and laughed.

"You needn't be afraid of speaking. *Condor*'s ours."

"Good God," blurted Mariet. "How could one man . . . you didn't need our help?"

Radis touched a particularly ugly lump high on his cheek with tender fingers. "Tyrees gave me all the help I needed. By the way, my friend, I hope you don't think *you* wouldn't be wearing some of these in ordinary circumstances." Tyrees only smiled. "Actually, it *was* surprisingly easy, after Flaan believed I was true blue again.

"He brought my devastated body to sick bay. When I 'regained consciousness,' I was raving. He had to restrain me physically from tearing off to kill you all. Soon, however, his calmer head prevailed. Besides, I was too weak to do anything but holler and spit blood. He told the medic to prepare a sedative, and sent everybody else away—it doesn't do, you know, for underlings to see their betters in such a state. Needless to say, he and the medic ended up with the sedatives. They're still snoring.

"The rest was even easier. I called the spacecrew in ones and twos to report to me in several locations suitable for lock-ups, until there were only a few running the ship. Since I had salted the officers away first, there was no one with the authority to do anything once the situation became curious. Then I sprung *Reacher*'s crew, armed them, and we marched the rest to the maintainance wardroom. *Condor*'s whole crew is there now, except for the pair dozing in sick bay.

"So," sighed Radis as he unclasped the neck chain of his cape, "your boys are now busy acquainting themselves with *Condor*'s systems. I saw no reason to disturb your rest."

"Holy jumping shit," said Mariet. "Holy jee-umping shit. *One man* puts a Battlefleet monster in his pocket like a toy."

"I accept your admiration, Captain, but remember"—he swept the cape from his shoulders—"this uniform inspires a certain automatic obedience. Right, *Mister* Tyrees?" With hands that had suddenly become gentle on the soft black cloth, he folded the cape neatly and held it for a moment before placing it ceremoniously on a table. "It'll be difficult having to get along without it."

"On the other hand, *Mister* Radis, you will be your own man for the first time in your adult life."

"Is any of us ever his own man, Tyrees?"

"What do you mean?"

"Well," said Radis, still looking glumly down at the folds of black on the table, "I might just be switching masters. Whose man are you?"

"No one's."

"Then why should I be yours?"

"Because you chose to be."

"Not quite. I chose not to be a part of . . . evil, I suppose, though that's a word I hesitate to use. I don't know what you are or where you're going. Where *are* you going?"

Tyrees's brow furrowed. "You're a traitor now, too,

Radis, however noble your reasons. The Chairman is our enemy. Help me to fight him. That should be enough.''

Radis shook his head. "Uh-uh. Nope. It's not enough. I have weeks to live, remember? I'm not going to squander it trying to wipe out one man for the sake of revenge.''

"You don't think that his elimination will be the best thing that could happen to the Regnum?" said Tyrees, now visibly irritated.

"Not necessarily. It would create a power vacuum that could result in all kinds of chaos, all kinds of suffering, especially as things are now, with the Regnum struggling for her survival.''

"Then perhaps she should be allowed to die a natural death.''

Radis's eyes turned hard. "You don't care what happens, do you? You just want to feel the Chairman's throat in your hands. Like I said, that's not enough for me.''

Bolla cleared his throat. He bent to pick up the cape, and stepping between the two, held it like an altar boy in the palms of his hands.

"You don't understand," he said, though it was unclear to whom he spoke. "Pol talked about noble reasons. The Cadre had a very noble one: to protect a galactic ideology that has given man a thousand years of peace. Amen. But a thousand years is not eternity; a thousand years is no more justification for keeping it alive after its time has come than a minute is.''

"I have some knowledge of your work, Doctor," Radis replied. "Certain economic factors, in concert with massive psychological tendencies, have recently had a corrosive effect on the Regnum. If that's true, why dump everything? Make some changes—get rid of the self-appointed barons in the Hub, for example.''

"No, no, no," said Bolla impatiently, bobbing the cape up and down for emphasis. "You miss the point. The system worked well for so long because it suited the social and economic conditions for the Great Diaspora beautifully. Those *conditions* have changed. The Diaspora is over. To oversimplify, it's like expecting the wild kids you sent out to conquer the frontier to suddenly become docile, suddenly begin using the proper table manners, when there is no more frontier. We need a *new* system to suit the new conditions.''

''Or a new frontier,'' muttered Tyrees softly. The others' eyes were drawn to his compellingly. They burned with a blue fire that consumed denial, that stamped upon his face the mark of the visionary who demanded, dared, others to follow. What they saw, they looked upon with clarity and passion, though it was not of the here and now. Each of his watchers, each in his own way and for reasons obscure, became his apostle. He took the cape absently, and absently dropped it to the floor.

''You are right, Doctor,'' he said, speaking with the fervor of divine revelation. ''We have conquered the outside universe, so now we turn against one another, because to strive is our nature. But there is another frontier—more vast and more frightening than any we have ever faced.''

A shiver ran like a quake through Bolla—because he understood.

Radis stammered, ''What are you saying?''

''There is a universe within. You must speak to Meta-sol. You must all speak to Meta-sol.'' He turned abruptly and left for the bridge.

The others looked as one upon the old man in the chair with the sparse white beard and the sightless eyes, still leaning on his gnarled cane. He was smiling.

So it came to be that a light-year beyond the flat plane of the spiral galaxy called the Milky Way, between the brilliant fires of its countless stars and the great darkness, a new frontier was born.

Condor's former crew was transferred to *Reacher*. The umbilical was cut, and with the cruel necessity that nature teaches so well, she was left to fly on her own. *Condor*, with a surge of heady power in her wings, soared along the intergalactic pathways, knowing truly the rich freedom of her namesake. She coasted the galaxy, occasionally swinging around to roost on a star. Each time, she left behind a very special birthing—a Tercian Seer with a calling, a message, a New Covenant.

Condor flew serenely, for she knew that only a few others like her could match her strength and none could match her speed. Time flew with her, but allowed Pol Tyrees enough to come upon scenes of Radis and Bolla and even Mariet and other spacecrew, children of enlightened technology, hunkering down to listen to the words of an old man who didn't understand the workings of a light-emitting diode. Gradually he took them as he had taken Pol-Nesol-Rast—into the wonders and terrors of the universe each contained in himself. He gave them tantalizing glimpses of unmined lodes of golden power there; some were able to chip out nuggets whose glistenings promised more to come.

None more than Radis dared deeper; none more than Radis despaired at the lateness of his find. Before very long he was a permanent resident of the sick bay. He lost weight and his skin took on the translucency of an ancient, infinitely fragile manuscript under glass. He refused the release of narcotics, but pain had etched the jagged edges of a storm-worn shoreline on his virile face. He spoke only in whispers, but he raged against the dying of the light.

He and Meta-sol had become close friends, cementing a bond that had begun to form many weeks earlier when the Tercian had pronounced his death sentence. Meta-sol had made it his sole concern in recent days to lend what peace he could to the man as he slipped, spiritual fingernails scraping on the slope, away.

Radis lay quietly with a thin tube plugged into his arm because he had trouble keeping food down and fell into long periods of coma when eating was precluded. Meta-sol sat beside his bed with a stillness much more profound than that of the dying man. They talked sporadically.

"You must have better things to do, Meta-sol."

"I do not."

"Your teaching. The others . . ."

"The others know—as do you, my friend—that they must teach themselves. From time to time they must be . . . invited to open certain doors. That is all I can do."

There was another short silence, because it tired Radis to speak, and because he wanted Meta-sol to stay with him in any case. He loathed self-pity, however, and thinking his eyes might be wet, summoned the strength to roll his head away.

He whispered to the wall. "That's what bothers me the most. I can see those doors. Some of them. I'll never get to open any now. It would have been better to die not knowing."

Meta-sol shook his head. "Not knowing is itself a kind of death, my friend. Certainly it is not living. We are made to know . . . to strive to know."

"Perhaps you are right. But we are not made to die. I'm not doing it well."

"Nor could I," said Meta-sol, though Radis did not believe him. "You did live well. Without you, Pol-Nesol-Rast would never have begun the New Covenant."

"Do you think they will have an effect, Meta-sol? There are so few of you. Each time we place a Seer, I feel like we're dropping a diamond into an ocean."

"I *must* believe. We must all believe. From that, all things will follow."

"Well, Doctor Bolla believes, and he is a skeptical pragmatist, if I ever saw one."

"Yes. He says the . . . conditions are right. I do not understand his . . . methods, but the strength of his mind is there to see."

"You two make strange bedfellows."

"I am sorry. I still struggle at times with your . . . way of speaking. You said . . ."

Radis lifted and waved one hand as if its weight were a newly discovered burden. "Never mind. Unimportant. You both have faith, something of value that I spent most of my life missing."

"My faith will live as long as Pol-Nesol-Rast lives," said Meta-sol.

Radis looked at him falling silent again and wondering for the thousandth time about the strength of Meta-sol's regard for Tyrees. Almost deification. Yet there was also fear. He was about to probe that regard, for as his breath shallowed, so did his reticence about such things, and so did Meta-sol's; but at that moment Tyrees himself appeared at the foot of his bed. Bolla was behind him.

"How is he, Meta-sol?"

"I can answer for myself," said Radis in his whispery voice. "I'm just peachy. How are you?"

"He draws near the Black Hole," replied Meta-sol. "But he fights its pull as I have never known a man could fight. He teaches me . . . defiance."

Bolla had always had great difficulty in the presence of sickness or death, so said nothing. That cold, curious part of him took over automatically, setting him apart in an observer's stance. Not surprisingly, there was nothing to see in Meta-sol's face, but he thought there was a deeper bow in the Tercian's back, a stretching of the spirit into perilous thinness. Bolla was convinced that Meta-sol had never fully won back the essences he had fed Tyrees after he had collapsed on *Reacher*.

Tyrees was different—as always. In the past weeks he had begun to take on the regal sternness of his grandfather. He lent the feeling that he could—perhaps obsessively—reach out in anger at any time to rip from whatever powers that may be, prerogatives that didn't belong to him. As he looked down upon Radis's spent reed of a body, that anger was in his eyes.

"I never thanked you for what you did for us, Radis."

"Well, don't start now," said Radis, the sounds graveling softly out of his throat. "Virtue is its own reward. I never thanked *you* for that beating I took."

Tyrees glared fiercely at Radis's ragged smile, and Bolla knew he was searching desperately for something to say, something to do. He touched the tube that fed Radis with a cloudy liquid, and traced it delicately to the now slack-muscled arm. His fingers hesitated there for a moment before moving to the side of Radis's neck. Puzzled, Radis began to turn his head to speak, but Tyrees suddenly used both hands to straighten it again, fingers probing the jaw lines high along the front of the ears. Bolla saw the invisible curtain fall—the same one that fell when Tyrees was in the command chair—across his eyes.

Meta-sol started violently in his chair as if from a charge of electricity. His cane fell from his hands and clattered on the floor as he reached for Tyrees, blindly.

"Pol-Nesol—"

"Doctor, get the Seers," said Tyrees. He released Radis and tore the tube from his arm. "There are two left. Get them."

Meta-sol shook his head, black eyes darting, looking for something that could be seen. "No, Pol-Nesol-Rast. We will kill him. I have seen what is there."

Radis's face took on a look of utter terror, but he said nothing. Tyrees turned to his mentor.

"We must try, Meta-sol. There is nothing to lose."

"That is not so, Pol of the hidden stars," said the Tercian, suddenly calm again. "Much may be lost . . . perhaps even you."

"We must try, anyway. Help me. I can do nothing but damage without your guidance."

"Try what?" croaked Radis, trying to sit up in the bed.

"Stay quiet, Radis . . . Meta-sol?"

During the silence that followed, Bolla expected, waited for, then saw Meta-sol's slow, sad nod. Stamped unalterably on a file in his mind was the image of the triad of Seers gathered around the unconscious form of their leader back in *Reacher*'s sick bay.

He ran from the room like a frightened boy on legs that forgot they carried an aging, very pudgy body. The corridors blurred by on both sides, but by the time he got there, his lungs were remembering very well, and he had to gasp out their names at the entrance speaker panel.

"Don-tar . . . Spel-sol . . . It's Doctor Bolla . . . quickly."

The door slid open and both were there. Bolla stood panting. It's absurd, he thought. The canes. The shawls. The beards. I'm a computer expert, a social psychologist, and here I am on a starship running around like a clown hoping for . . . what? More *magic*? Will it be white or black? Miracle or tragedy?

"Meta-sol . . . Pol-Nesol-Rast. They need you in the sick bay."

There were no questions, no wasted words. They spent a half second looking at each other and came immediately. Bolla followed; they were older than he—all the Seers were—but he had trouble keeping up. One, Spel-sol, was tall and gaunt; Don-tar was a stubby block of hard leather, but carried no flab. No Tercian, let alone a Seer, ever owned an extra calorie.

At the sick bay nothing had changed except that Radis

had been moved in his bed. Now his head was at its foot and away from the wall.

Spel-sol was a majestic figure, his full beard still largely black but slashed with lightning streaks of white. Among the Seers he was second to Meta-sol, but he had the imperial gestures of a king and a bearing that inspired reverence. Nevertheless, in the presence of Meta-sol and Pol-Nesol-Rast, he was humble and deferential. When they were told what was to be done, it was he who cut short the anxious inquiries of Don-tar with a simple touch of his hand.

"We must . . . ride with you," Meta-sol was saying to Tyrees. "Your touch, your force, our direction. You must concentrate on . . . control. Control only."

"I understand," said Tyrees. "Let's get on with it. I'm ready."

"No. You are not, Pol of the hidden stars."

Tyrees opened his mouth, obviously to object, then stopped himself and nodded. He pulled a chair to the foot of the bed and sat, forearms resting on his knees. Soon Bolla could see corded neck muscles slacken and disappear beneath the skin. Wrists slackened. Lines of tension that Bolla had not recognized as such melted from the face. Chin fell to chest. Beside him Radis lay, only semiconscious now without his umbilical tube of sustaining chemicals, breathing in tiny, shallow rasps.

"All right," said Tyrees, raising his head. Bolla saw a different man looking out of those terrible blue eyes. He had more of Meta-sol in him now—still, pacific, utterly contained. His voice had lost its hard edges.

"Doctor, we might need the medic, but don't call him until it's over."

"He can't help Radis now. Why should he be able to help him after—"

"Not Radis. Me and the Seers."

Tyrees moved to stand to one side of the narrow bed. He placed his hands as he had before, fingers along the high jaw line. Meta-sol came to the foot of the bed over Radis's head, and laying his cane beside Radis's body, reached out both hands to take Tyrees by the wrists. Spel-sol and Don-tar put one hand on each of their shoul-

ders. The configuration struck Bolla as arcane, suggestive
of some primitive religious rite, something to tempt the
eye of a sculptor. It also conveyed function: Tyrees the
power; Meta-sol the guidance; the others support.

Very soon—and though Bolla expected it, his neck hair
still lifted at the sight—the red glow he had witnessed on
Reacher began to rise out of their bodies, growing stronger,
higher, redder, until the whole room pulsed with its light.
Unconsciously, Bolla breathed uneasily to its rhythm.

A million light-years away, Pol Tyrees was riding a tide
of energy so overwhelming that it was difficult to recognize as his own. But like a boy bouncing with fearful
delight in wild surf, he felt his father's hands take hold to
steady him for the swim. He could sense it all—the buzz
of power he could only think of as electrical, the delicate
but disciplined hands of Meta-sol, the more distant, more
discreet presence of the others—all bobbing in the heaving
surf of their own mingled essences.

For a time he just enjoyed the feeling of release, the
sensation of being unleashed from restricting shores. Then
the lightly stern hands gave him a direction, and he surged
along its line until he felt another presence, unlike the
others. It was diminutive, but foreign. It had no buzz or
crackle—it spurted with a haphazard whine which was
irritating. Because he was still a child in the surf, he
started to veer away, but the gentle pressure of the hands
brought him back.

Radis.

It was Radis. The whine was small and weak and somehow disgusting. It nipped at the ankles like an ill-tempered
lap dog, jealous because his mistress's attention had lagged—
but it was the whimper of a strong man dying.

When he knew, he began to drive for its source; but
again he felt the hands, this time restraining. Caution.
Caution.

The waves upon which he rode were impelling, but
rhythmic and somehow secure; what he approached was
sporadic and insidious, like the eddies formed on a shoreline when a heavy river disgorges itself onto submerged
rocks. He slowed, obeying the hands, and with careful

power cleaved through its spill and up the river's narrow maw.

Once past its mouth, the resistance was weak. Almost, it seemed, the river reversed itself and began to pull him inwards. Until then there had been no particular sense of light, but now the waters were turning darker. Before, he was a swimmer breasting the waves; now he was under them, beginning to panic, beginning to tilt for air and light.

Then he felt the hands again—less strong, but steady, reassuring. "This way," they said. "Go on. Go on. Leave the light. Follow the shadow."

He did. The going was easy, though the darkness frightened him. His sense of the presence that was Radis grew, and so did the pulling inwards, but his recognition of the man was blighted by a peculiar odor. It was inseparable from the presence itself, and it hinted of putrescence, of a hidden tomb.

It, too, grew stronger, until it pervaded the ether in which he moved, making it rank with the vomitous stench of decay. Radis was it, it was Radis. Though he had no body, he felt his throat constrict, his gorge rise. Everything in him rebelled against the sense of contamination. Again he started to turn back, when the strength of the poisonous current seemed about to become irresistible, the darkness about to swallow him up; again the hands, barely perceptible now, trembling, urged him on. Nevertheless, he soon got to the point when his senses demanded escape; he was about to slap the hands aside and tear back against the insidious current, when he was suddenly upon it.

There.

A shadow, a blob of blackness—deepest black—outlined by the paler dark. Throbbing, voracious, it was sucking in the ether that was what remained of Radis. It was sucking in *him*.

NO!

Terror exploded. He turned, dragging the feeble hands with him, kicking with mad strength back toward the dull light. Then, as his frenzy abated because he had found the hideous suck less than his will, he felt the pain. It came from the hands, from Radis, from cries in the far distance;

it came to sting eyes he did not possess; it came, and it *be*came—*him*.

With a scream of outrage he turned once more. No one, no *thing* had the right to inflict such anguish upon beings condemned to measure their lives by the number of heaves in their lungs. He added his own speed to that of the suction. He was an arrow of anger and he pierced the glutinous black like a desert sun pierces the crevass of a night crawler. When he was completely enveloped, totally within the embrace of its negativity, he threw out all the burning energy, all the light-craving anger of those who must die, against its black horror.

It felt the light, drew it in; felt the heat, drew it in. It drew in the burn of life until it could take no more.

CHAPTER SEVEN

It had been more than an hour, and Bolla had settled himself on a surgical bed long before the first scream came. The five figures were a frozen tableau until then, the pulsing red glow all that suggested life.

The scream came from Tyrees. It was a sound carrying such a purity of terror that Bolla's heart leaped and crashed painfully against his rib cage.

"NO!"

The red glow flashed white. Meta-sol's hands trembled violently on Tyrees's wrists. The fingers became claws that fought to hold against the shaking, but could not. Bolla jumped from his bed as Meta-sol fell.

The second scream was different. In a way, it was even more terrifying to Bolla because it contained no fear. What it did contain, in measureless proportions, was all the killing hate, all the raping blood-lust of which only the insane are capable.

The light flashed madly. First Don-tar, then Spel-sol toppled over like marble statues. Tyrees, hands still locked to the sides of Radis's head, his own head thrown back, wore an impossible expression of feral, violent loathing.

The light died as abruptly as Tyrees's scream. Bolla blinked. His heart was racing—he still had the presence of mind to worry about it failing. He approached the bed like a very old man approaching the scene of a gory accident.

Tyrees was the only one on his feet, but there was nothing in his eyes.

"Pol?"

No response.

"Pol . . . what happened? What's wrong?"

He stepped over Meta-sol's body to take Tyrees by the arm. He shook it.

"Pol!"

This time there was an answer—but it came from the bed. "Is that you, Doctor?" Radis sat up.

Bolla's laboring heart took another jolt. Radis sat there rubbing his eyes like a little boy on a school morning.

"You know, I'm damn tired," he said.

Then it was Tyrees's turn to fall, almost taking Bolla with him to the floor. His eyes remained open after he hit, but Bolla could detect no breathing. He checked for a pulse and found none. He put his ear to Tyrees's chest. From his sitting position Radis peered over the side of the bed and discovered that he was surrounded by a tangle of bodies. It looked like the carnage of a mass suicide.

"What the *hell* is going on?"

Bolla could only shake his head.

"How are you?" Radis asked pleasantly, as one might greet an old friend after a long absence.

"Medic," said Bolla.

"What?"

"Medic!" Bolla pulled himself to his feet and stumbled for the intercom.

Pol Tyrees and the Seers were in deep comas varying in duration from two days to a week. The toll exacted for Radis's life was paid for most dearly by Meta-sol. He was the last to surface, and he came up carrying signs of invisible scars. His walk was slower, his silences longer, his voice more distant. In contrast, Tyrees emerged newly born, confident and begging challenge. The changes in Don-tar and Spel-sol were marked only by attitude. Near Tyrees, they behaved as if in the presence of a god. Bolla overheard them use a whispered additive to his Tercian name: Pol-Nesol-Rast, *Vitar*. The full translation was now, "Pol, son of Meta-sol, out of the darkness, *life giver*."

Radis, of course, was Lazarus—at least to himself. There had been a rare clerical error made by those charged with the records of fate, and he had been left off the ledger. For this his gratitude, and his delight, were unbounded. He was not a vital man in his prime given back what was rightfully his; he was a fortunate man, fortunate beyond all reasoning, because he had been gifted with a second life, with each tick of its time precious and unexpected.

Condor flew on. She soared to carefully chosen roosts now, from one spinning edge of the galaxy to the other, because she had only two more birthings—Don-tar and Spel-sol. None of the Seers left *Condor* with more fervor than these.

When the last had been left behind, Tyrees called a meeting of Bolla, Radis, and himself. That triumvirate constituted the leadership of the small band of dissidents, though no one questioned the supremacy of Tyrees. Meta-sol and Mariet were often present—through their own choice—at such meetings, but said little. The former, perhaps because of the loss of his Seers, had withdrawn more and more into himself; the latter, by necessity and preference, was most often on *Condor*'s bridge instead.

"Well," said Radis, stabbing buttons for his coffee before settling in. "I hope we're going to get into some nitty-gritty about future plans this time. Coffee, gentlemen?" Bolla nodded, Tyrees declined. "Oh, I forgot you don't take stuff like this, Pol."

"I've got all the chemicals I need for uppers and downers right here inside me," said Tyrees.

"Yeah, but to put it mildly, you've also got better access to them."

Tyrees smiled. "It's harder to *gain* access if you depend on the stuff from outside, Radis. That's why your teacher is blind."

Radis looked ruefully down at his cup and sighed, "Ah, well." He poured the coffee down the drain.

Bolla chuckled and reached for his own. "I'm a devout convert, too, gentlemen, but not *that* devout."

Radis laughed. "You will forgive my skepticism, Doctor, but I hope our Seers generate more commitment."

"Ah, but they will, my young friend. After all this

time, I see that you still don't understand. You assume that people will believe because what they are asked to believe is worthy. Unfortunately, that is not the case.'' Bolla had lapsed again into his professorial mode. Both his listeners recognized it and suppressed smiles; nevertheless, they listened carefully.

''There is a very ancient saying: nothing can stop an idea whose time has come. That old saw is an intuitive expression that lies at the very heart of probability theory in terms of mass human behavior. The validity of the idea itself is irrelevant; it's the *timing* that counts. Our Seers are trying to deliver the same simple message that Pol just did to you: look inside instead of outside.'' Bolla paused to sip his coffee and smack his lips. ''Oversimplified, I know. But the message will spread, faith will grow, not because of its *truth*, but because it is being said when the people are ready to hear it. The same would be true for many other messages. That is why I remain optimistic in spite of our small numbers.''

''Yes,'' said Tyrees, ''but those numbers remain our largest drawback. People can't believe what they don't know. Radis, how goes your project?''

''It goes well, so far. Our evidence against the Chairman is now in the hands of his strongest political enemy. As you know, he is president of Caanon—Spel-sol's new territory—and Caanon's been squirming uncomfortably within its Regnum membership for years. If he uses it well, that information will add a light-year jump to our movement. The key is getting at least some of it into the public communications net. The president assured me he can, and will.

''It's also very important that a great number of the public come to know of the existence of the Seers quickly— otherwise, the Chairman could get to them before anyone would react to their 'disappearance.' In time, they should be safe.''

''Couldn't the Chairman trump something up—treason, sedition, perhaps—and simply lock them away?'' asked Bolla. ''We know the lengths he is capable of going to.''

Radis shook his head. ''Only in secret, Doctor. We still have laws he just can't flout publicly. The Seers can say anything they like, short of libel. They aren't going to *do* anything seditious, that's for sure."

"If they're going to be such model citizens, why should the chairman want to do anything at all?"

"He will," said Radis. "When the president of Caanon throws our stuff at the proverbial fan, the Seers can corroborate it—at least the planetary genocide. That particular tidbit will emerge later, though, when the pressure on the Chairman has started to mount."

"There's a better reason," put in Tyrees. "It may be enough to panic him into throwing caution to the winds, so don't underestimate the danger to the Tercians, Radis."

"Am I missing something?"

"I hope not. But the Chairman is a shrewd powermonger. He knows what the Tercians are and what they can do. He knows we're on the loose—two ex-Cadre Ones and a Regnum Special Commissioner, not to mention a Battlefleet starship. Should the Seers gather a popular following, as Doctor Bolla predicts, especially with an inaccessible leadership guiding them, the Chairman will ultimately come to the obvious conclusion: a power base."

"Power base?" said Radis under knitted brows. "I thought that . . . what are you . . . ?"

"You wanted to talk about the future. Ask the doctor."

Radis stared at Tyrees for a long moment. The man who gave him back life was still a total mystery, not as a stranger would be, but as unknowable as the fictitious alien. He turned to Bolla, who was fingering one of his jowls.

"Doctor . . . ?"

"You know, when my wife died—"

"*Doctor!*"

"When my wife died—not long before I got into this quixotic affair—the quidities of human behavior interested me less and less. Maybe it was because it just didn't seem to matter as much. Until I met this man." He made an unnecessarily precise, forefingered point at Tyrees. "This man constantly surprises me. Now I simply expect surprise. That's much easier." He sighed.

"So, he's done it again. But yes, I think I know what he's up to. You want it *all*, don't you, Pol?"

Tyrees said nothing, but the blue eyes seemed to deepen and intensify.

"You're not content with enlightening the masses and dumping the Chairman. *You want the Regnum.*"

"Yes."

"The *galaxy* perhaps."

"Yes."

It took a moment before Radis realized how deadly serious both men were. When he did, his heart raced.

"My . . . God. Oh, my God," he breathed.

"God indeed," said Bolla.

Tyrees steepled his hands and looked over them, visiting each man with a slow, scrutinizing wave of blue. It was the taking of a measure, and both knew it; neither knew the results, nor what he wanted them to be. Finally Tyrees lowered his hands and leaned his elbows on his knees. He spoke softly.

"You are both accustomed to . . . large ideas. Especially you, Doctor. Don't let its size daunt you. No, hear me out," he said with a raised hand, as Radis was about to interrupt. "It is a logical extension of our actions now. If we succeed in ousting the Chairman, he will be replaced by his clone—or worse. Bolla said it—the *system* is rotten at its foundations, so nothing would be gained except my revenge." He allowed himself a small smile. "The Trade Wars would escalate even more, and the Regnum would take a long, painful time dying. We have something to replace it.

"There is no alternative, when you think about it. If we should *fail* to exterminate that vermin, we would be dead anyway. So there is no half way. Even now. All that remains is to accept our destiny."

"Large idea, large word—destiny," muttered Bolla.

But by this time Radis had sprouted wings. The man who had given him life now offered him a saint's cause to fly for. "I like it. I like the idea of it."

Though he knew it would soon claim him, too, the "idea" was still too big for Bolla. Besides, he was too old and venerable for quick-winged enthusiasms. He cleared his throat. "Ah, you said we had no alternative, Pol. We do."

"Oh?"

"Yes. The intergalactic pathways."

"Oh." Tyrees looked at the floor like a boy caught with chocolate on his face. "I didn't think you'd even consider that."

"Why not? Find some more women, go a-wandering, begin a brand new utopia somewhere out there in the wild blue yonder. It's an attractive notion."

"Wild *black* yonder, you mean. It did tempt me for a while, but I rejected it because it smacked of escape . . . of death, too—the big escape." He looked up from the floor and smiled at Bolla. "Stop diddling with me, Doctor."

"Come on, Doctor!" said Radis, flying high now. "Why not? Pipes and slippers! Take the pipes and slippers whether you're seven or seventy and . . . and you're finished, *anyway.*"

Bolla nodded indulgently. "Fine sentiment. Laudable. Perhaps even true. But tilting at windmills is still the mark of a fool. I have less to lose—at least in terms of years—than either of you. But I'd rather opt for slippers and a pipe than waste the time I have left on juvenile dreams." He fidgeted in his chair. He seemed, with incongruous swats at the air, to be trying to rid himself of pesky mosquitoes.

"What does Meta-sol think of all this?" he blurted.

"He ignores politics. He cares only about the spread of the New Covenant."

"And your well-being," added Bolla. "Ah, well," he sighed, "in for a penny, in for a pound."

"What?" Radis was irritated by Bolla's perambulations, his withholding of enthusiasm.

"Forget it. An archaism—like me." He sighed again. "All right, Pol, what's the next step toward our divinely ordained destiny?"

"Allies," said Tyrees. "It's time we visited with the ruffians in the Hub."

CHAPTER EIGHT

Condor flew on.

Following the pathways that bent like rainbows out of the Void to chance upon the tiny spiral spray of stars glistening in the darkness, she swung high and wide. Feeling her wings, reveling in them, she swung into one leg high enough to see for the first time how delicate, how beautiful, how alone, was her sparkling home, a few precious, tentative millions of light-years across. The galaxy lay in a deep well of darkness below—a misted jewel, a distant melody whose sweet notes left pangs for fear they would be lost.

Condor ached with the soundsight of its beauty. She was thunderstruck by her need to protect it, by the thought of the ravages with which time would visit such a wisp of butterfly's wing. Driven by that need and that thought, she chose a plummeting rainbow, folded her wings behind her, and dove passionately down the sharp curve toward the densely clustered sparklings at its heart. . . .

At the time *Condor* was stooping to the Hub, she was the subject of intense deliberations on a small planet out on one of the spiral arms. Regnum was the seat of galactic government. It was here the Council sat and the many arms of Regnum law had their source. Their power to hold was eroding, but like the tendrils of a dying and angry monster whose writhings still had deadly potency, they groped for an enemy.

The Chairman sat at the end of the huge slab of mahogany, not in state, but in anger. Everything about him bore the stamp of the bull: massive chest and neck; shoulders that hunched forward when he saw red; powerful, stubby arms; heavy head with a lowered chin and small, pinched eyes.

It was his practice to glower and wait, wait for the shufflings and lowings of the others to place themselves in a head-to-tail circle of bickering recrimination. Then he would lower his chin an extra notch and charge. And charge. And charge. Each was a short burst, horns slashing, the target changing unpredictably. The thrusts were rarely deadly, however; they were meant only to break the skin, inspire fear or panic through the sight of one's own trickling blood.

A very few of the more perceptive among the members of the Council of the Regnum watched carefully for that jaw to slip below the line. It was drawing close, so their silence came sooner than that of the others, and they, too, waited.

"Surely you are overestimating the influence of a few stone-age preachers, Raaf," said a hard-bitten councilwoman laconically. She had mastered the technique of assuming an air of bored but knowing cynicism when those around her grew excited. It had won her a reputation of tough decisiveness and a large following. The Chairman loathed separately each one of the myriad wrinkles that webbed her face. "We've had our mystics before—still do—and in time they always turn out to be ineffectual neurotics."

"But their popularity is growing with unbelievable speed!" cried her antagonist farther down the table. "What they call the New Covenant is becoming a powerful movement!"

"So? People are just fascinated by their origins—the thousand years of isolation from the galaxy, and the Black Hole bit. It'll die like a thousand other fads this year."

"I don't think so. It's already spreading off their base planets like a contagious disease. Every starliner carries a new disciple."

"I still can't see the harm in—"

"Look at the pattern. Every one of those base planets has a record of troublemaking. They're not loyal members."

"You're being alarmist, Raaf. Those—what do they call themselves? *Seers?* They're just spouting some nonsense about 'knowing thyself.' Not even new, let alone seditious."

"Except that their leader *is* a traitor. Self-proclaimed subversive. Ex-Cadre to boot. He's god to them. 'Life-Giver,' they call him, and they tell ridiculous stories about his miraculous powers. Now I call that dangerous, especially when we can't get at him."

"Just a minute, Raaf," came another voice from the Chairman's end of the table. "What did we find out about this character, anyway? Why the big revolt? And how the hell did he get hold of a Battlefleet starship?"

The Chairman's jaw fell another notch, but all that followed was a slight turn of his head, allowing him to take in the figure immediately to his right. Black cape. Solid black piping on the high collar indicating the highest possible rank—which held one man: the Cadre Proctor. He spoke curtly.

"I can't tell you any more about Tyrees than we knew a month ago. On Tercet he became a convert, then a Seer. He renounced the Cadre. He was joined there by ex-Councilman Leeth, who apparently was mounting some sort of opposition to this council. As you know, he was accompanied by Doctor Hans Bolla, the Special Commissioner. A Battlefleet vessel was sent to investigate, but too late. Leeth and his ship were later destroyed when he refused a boarding party and fired on one of ours.

"As for the capture of *Condor*, two reasons: an incompetent captain, and another defection—Officer Radis, Cadre One." The Proctor offered no apologies or explanations for the unthinkable actions of two of his officers, but cold outrage was stamped on his face. Another querulous voice came hard upon the last of his words.

"But *why*, damn it! *Two* of them. I've never even *heard* of a Cadre One turning before now."

The Chairman spoke before the Proctor could. His chin had dropped to his chest, and his small, ball-bearing eyes stared out from beneath jungle-thick eyebrows, like a viper's from its hole.

"I'll tell you why," he said, voice low and menacing. "The *time* has come. With the Trade Wars gnawing at our innards, the time has come for the snakes to crawl out from under their rocks because they think they can coil around our soft spots while we fight a life-and-death battle in the Hub."

"You are absolutely right, Mr. Chairman," said the councilwoman enthusiastically. "The Trade Wars are the overwhelming priority. Tyrees and the Tercians are just a sad bunch of yowling misfits who seized an opportunity. Not worth wasting our resources on now."

"And you are absolutely *wrong*, Councilwoman Sheek." First charge, first blood. "They're *inside* us. Like parasites, like worms. Only an idiot would fail to see it. They work on people's *minds*, for God's sake! They're hypnotizers who nibble away at beliefs and values and thoughts! They're carrion who feed upon blood and souls. . . . No, I don't hesitate to use the word—*souls*."

Councilwoman Sheek fell back in her chair, one arm across her meager breasts as if she had literally caught a horn. Her influence was such that the bull rarely took a swing in her direction. The issue must be important to him—or he had seen a red flag.

"Mr. Chairman," she gasped, "surely you don't—"

"I don't ignore sparks that could turn into a holocaust. Listen." Now the lowered head began to cast slowly, the hard round eyes taking all of them in. "They preach selfhood. Ego-centred individualism. Everything that denies the spirit of community that keeps the Regnum alive. Tolerate them now, and you will regret it as you would regret harboring the cubs of a wolf."

The Council was amazed at the vehemence of his attack. Even Raaf, who had taken a similar position, was taken aback. The more thoughtful among them were doubly disturbed because with each new crisis, the Chairman was able to gather more powers to himself— already, his prerogatives were becoming kingly. To oppose him too strenuously brought their patriotism into question.

One of that small group spoke up. "You imply strong measures, Mr. Chairman. What did you have in mind?"

"For the Seers—immediate arrest. Detention, that's all."

"The charge?"

"Treason."

"It won't stick."

"Without a trial."

"Oh . . . you realize that's illegal, of course."

"Emergency Measures—so stipulated by this Council."

Councilwoman Sheek, still smarting from the Chairman's cut, wanted some of her own back. She had two qualities the others lacked: total disregard for consequences once she set upon a course of action, and total fearlessness. She used her quietest, most cynical tone.

"Mr. Chairman. Should the Council grant Emergency Measures—an absurd piece of overkill, I assure you—and those preachers are locked away, you will achieve precisely the opposite of what you intend." The Chairman's chin remained dangerously low, but there were many small nods around the table.

"I beg your pardon?" he murmured.

"Martyrdom," she intoned. "You might as well kill them."

The Chairman was forced to witness the rare phenomenon of momentum gathering against him. There was a crucial moment when he gripped the arms of his chair and it looked as if his next charge would be literal; it passed, however, when Councilwoman Sheek demonstrated some uncharacteristic diplomacy.

"*Condor* is another matter, Mr. Chairman. They are proven criminals and out of the public eye. I don't think you need trouble yourself or the Council with the niceties of *their* disposal. Religions are full of dead gods, eh?"

CHAPTER NINE

Condor had come to rest in the Hub, where the night skies shone with a profligacy of stars. As if in a fit of spendthrift joy—or perhaps it was anger at the screaming blackness—the Maker had cast vast handfuls of those most precious of cosmic gems into the Void. Their rich and colorful light filled the hearts of *Condor*'s small band with new hope and new resolve. Such splendor inspired a sense of destiny, and they—each privately—were beginning to think without embarrassment in precisely those terms.

She was in a severely elliptical orbit around Kang-gor, the seat of a small, young empire of a few dozen planetary systems loosely allied to buttress their defiance of the Regnum. *Condor*'s orbit was swift, and stretched into a long, flattened egg so that she could approach Kang-gor's star in some safety, fire a message burst, and retreat to allow the receiver time to consider. These were paranoic times in the Hub, which was in constant flux and warring internally as well as against the Regnum, so the nature of their reception was not predictable. Kang-gor had been chosen, however, because of her relative stability, and because she had emerged as the closest thing to a leader that the Hub could boast of.

Condor's message told them the basic story of their recent history and requested a meeting to discuss common goals. The problem was *Condor* herself—one of a half-dozen Regnum vessels requiring a generation to design and

74

construct as an interstellar fortress of massive destructive capability. She was not a machine that encouraged trust.

They were wheeling around the tight curve a light-day from Kang-gor and heading back. Mariet was in the command chair, keyed up by the role he was finally playing—every boy's fantasy, but his especially. A Transport captain might possess the skills and the knowledge to live such a dream, but never the opportunity. In the months since Tercet, he had made *Condor* his baby, and he ached like a loving, usurped nanny when Tyrees sat in the chair to guide her along the pathways.

"How long?" asked Bolla, who was sharing one side of the chair with Radis. He directed the question at Tyrees on the other side, but it was Mariet who answered.

"I'm decelerating, to make us less threatening. We can take a message in . . . just a few minutes. At least an hour before anything hostile is possible physically. Does anyone know what these characters possess in the way of defense?"

"Plenty of armament, certainly," said Radis. "No idea what they're carrying it around in. Probably transports like your *Reacher*—modified, of course. Nothing like *Condor*, but numbers alone can make up the difference."

"We'll know soon, if they decide to get cute," said Mariet.

He swiveled slightly in the direction of the space technic in charge of the console devoted almost exclusively to *Condor*'s offensive weaponry. It was a complex system involving every kind of projectile from light to sound waves as well as conventional missiles—all further complicated by subsystems that controlled targeting, tracking, firing, and field-media selection. It was perhaps the most difficult of *Condor*'s functions that Mariet and his crew had to master. They seemed confident, even delighted with the sophisticated gadgetry, as only spacecrew tinkerers could be. Bolla, who knew best the capricious literal-mindedness of even the mega-byte machines, felt less assured. The ex-Cadre Ones worried about the unpredictable behavior of men who had never fired a shot in anger, let alone stood in one's path. Nevertheless, in spite of the sprung-tight tension Tyrees read in their bodies, Mariet's men shared their captain's bright eagerness.

"FIRECOM."

"Yes, sir."

"Readiness Report."

"Yes, sir. Four laser cannon bearable—ready, but not targeted, maximum range. Two vibrarifles set, defensive frequency, intermediate range. Twelve short-range photon missiles brought to subreadiness, unarmed. Shields up, half power."

Mariet's response was immediate, decisive. His wired greyhound of a body pointed like a dog born—though not trained—for the hunt. There was a new burning in his eyes, kept aglow by the volatile chemical mix of fear and glee.

"Arm the missiles. Bring the shields to full power—we've decelerated enough for it. Compute for multidirectional attack."

"Yes, sir . . . missiles . . . armed. Multidirectional . . . in. Shields are . . . shields won't come full, sir. About ninety percent."

Mariet spun the chair angrily with his spidery legs. "NAVCOM!" The word was a squeaky scream.

Tyrees frowned and opened his mouth to speak, but Bolla's hand on his elbow stopped him. They exchanged looks, and Tyrees nodded reluctantly.

"Sir?"

Mariet took a moment to regain composure. "Status report."

"Still decelerating, sir. Rate—point zero five lights per hour."

The captain, very slowly, half rose from the command chair. "NAVCOM, the order was point zero five *five* lights. Do you have the smallest notion—*any idea*—what an error like that could mean in our situation?"

"I . . . I . . . sorry, sir." The technic was having trouble breathing. "I must have . . ."

Mariet settled back into the chair and took a deep breath. "All right, all right. I should have confirmed. We are not yet a battlecrew." Then he did something that impressed the worried trio around the chair. He smiled. "But if we live long enough, we're going to be." Nervous titters filled the bridge. "Reset zero point five five, if you please.

FIRECOM." He swung back. "Let shield power build to max."

A long silence followed. In spite of the break in tension, every man on the bridge thought upon the terrible fragility of their grandiose dream—one that could be shattered by mishearing a single, silly little number. No one thought about it with more anxiety than Pol Tyrees. He stepped off the dais that elevated the chair and walked to the observation bubble in a dark corner of the bridge.

Bolla took careful note of the action. He had watched the naturally reserved Tyrees in the last few weeks—amidst the awesome loneliness of deep space, where most men craved the tender balm only a woman could bestow—fall away, withdraw into that infinitely isolated limbo inside. It was a place of dark, forbidding comfort that Bolla had come to know, with the help of Meta-sol, as a night crawler fearfully peeping through small cracks along its perimeter. Tantalizing. Dangerous. He suspected that Radis felt something similar. It was a barrier—a frontier—that, like some of the legends of ancient magic, seemed to bring a curse with its knowledge. He sensed, out there at the furthermost periphery, a soft, alluring boom—a pulse, a chant—heaving forth the same, irresistible message over and over and over.

Power . . . Power . . . Power . . . Power . . .

Was that pulse akin to the thrum of the web strands felt by the tremulous, virginal male spider? Bolla didn't know, and he didn't know if he wanted to know.

But Meta-sol had been inside, and he was no monster. One must, after all, only meet oneself . . . one's self. Self.

"UI's! UI's! Three . . . no five! Five UI's—four quadrants, sir!"

The cry from SCANCOM broke Bolla's anxious reverie. Tyrees returned to the command chair on the run. Mariet again began to rise from the chair; then, as if touched suddenly by some divine hand, he settled back and actually crossed his legs. He assumed an aspect of noble boredom, looked from under half-lowered eyelids down his long nose at SCANCOM, and spoke laconically.

"Please complete your report, SCANCOM."

"Uh, yessir. Five unidentifieds. Maximum scanning range. We're targeted. Wide funnel approach. Collision speed . . . zero point nine one light. Still out of firing range, perhaps . . . six minutes."

"Thank you, SCANCOM. Stand by." The captain rubbed his nose idly as he thought. "Hmmph," he said conversationally. "Must have projected our orbit—setting up an ambush even before they could see us."

The maneuver was straight from the book for superior numbers against a single, more powerful enemy: the lines of attack formed a wide, shallow funnel descending on the target. The tactic allowed them the widest possible dispersal while at the same time concentrating their power without the possibility of getting caught in their own lines of fire.

"So much for our friendly message," muttered Bolla. "Should we run?"

"We don't run unless we have to," said Tyrees. "We've been running long enough." Bolla was startled at the depth of bitterness in the voice. "What are our chances, Captain?"

Mariet looked at Tyrees coolly. He seemed to take pleasure from his newfound calm, delivering a studied answer while the nerves of Bolla and the bridge crew jumped with each tick of the clocks in their heads.

"Hmmm. Two variables there, I think. Difficult to estimate the capacities of those hybrids coming at us—my guess is that they've concentrated on improving firepower because speed, defensive mechanisms, and so on, would require radical changes in the basic transport design. Not probable. In which case, we eat them for breakfast.

"The more serious concern is their desire." Mariet smiled his two-toothed smile. "If they *really* want our hides, they can probably get them. At the cost of at least three of their five bumblebees."

"Laser cannon, sir! A shot from each of the five!"

Mariet blinked rapidly, but there was no other change in his demeanor. "Thank you, SCANCOM—stand by. . . . You see, gentlemen? They've increased their firing range somewhat. . . . NAVCOM."

"Sir!"

"Cut deceleration, release engine power. FIRECOM."

"Yessir!"

"Put all available power into the shields, please."

"Yes, sir. Firing orders, sir?"

"Stand by, FIRECOM. . . . Well, gentlemen? We can still show them our tails."

Tyrees slammed the chair arm with his fist, increasing the frequency of Mariet's blinks. "Our message—they simply didn't believe it. Send them a more dramatic one."

Mariet inclined his head. "Beg pardon?"

"Can we take those five shots?"

"Yes . . . probably. Damn little more, though."

"Take them, then. If they keep coming on, take *out* one of their ships. Only one. Then wait."

Bolla did not like what he was hearing. "Pol! These are human lives, not chess pawns! We can get away—without bloodshed—and try . . ."

"No." Tyrees turned his eyes on Bolla with a blue burn. "Read your own work, Doctor. 'The more passive the action, the less significant the results.' Your words. Do it, Captain."

Before Mariet could do anything, *Condor* convulsed. She was struck by a tremor so deep and violent that her passengers felt it to the roots of their teeth. The silent vibrations strummed at their eardrums, too, forcing them to open their mouths and work their jaws around the pain. It subsided in a few seconds.

"Damn it, SCANCOM!" yelled Mariet. "Don't you have the sense to warn us?"

"Sorry, sir, I . . ."

"Never mind. FIRECOM, how are the shields?"

"Down to twenty-five percent, sir. Rebuilding now."

"SCANCOM. Those ships exactly the same?"

"Uh, no, sir. One is somewhat larger."

"Coordinates?"

"Point zero zero seven slash, nine point one four slash, three three point one zero nine."

"Lock in, FIRECOM. A whole cannon salvo—now."

"Yessir," said the nervous technic. "But the power—I won't be able to build the shields back until—"

"Now!"

"Yessir . . . salvo of five . . . ."

There was a series of rapid clicks as he set the program and unleashed electrons into the invisible channels that unlocked the firing key. Even then he could not send the salvo—enough destructive energy to mutilate the face of a coastline—by himself. His efficient fingers flew over the touch pads for a few seconds before a light came on his board and a soft beep oozed from the walls of the entire bridge. A key cover began to flash. The hand that lifted it and settled on the key was steady—the voice was not.

"Ready, sir."

Mariet swallowed, the prominent Adam's apple bobbing half the length of his turkey's neck. He hesitated only a second before flipping another cover on his armrest and turning a key.

"Fire."

"Fire," repeated the technic, turning his own key. The beeping stopped. "Salvo's gone, sir."

Though the bridge crew knew it would be several minutes before anything could happen, all eyes went to the screen, where five winking blips formed an almost perfect pentagon. "Which one?" someone whispered.

"Watch your consols!" roared Mariet. "You're not bloody cargo boosters anymore, you're soldiers! Keep discipline or you won't be for long."

White faces looked at the captain for a moment like so many chastised and frightened children, then fell to their boards. Illumined from below by the instrument lights, the faces became ghostly, disembodied. They had let fly a spear at a killer prowling in the darkness, but there was no grunt of release, would be no cry of pain or spurt of blood should their spear strike home. Only a dying light. Soldiers they might be, but the newly proven, blooded warrior remembered in their genes could not surface here. Somehow that made it more frightening.

"Can they evade?" asked Tyrees.

"Too late already, I think," said Mariet. "*Condors* they're not."

"Will they fire again?"

"They can't—not laser cannon. They don't have the

power and they won't be able to regenerate until long after
our shot.''

"Our target—can its shields—"

"Against our salvo?" Mariet smirked. "Like a turtle
under a sledgehammer." Bolla winced. "But don't take
my word for it. How long now, SCANCOM?"

"Should be right about . . ." One of the blips on the
screen flared and disappeared. The technic's voice faltered. ". . . now, s-sir."

So it was that the first blood was let by the movement
already known as the New Covenant. A few dozen lives,
perhaps, probably insignificant even in the human scheme
of things; certainly so in terms of their mark on the Void
they fought in. There were no riven bodies, no grotesque-
ries of bone and viscera, no terrible death throes or cries of
agony. In a measureless instant they simply became part of
the great nothing.

The men around the command chair were affected in
very different ways. Tyrees and Radis had killed before,
and found no zest in it; but the scale was larger this time
and the deaths more a function of choice than duty. Tyrees
stood in the semidarkness rigidly, blue eyes aflame—to
him it was, finally, a prisoner's first strike back at a
jailer/torturer. More obscurely, it was also his claim to a
right to be—to become—whatever he was meant to be.

Radis had been virtually silent through the engagement,
and still remained aloof. His training demanded silence in
a crisis unless words could make a difference. To him it
meant two clear, simple things: necessary evil in a worthy
cause; and an unequivocal loyalty to the man who had
given him a second life.

To Bolla it was the headlong fall of a nightmare. No
feeling man's contact with death can be mundane, but
Bolla's life had not been that of an ordinary man. He
thought of the uncounted times he had used superscripted
figures to number snuffed out lives— real or probable—for
his calculations, his projections, his theories. Games. Silly,
blind, cocoon-wrapped games. Who could justify death?
What could justify death?

To Mariet it was vindication—pride, glory. Victory. His

beaver smile was back because part of the victory was over his own fears and uncertainties.

"One bandit down," he said matter-of-factly. "Shields, FIRECOM?"

"Forty percent, sir. Building."

"Watch for changes, SCANCOM."

"Yes, sir."

"What they do now should tell the tale."

"Can we take a four-shot salvo?" asked a shaky Bolla.

"Probably not, but we'll see one soon enough to evade . . . I think, but with this collision speed, the field is reducing rapidly."

"Cut speed, then," said Tyrees. "Give them time to think."

"That's deceleration. The shields—"

"We're delivering a *message*, Captain—'We can destroy you, but we'd rather talk.' "

"The first part of the message isn't true," Mariet replied. "We can't take them all."

"They've had ample evidence to think it's true. Cut and run now, and we've just killed a lot a people for nothing."

Mariet looked at Tyrees as if he had just realized for the first time what a blip vanishing from a screen meant.

"Full deceleration, NAVCOM."

"Yes, sir."

Condor's passengers could feel nothing, but off the pathways—where only conventional speed and power were possible—a nuclear fusion engine, the most powerful ever built by man, was tearing space apart to slow her dive towards the Hub vessels.

Radis put a hand on Tyrees's shoulder.

"You have a suggestion, Radis?"

Radis nodded. "Repeat our other message—the verbal one."

"Yes . . . of course. Captain?"

"TELCOM, send—"

"Sir!" The cry came from SCANCOM. "Simultaneous cannon fire. Salvo of four!"

"Evasive action!" screamed Mariet. "NAVCOM, evasive action!"

Condor had been decelerating in the manner of a hawk

with wings fighting a ripping wind to break her dive at sea level; now she was called upon to bank away—a maneuver requiring a parsec's distance—and her dropping speed made that an excruciatingly slow process.

SCANCOM was counting down. "Nine seconds, eight, seven . . ."

"Send that message burst!" hissed Tyrees.

"G-gone!" stuttered TELCOM.

"Three, two . . ."

A quake hit *Condor* for the second time—stronger. Had one come, none of the bridge crew could have carried out an order because the vibration rattled their fingers over their boards like epilepsy. Teeth clattered together and chipped. Tensed muscles were torn at socket joints. Many of *Condor*'s circuits snapped closed, and the lighting wavered. FIRECOM's technic screamed and fell from his chair, hands clawing at the sides of his head as his eardrums burst. His nose was bleeding. Those who had been standing around the command chair were writhing on the floor.

Only Mariet's pain was tempered—because he realized that with each passing second their chances of survival were increased.

When it was over, the bridge was strewn with traumatized bodies in various stages of shock, but Tyrees was at the FIRECOM console hollering at Mariet.

"The shields are gone. Captain! Release the fire switch. Captain! . . . Bolla, Radis . . . somebody! Release the fire switch!"

Radis was the only one capable of willed movement. He hauled himself off the deck using the command chair arm like a spent swimmer scrabbling at a rock. Mariet was still sitting, moaning and weakly waving something away from his face with limp and fluttering fingers.

Radis was fighting with the fire-key cover when the message beep came.

"Hold it!" Tyrees leaped over bodies and pushed the semiconscious TELCOM technic roughly to the side. He hit the Receive pad.

A beautiful woman appeared on the screen. A . . . beautiful, beautiful . . . woman.

"*Condor*," she said, "this is *Spacehawk*. I am Shaamlik. You are unscathed. We have lost our flagship. We accept your message and ask that you cease fire and accept impasse. We request a parley. Please acknowledge."

Her hair flowed loose and long like honeyed water. Her mouth and forehead were full and wide and handsome. Her eyes were deep and black and lustrous. Her words were chips of ice.

"Well . . . shit," said Radis.

Tyrees hit Send/Audio Only, knowing that the Hub ships could not fire again soon and there was no point in displaying the condition of the bridge crew.

"This is *Condor*. I am Pol-Nesol-Rast, Seer of the Gathering. I acknowledge your message. A pity you did not acknowledge mine, for the blood of your brothers will forever disturb your dreams. We will talk in peace only when you bring your vessels to rest. My lieutenants will discuss details with you then. Come in innocence."

Tyrees tapped the End Transmission pad without signaling off. Radis and Bolla had recovered sufficiently to regard him with mouths agape. Almost without thinking, he had adopted the formalized and lofty language of the Tercian Seer and their holy book, *The Teraac*. Now that he was finished, he felt sheepish, but decided his intuition was valid; it would strike the Kang-gorians as strange, but more impressive. Besides, he enjoyed the poetic cadences and metaphors of Tercian rhetoric.

"The prophet cometh," said Bolla, raising eyebrows under a large welt on his forehead. But his sarcastic tone fell short of purity.

Radis only smiled broadly and nodded. "Good technique. You sounded just like Meta-sol." He turned to the still form of Mariet sprawled in the command chair. "We'd better get the good captain back into shape and mop up around here before we play prophet for our touchy friends, though."

"We can not prepare for such things."

The soft voice came from the entrance of the bridge. They looked up to see Meta-sol standing there, leaning more heavily than usual on his cane, smiling more sadly than usual behind the white filaments of beard.

"Huh? Of course we can, Meta-sol," said Radis, misunderstanding his words. "We . . . is there something wrong?"

"Yes . . . it has always been . . . wrong. We were made for it, but we were not made to . . . *prepare* for it. I do not know why."

He moved toward them, his cane held tentatively half up its shaft, like a noble soldier in defeat offering up his sword. His blind eyes stared fearfully at the black screen with its four tiny blips of light. His free hand emerged from under the shawl, also tentatively, and touched Tyrees on the sleeve.

"We have . . . caused many people to die?"

Tyrees hesitated, then he, too, looked at the screen. "Yes, Meta-sol."

"Yes . . . It allows no preparation." His hand moved from Tyrees to rest gently on Mariet's arm, which hung like a scarecrow's out of the command chair.

"Your captain is also dead."

CHAPTER TEN

Captain Mariet received the spacefarer's equivalent of a burial at sea. The medic pronounced the cause of death to be a massive coronary, which Bolla found morbidly ironic. Given his age and obesity, that was his pet fear—and this relatively young bone-and-gristle man had succumbed to it.

The crew had formed a strong attachment to their fussy, waspish captain, something they would not have admitted when he was alive. Tyrees felt his absence in a peculiar way. He had watched the man growing quickly from a whining bureaucrat into a decisive, daring leader—though that process had been cut short. Mariet himself had just begun to make the discovery of this metamorphosis, and for the first time in his life was beginning to feel a pride that was unaffected. Had he died earlier, there would have been less reason for feeling a sense of loss. Perhaps that was enough. Mariet might think so. Amen.

The meeting with the beautiful Shaamlik had taken place aboard *Condor*. She appeared with a voluptuous body and a burnt-crust expression. It turned out that her command of the Kang-gor fleet had been a field promotion because her admiral had perished with the ship *Condor* destroyed. It also turned out that she was the daughter of the Baron Mace, ruler of the young empire. She was in constant communication with her father, and a second meeting was set up to take place on Kang-gor itself two days later.

Tyrees did not take part in the negotiations; they were conducted by Bolla and Radis, who acted the part of trusted lieutenants dedicated to a cause and awed by their leader. The acting came easy because most of it grew untended in their hearts anyway.

Tyrees spent that time with Meta-sol—a time of searching and struggle for both. Each was alone on the brink of things, astride the sharp edge of perilous decision where past experience was a net that no longer looked secure, no longer promised safety. In consequence, Meta-sol clung to old values that had never before been threatened—and to his instinct; Tyrees clung to the certainty that he must be allowed to follow the path of his own burgeoning—and to his instinct.

"Do you understand fully what is going on, Meta-sol?"

Meta-sol sighed deeply. He ran fingers that were no longer supple, no longer so clean of the usual signs of age, over his burnished cane. He had been the master—in every sense of the word but physical strength—back on Tercet when he'd seen in this man a miraculous power, something . . . incredibly packed with . . . what every man *should* possess but never did. Unrecognized, untapped, undeveloped—unknown. Now, already, in this place, at this time, he was no longer the master, and he was afraid. He still believed with a passion that no man whose passion is tied to the senses can know—that Pol-Nesol-Rast was the test gift sent to mankind to determine their worthiness for the privilege of continuation. He also believed that the outcome depended less on Tyrees himself than on how his own received and shaped him. So, like all true saints, he was filled with the terror of uncertainty; like all true saints, he would not allow uncertainty to paralyze him.

"No. I do not understand . . . fully. In the galaxy, in this ocean of blackness specked with the light of many suns, Tercet is a grain of sand. We accomplished much there . . . so much. Desert tribes with no thought but to live . . . to live. Only animals. Strong and noble . . . animals. The first Seers and *The Teraac*, they brought us . . . light." Meta-sol's fingers shuddered slightly on his cane. Then they gripped it, hard. Eyelids that never had reason to close, closed tightly, shutting out a light more painful than any darkness.

"But we, we and our thoughts are so . . . *small*!"

"Meta-sol—"

"And you, Pol-Nesol-Rast, are our child, and I do not know what you . . . have become."

The emotions that charged softly through the heart of Pol Tyrees were as ancient as those burning through the breast of the first son yearning for understanding from the first father. To him they were just as new, and perhaps more agonizing, because he had had the rare privilege of *choosing* his father.

"You disapprove of the . . . deaths."

Meta-sol nodded, his head bobbing up and down like a chip of wood on windblown water. But he stopped abruptly. "No, Pol. No one can keep his mind . . . flowing, and disapprove of the inevitable. No, not the deaths. The killings."

"Killings?"

"*Willed*, Pol of the hidden stars. The willed taking of life, as if it had little value, as if the takings of the Black Hole were not enough."

"Tyrees bridled. "The Kang-gor ship? I did not will it, Meta-sol."

The old man resumed nodding, his head almost tapping the head of his cane. "No? Whose will was it, then? The Maker's?"

Tyrees winced at the sarcasm—a turn of mind very foreign to Meta-sol. The Tercian Seer is learning from *us* now, he thought.

"Theirs," he replied. "Did you imagine that the New Covenant would come about gratuitously? Without blood?"

"I imagined that it would come about without blood . . . on *your* hands."

Tyrees stood. He whirled and strode to the door. But before leaving he looked back at the one man yet alive who could touch him deeply with anything but anger.

"I am only a man," he said.

CHAPTER ELEVEN

As planets go, Kang-gor was opulently rich. Her defiance of the Regnum many years earlier had begun because she could not tolerate a paternalistic system that enshrined the status quo and attempted to regulate her into mediocrity. She demanded, and had won at some cost, the right to grow as she would. She was consistent enough to allow those who joined her empire the same right, so long as they shared her defiance. As planets go, she was young and filled with the headstrong self-importance of youth, and she was led by a man whose personality shouted out the qualities of the rebel: bellicose, passionate, daring, iconoclastic, avaricious. His name was a single syllable, a fist of sound—Mace. Of middle years, physically and spiritually robust, he was consumed less by power itself than by a sense of what was possible when it throbbed in his hand. He was a buccaneer whose goals would forever lack hard definition because it was the striving, the movement rather than the direction, to which he was addicted.

As *Condor* circled his world, a bird hovering for a worm, Mace entertained her strange and lethal masters.

Tyrees sat aloof, a high priest in confident possession of immortality. He was garbed in a simple black tunic that kept reminding Mace of the Cadre—his most potent enemy and this man's spawning ground. What he had been hearing about Tyrees from beyond the Hub—even before *Condor* pierced Kang-gor's bubble of space—was variously con-

fusing and incredible. His spies sent news of a growing fad
among the populace, a religion called the New Covenant
whose apostles were supposed to possess miraculous powers and whose founder could actually bring the dead back
to life. There had been stories about Cadre rebels (unthinkable by itself!) capturing a Battlefleet warship and causing
the Chairman to ignore the Trade Wars with his maniacal
effort to find and destroy them. There were rumors of
documented evidence circulating in high places of outrageous crimes committed by the Chairman himself.

In most of it, sometimes buried in trivia or literally as
part of a footnote, the name Tyrees popped up. It happened with such subtle regularity that it took a computer
data analysis to make the correlation and flag him for
further investigation.

Now *Condor* was here. Now *he* was here. What the hell
was he? What did he want? Could that original message be
believed? Simply an enemy of the Regnum looking for
allies? Mace was certain of only one thing—that killer
machine a few thousand miles over his head could rip
Kang-gor open like a hawk on a mouse.

Tyrees had shown little inclination to talk, but the other
two did. The fat one especially. No fool, though. No fool.
Insane story. Crazy. Grandson of a Cadre Proctor. Tercet.
Alien hoax. Planetary genocide (he'd believe anything of
the Chairman). Seers? *Condor*. The New Covenant. Radis,
ex-Cadre One as well (believable—he did have all the
earmarks).

Out of the corner of his eye Mace could see his daughter, still smarting from her defeat in space, but listening
intently. He was proud of her courage, but soon she would
have to admit responsibility for the loss of their flagship:
her tactics had been too impetuous. He noted that while
she listened, she never took her eyes off Tyrees. Just as
well. He always made it a careful point to be honest with
himself—and he was afraid of that man. The more he
heard, credible or not, the more he was afraid. He had a
sickening premonition that the flux of things was about to
turn and carry him away.

The fat man, speaking affably—an uncle with the best
of intentions—was finishing the story.

"So you see, we had no choice but to fire on your ship. I assure you, your losses would have been much greater were our intentions not exactly as we have stated them. We want you to join us."

Bolla folded his hands over his paunch and settled back with a benign smile. Mace shifted in his chair, staring at his well-shod feet. He twirled a ring around his pinky finger; it clutched a diamond the size of an acorn, which flashed with each revolution. The silence was drawing thin before his head lifted to take in his three closest advisors. They sat stiffly, like reluctant eavesdroppers, at the periphery of the group. As his hard eyes rose, theirs fell. He snorted and turned to his daughter.

"Shaamlik? Are we hearing the truth?"

Shaamlik still gazed at Tyrees, who seemed oblivious to her and everyone else. She placed her index finger on the tip of her nose and moved it slowly up and down its long, perfect bridge. Then, with equal slowness, she nodded.

"I think . . . so," she said. "But how *much* of it are we hearing?"

Mace stopped twirling the ring and cocked his neck at Tyrees. "What if I just reject you out of hand? What happens then?" He pointed the bejeweled little finger upwards.

Radis answered. "*Condor* is our protection, not our threat."

"What *is* your threat then?"

"We have none."

"Oh? I simply say no and you go on your merry . . ."

"We have a threat," said Tyrees quietly. Everyone in the room was startled. He spoke as if to himself. "We have a path to follow. It is clear before us. The light brought by the New Covenant grows in brightness each hour. Those who do not follow will suffer a darkness of their own making."

Mace's fear jumped a notch higher. He was certain these were the words of a mad zealot.

"You may find *yourselves* in darkness," he said harshly. "I can have you killed now and take whatever your space monster can dish out. We'll survive in the end." He rose, not knowing whether or not he was bluffing.

"Please, Father." Shaamlik held up a cautionary hand. "Please." Slowly, gingerly, Mace sat again. "You condemn us with 'darkness,' Mr. Tyrees. Be specific. Darkness is . . .?"

"Ignorance. A place which allows no survival."

Mace's nerves were stretched to the point where his response was totally spontaneous. He laughed. It was pitched high and shrieked with uncertain relief; it whooped with fear and ridicule, and continued until he was gasping for air.

"Sit still," said Tyrees as Mace raised a hand to wipe his eyes.

"Whaa . . . ?"

"Do not move, please."

The tone took obedience for granted—and Mace obeyed, lowering the hand to his lap. "Look, I've had just—"

"Do not speak."

Once again, Mace obeyed. He sought Tyrees's eyes and realized that the man was staring at his ring. He, too, looked down at it, irked by his own compliance. The stone was brilliant, dazzling with light, and the ring beneath it . . . grew warm . . . warmer . . . warmer . . . hot!

"Aggghhh!"

Mace tore at his finger, frantically trying to remove the ring. Tyrees's voice cut through his hysteria because he was hearing it with his mind rather than his ears.

"No. Do not be afraid. There will be no more pain. Calm yourself."

Mace fell in upon himself like a man taking a stunning blow to the head. Breathing deeply, he sagged into the chair; the diamond dangled between his legs, danced to the tremble of his hand.

They all watched. The terrible concentration of those coldly burning eyes. Violent blue. Violating blue. Blue also was the fire that began to erupt from the diamond on Mace's finger. Tongues of white-blue light shot out and up, flared into walls and ceiling and pale, disbelieving faces. The room became a fishbowl of mad, flaring energy—bulleting, chaotic ricochets of trapped light spears boomeranging into an intensity that threatened to tease out, unleash the wild, kindred pulses closed fearfully in the darkness behind the watchers' eyes.

"Pol!" screamed Bolla.

The lightnings died suddenly. The Kang-gors were so frightened and disoriented that they didn't notice Tyrees slumping. He was ash gray, and would have fallen from his chair had not Radis leaped over quickly to hold him with a hand on his shoulder.

One of Mace's advisors was on his knees, hands clasped in desperate fervor. "Oh, oh, ohhhh," he cried.

Radis bent over Tyrees, cutting out the others' view. Bolla recaptured his look of benign solicitude, got to his feet, and stepped to the group's center with arms outstretched.

"Please, don't be afraid. Everyone is quite all right, I trust? I apologize for the . . . drama, but I'm sure you understand. Pol . . . Pol-Nesol-Rast knows how difficult it is to accept on . . . on faith alone, yes? We will take our leave now, to give you time for discussion and deliberation." He bowed deeply. "Take all the time you wish. We await your pleasure."

With that, he turned to his companions. Tyrees was already standing, but supported unobtrusively by Radis. They left quickly. Mace was gazing with stupefaction at the raised blisters around the ring on his little finger. His shock obliterated the pain he knew must be there. And the diamond was *black*.

"My God," he said. "My God."

"He *is*!" whispered the advisor, who was still on his knees, shaking now. He wrung his clasped hands, and his mouth became a rictus. Shaamlik rose, strode forward, and struck him full in the face with a wide, robust, open-handed blow that shattered their collective awe and toppled the man to the floor, where he mewed quietly.

"A magician, perhaps," she said calmly, turning her back on the others. "But a man to be reckoned with, Father."

Mace nodded, though he could not take his eyes away from the ring. "How . . . how could he do that?"

"What does it matter?" With an abstracted toss of her head, Shaamlik threw a soft billow of silk-smoked hair back over one shoulder. Her less than average size, the soft, sensuous curves of thigh and hip and breast and mouth, were obscured—like a finely etched postage stamp canceled with a smear of bureaucratic ink—by the captain's uniform and her air of cold command. At this moment, however, some of the lush wonder suggested by her body crept unbidden into her voice.

"What does it matter? He's more than . . . than a bag of cute tricks. He . . . he's going to make things happen, Father. That man is stamped out for something special." She walked to a window and looked out.

Mace was finally able to take his eyes from the ring. He stared at her back for a long time. "Get out!" he shouted.

Two of the advisors scrambled for the exit, hindered by the necessity of half dragging the third. Mace continued to stare at his daughter's back, his face suddenly older, sadder—the face of a man who has accomplished much, but recognizes the nether end of stretched limitations and takes the measure of heights above him that he had never imagined were there.

He sighed. "If we follow him, Shaamlik, the Chairman will do no more diplomatic dancing, no more fainting or blustering or shadowboxing. The gloves will come off. Regnum law has always been a shrine that he had to bow before in public, but if we take up with this man, the Trade Wars will turn into one killing, blood-spilling mess— law be damned. I've just realized why things have been so comfortable lately for us. He's after something more dangerous—something that scares the shit out of him. He's after that man."

Shaamlik looked at her father in a way that no one had dared look in many years. "So," she said. "So. The man who once had the gut to give the finger to a galactic tyranny now *shrivels* when the bets are all called in? Are you afraid of the Chairman—or of *him*?"

Mace opened his mouth to say words that would blow her back like a leaf before a storm, as he had in the past. Instead the mouth closed and his eyes began to water. He swiped at them. With weak anger he swiped at them like a child pushing away tears.

After a time he turned away from her, but spoke in an even timber. "No. I am not afraid of him—at least not as a man." His voice was so low and tentative that Shaamlik turned from the window and moved closer to listen, because in spite of a newfound and burning need that was a surprise even to her, she was hearing a tone from her father that was never there before. "I'm afraid of . . . of losing hold of things. Control . . . keeps me alive, I guess. Second fiddle . . . *He's* the one now. I feel old, Shaamlik."

She was disappointed. Ashamed. "Shit," she said.

"Shaamlik?"

"Take a rest, Father. *Follow* for a change. Join him."

She headed for the wide, impressive doorway, but turned on her heel at its threshold, an actress delivering a last order to a makeup lady. She smiled radiantly, graciously, and cocked her head.

"On the condition that I go with him. *Condor* needs a captain."

CHAPTER TWELVE

Condor flew on. For a long time she ranged the Hub, and her cause gathered momentum. It helped that the largest faction among the rebel worlds—Kang-gor—was already an ally, and that a Kang-gorian was her Captain. Shaamlik flew *Condor* as if the mammoth plasteel bird were horse-flesh between her knees, as if skill and intuition were one.

The hybrid crew was forced into yet one more metamorphosis. They had begun as the milk-run crew of a transport ship, and had been transformed by Mariet into soldiers of a sort, soldiers of some dedication, but little art. From the beginning of her training, Shaamlik's mind-set had been military. Decisions were life-and-death, speed essential, fear an invisible enemy. On the bridge she was a ruthless surgeon slicing out weakness. She excised the old, un-ranked, and unwritten hierarchy that every ship possesses, and switched duties among the crew until she had a mix of talent and function that pleased her. At any particular station she preferred an inexperienced man who showed high potential over an old hand who was simply compe-tent. At first her beauty cowed and discomfited them; then they grumbled and chafed when the scalpel appeared, and were soon shocked by the easy mercilessness of its cut.

But there were incidents not unlike the one in which *Condor* clashed with the suspicious Kang-gorians. In these, her natural impetuousness was tempered by Bolla and Tyrees, so her gifts as a flier of interstellar birds was unsullied by rashness, and the crew came, reluctantly, around.

As news of *Condor* began to precede her, these incidents grew infrequent, and there came a time when she rode a high wind over a clean plain. A time for new directions.

By then Mace coordinated a loose polyglot alliance of Trade War rebels who saw in the New Covenant an opportunity to outface the Regnum boldly. Hitherto, usually singly, they shadowboxed with their mother federation by ignoring trade regulations, claiming independence, and closing off communications. Because of distance and numbers, individual rebel worlds could indeed function autonomously for a time; inevitably, however, the Regnum would get around to staging a direct—often military—confrontation, and this always forced their capitulation. Now they had a charismatic leader, admittedly dangerous and inscrutable, whose only design seemed to be to destroy their enemy.

From the spiral arms came news of the work of the Seers—vague, undetailed, but certain in terms of the explosive spread of their teachings.

Condor poised once more at a turning point.

Pol Tyrees had called a conference in the officers' wardroom. Bolla, Radis, Shaamlik—even Meta-sol—attended. The old Tercian seemed more ethereal than ever, more aura than substance. His skin was translucently white, with blue veins standing out from the backs of his hands atop the cane. His beard had become so sparse and white that it was invisible in strong light. The long silences to which his companions had become accustomed had grown even longer, and the blind eyes rarely opened. Nevertheless, his presence was still felt—perhaps even more strongly. To all but Shaamlik he was a comfortable ghost—should he leave a room, a warmth left with him; but the new captain shunned what she regarded as the mystical hocus-pocus surrounding Meta-sol, and felt hair on the back of her neck quiver when he was near. Nevertheless, on the rare occasions when her mind was off her duties and an opportunity such as this presented itself, she ignored everything but Pol Tyrees.

She devoured him with her eyes. Not mooningly, like a

sentimental lover, not entranced like a Svengali slave; but
with the calculating voraciousness of a cat watching a
caged bird. She saw on him the mark of mystery, of
shackled power. Perhaps those psychologists who had always been fascinated by strong, sensuous women whose
passions were dissipated only while atop half-wild stallions
would have recognized the look. Those psychologists would
not be able to penetrate the brittle shield that Tyrees held
before her, however. It was too perfect. It was fashioned
with such functional artifice that even he didn't know it
was there, but it denied her beauty, her gender, even—
when she wasn't in the mode of *Condor*'s captain—her
existence. Perhaps only Meta-sol could know that fear
quaked behind the shield.

Fear.

Under the sharp current of expectancy that hummed in
the room's atmosphere, then, were other, more subtle
currents: Tyrees's buried fear; Shaamlik's raw and homed
cupidity; Radis's resurrected vitality throbbing with the
need for action; Bolla's computer mind at war with his
own mortality; Meta-sol's silent despond.

"Well!" said Radis, rubbing his hands together in mock
imitation of a greedy shopkeeper. "What's next? Shall we
turn off a few stars? No. That would be vulgar. Let's have
Condor lasso the galaxy, pull the rope tight, and then we'll
always have enough light to read by!"

"You know, Radis," said Bolla, exhaling a long sigh,
"I find it hard to reconcile these boyish enthusiasms with
the buttoned-up Cadre One I had come to love so well."

Radis grinned sheepishly, but there was no apology in
his response. "Born again. Like my leader, only more
literally."

At these words Tyrees came out of his private place, the
deep, blue fire returning to his eyes. Radis made the connection between Tyrees's increasingly frequent habit of
submerging within himself—like a photographer ducking
into his darkroom—and the Tercian's. He knew they both
"worked on things," but how or what was beyond him.
He was a man of many accomplishments, but here he was
the lowest apprentice to ancient sorcerers, one who scoured
the mortars and petals of necromancers. Living with un-

leavened awe, he knelt to their altar and yearned to gather in the secrets of their magic.

"Sorry," muttered Tyrees.

"Where do you go when you leave us, Pol?" Bolla was the only one who reserved the privilege to call Tyrees by his first name, though he never indicated a preference. Perhaps because of this he now had many names: to Meta-sol he was always Pol-Nesol-Rast; to Radis, Tyrees; to Shaamlik and the crew, simply Sir, though "Black Rast" could be heard in the enlisted men's wardroom, because in spite of his heretical rift with the Cadre, he never wore any other color. Unknown to those on *Condor*, out in the spirals his names were already legion.

He shook his head at Bolla. "Hans, like you and everybody else, I dream."

No one noticed that Meta-sol smiled.

"In other words you don't want to talk about it," sniffed Bolla, shifting his bulk into a more comfortable position. "I know you play weird games in your head—like the old master here." He nodded in the direction of the old Tercian. "You go in there with the workout sweaties on, close the door, and have a jolly old time flexing neurons and bouncing synapses off the inside walls of your skull. Dreaming it is *not*."

"I'd talk about it if I thought you'd understand, Hans," said Tyrees quietly. "I'm still learning myself. So is Meta-sol."

They all looked, each through different eyes, at the figure in the chair—as always, leaning lightly forward on his cane; as always, sitting apart from the group. He was a blatant anachronism: shawled, bearded, bereft of technical knowledge, and as remote and unknowable as an oddly shaped and distant galaxy. His appearance—and his stillness—suggested an antique painting in which form and color had faded, diffused, until he blended into his surroundings, all soft shadow and soft light. They were mildly surprised when the figure nodded.

"Yes. We must learn . . . or die."

Radis, of the many on *Condor* who had taken instruction from Meta-sol, was his most devoted student, and he had progressed the furthest—which is to say he was the most

frustrated. He had devoted all of his spare time to the old
Tercian's "learning," practicing simple exercises, knowing just enough success to keep him at it. A month of
concentrated effort recently had brought him to the high
pinnacle where he could move each of his toes individu-
ally. When he first succeeded he let out a whoop of joy
and almost called the ship's complement together for a
demonstration. Then a sobering image popped into his
mind: a former Cadre One, trained to kill in a hundred
subtle ways, versed in the lores of hunt and capture with a
few others of that legendary rank, renounced for his powers of intellect—a respected and feared leader of men
sitting barefooted before a starship crew in intergalactic
space . . . twiddling his toes. Now he shook his head
ruefully and spoke to Meta-sol—a boy who never let slip
an opportunity when his grandfather was in a talkative
mood.

"But the kind of learning you talk about, Meta-sol, that
. . . that must require a lifetime!" The old Tercian's sad
smile spread like a flooding river into familiar channels.

"No . . . it requires *more* than a lifetime. Much, much
more. So it is written. Such is our . . . lot."

"But then there's no time for anything else!"

Meta-sol nodded again. "If one chooses to follow the
path of the Seer, there is no time . . . and there is *only*
time," he added wistfully.

"Well, if we had all followed it, we wouldn't be travel-
ing between the stars."

"That is the other path, the . . . *outside* path."

"Space?"

"All that is outside the body. You of the hidden stars
chose that path, long before Tercet." Meta-sol "looked"
upwards and fingered his beard absently. "You had come
. . . so far with your machines, that you could defy the
Black Hole and became our fathers. One thousand of your
years passed before we, your sons, could join with you
again. Yes, to travel between the stars." Again the nod,
heavier this time. "You have accomplished much."

Tyrees spoke then, his voice rough with bitterness. "Technology has rendered us moribund. One man has no more

significance than a decimal point in one of Doctor Bolla's probability runs. *That* is what we have accomplished.''

There was a long silence.

Radis thought he understood something of the thing that drove Tyrees and saddened Meta-sol. ''We have become an extension of our machines, then? We think we control them but they control us?''

''Yes.'' Tyrees hissed the word.

''No.'' Meta-sol raised his head. ''No, Pol-Nesol-Rast. You . . . *choose* to be controlled. You make the machines. They are not . . . evil. You make them. On Tercet we make buckets to carry water. But I do not carry water. I do not even cut the wood that is burned to cook my food. On the outside path, I am . . . useless.''

Tyrees was the closest to Meta-sol, but he now saw something in his old mentor for the first time. It had always been there, but in *Condor*'s plasteel womb it was forced closer to the surface. To the Seer the physical universe was intimidating . . . no, alien! He dwelt so much within.

Radis saw some of it, too. ''So you choose control of the inside, uh, path, but it makes you dependent on others?''

''Yes, that is the Tercian Covenant. Most labor so that a few may spend their years . . . seeking within. That is why Seers are blind. That is why the faith of our followers fills us with gratitude and . . . humility.''

Meta-sol never rested body weight on the arms or back of a chair, but as he spoke his back curved deeply under some burden. Fingers fluttered atop his cane. His gentle voice took on baggage, too, for it lagged softly.

''I am old, much older than you of the hidden stars are expected to live. You travel between the stars, and the galaxies . . . beckon. My universe is larger, perhaps. . . .'' He paused to moisten his thin lips. ''And I have taken only a few steps.''

''I see what you mean,'' muttered Radis. ''Shit. I'm a little boy with a toy space ship. I can move my toes. I'd need immortality to get as far. . . .'' Radis's head jerked up. ''Is that what you're after? *Immortality?*''

Meta-sol only blinked.

Radis leaned forward, a wild look in his eye. "Meta-sol? Please answer me!"

Tyrees was about to interrupt, had even begun to rise from his chair, but before he could speak, the blind man had lifted a hand, palm outward in his direction. Tyrees hesitated, but settled back.

Bolla and Shaamlik stared at each other.

"It is not written," said Meta-sol with the halting tones of confession. "It is too much an . . . admission of pride to be held within the sanctity of *The Teraac*. But every Seer . . . harbors it deeply, silently."

There was a soft snort from Shaamlik, but Radis ignored her. "But . . . why? Everyone wants to live forever, but to set immortality as a *goal*! It's so . . ."

"Yes. It is. It is . . . all of the things you are thinking. Nevertheless, a Seer always comes to be . . . tempted by it because it is a . . . I think you would say a 'logical extension' of what we are and what we do."

"How is that?"

"I don't think they're ready for this, Meta-sol," said Tyrees. Meta-sol "looked" at him a long moment, like a painter before an illusive subject, holding a hesitant brush over his canvas. Finally, his head bowed down and his words were so without volume that all but Tyrees leaned to them.

"Perhaps not. But it is necessary." He stood then, stood leaning on a wavering cane—and as if he had just become conscious of an unfamiliar and distasteful weakness, thrust it away to clatter on the floor. He took two steps forward, bringing himself to the center of the group, and drew himself up. Radis could see the hem of his shawl trembling, and became alarmed.

"What's . . . ?"

"*Control!*" shouted Meta-sol.

The word boomed out, a heavy hammer striking iron. Shaamlik instinctively covered her ears. The slight figure before them had suddenly lost all frailty. With a long pull of air he filled his lungs until his chest was doubled in size. He threw back his head.

"CONTROOOOOOLL!"

A glass shattered at Bolla's elbow. The plasteel bulkhead—

and their ears—hummed with vibrations long after the assault of sound was over. Meta-sol seemed invigorated by the effort, though he was breathing heavily, and strode with gusto back to his chair. With an air of satisfaction he cocked his head toward Radis. His voice resumed its gentle cadences.

"You see? I still have some . . . power. We seek control. First, control over the body. *The Teraac* says that the cosmos is a single onion with many . . . layers. The mind is its core, and the body its first layer. The second is what we have been calling the outside path."

"You said many layers, Meta-sol," threw in Bolla, whose interest had soared at the word *immortality*. "There doesn't seem to be anything left."

"There is," said Tyrees quietly, emphatically. "There is a third."

"Damn!" Radis slammed a fist into a palm, wild eyes shining. "Can it be true?"

"Can *what* be true?" sputtered Bolla, exasperated. "What's the third layer?"

Radis was on his feet now, pacing like a caged jungle cat. "Don't you see? Don't you see? My God . . ."

"Radis—"

"Time! It's *time*, Doctor. Meta-sol is saying we can control time!"

For a brief moment the savage light that burned in Radis's eyes flared in Bolla's. His breathing quickened. He opened his mouth wide instinctively to draw a long, dampening draught of air. When he was through, the light died in his eyes and his jaws closed with an audible snap of teeth.

"Absurd. Hubris. With all due respect, Meta-sol—"

"Come on, Doctor!" said Radis excitedly. "You're still tied to your machines. You've seen what these two can do. Why the hell not? Extrapolate! What are the limits?"

"Extrapolate," muttered Bolla derisively. "Please don't use such . . . such clean, scientific terms in the context of folly." He turned his bulky frame to address Meta-sol directly. His voice was full of compassion, and something else as well—a deep, yearning sadness. "There's a flaw in your thinking, Meta-sol, a flaw born of . . . of desperate, very human, *hope*."

Radis had retrieved the cast-off cane, and the old Tercian was back on the faded canvas, sealed eyes and filmy beard etched into stillness. "Please, Doctor," Meta-sol whispered. "Tell me."

"Your onion. And its layers. At its core you put the human mind." Meta-sol nodded. "That is the agent of your control—of the body, of the physical universe, of . . . of time itself, you claim." Another nod. "That means that everything—*everything*—is a construct of the human mind. That means, a priori, that those stars out there"—he pointed dramatically above—"and *Condor*, and space and time and my friggin' false teeth exist because we want them to!"

Shaamlik and Radis watched the crimsoning face of Bolla subside slowly into its jowled flaps. What began as empathy was now bitter anger.

"Don't hold out to the ignorant such charlatan promises. All things *die*. That may not be written in *The Teraac*, but it's written on your face, and mine."

Meta-sol shook his head slowly. He "looked" at Tyrees, who only pursed his lips and held his silence. When he didn't reply, Bolla continued, his tone undergoing yet another shift into smug despair.

"I've made psychology, in one form or another, my life's work." He pointed a rigid forefinger, first at Meta-sol, then at Tyrees. "And you, and you, are incredibly gifted men who have fallen prey to the most tragic of human delusions. It is unvoiced and unconscious, but you feel it is *unjust* that you were born to die, so you assume the prerogatives of the gods. You claim immortality. You even demand the function of creation! You refuse to accept the fact of your insignificance!"

"It is not . . . unconscious," said Meta-sol in a voice filled with ancient fatigue. "But you are . . . accurate. We are in a universe of our own making. We are its . . . creators."

Bolla threw up his hands in exasperation. "That is patently absurd! On the face of it. How can you—"

"All things are . . . energy. All life is . . . directed energy, energy under some control. That control is . . . limited only by the power of the mind. Extend that power.

Expand it. You will control the universe. You will *be* the universe. So it is written." Meta-sol's cane tapped the floor gently with the rhythm of his conviction. "You see, Doctor, we cannot really create, as I said, because it is already there. It is . . . us. If we but touch it with our mind."

Bolla stared wide-eyed at the old Tercian, but did not interrupt. For a time he listened like a child before a warm fire at night would listen to a wise old man telling fascinating stories whose verity is taken for granted. Meta-sol was the narrator of a grand and outrageous dream. Give in to its lure, and reality receded, becoming itself a dream hazed by distance, tarnished by the memory of its meager, demeaning possibilities.

"So we must seek control," said Meta-sol in a voice full of wistful faith, yearning conviction, a voice that comes naturally to all great teachers. "Control of the mind. We use as much of its . . . potential now as *Condor* uses its mote of space in the cosmos. We lack time . . . only time. That, too, is but a skein of energy we have not yet touched." Then a hint of anger surfaced. "You accuse me of . . . of unholy pride, Doctor Bolla."

He paused to lick his thin lips, and the weighty inflections of confession returned to his words.

"That is just. I resent the . . . mote of time my small powers have been able to control. So little remains." He "looked" at Radis and smiled. "So I must use it to teach." Then he turned his head to the man in black, and the smile quivered on his lips. He rose from his chair, slowly, lifted his cane, slowly, and pointed it at the dark and silent man named Tyrees.

"He will go where I may not. That is why he is my savior." He turned and walked, slowly, from the room.

CHAPTER THIRTEEN

As Meta-sol walked from the wardroom, *Condor* ripped noiselessly through the fabric of normal space into a dimension that disdained old concepts of time and distance, but still baffled the minds of pure mathematicians—even though less fastidious, more practical scientists had for millennia taken advantage of the simple principle that if certain switches were flipped, it happened. Ancient farmers puzzled little over the miracle of the light bulb.

Still, *Condor* was flying to new heights, and all were aware of it, heady with it when the contemplative mood struck. To the men of *Condor* the galaxy had become a neighborhood block; with Tyrees and the intergalactic pathways, the light-years journey out to the spiral arms was a stroll to the corner store.

Condor had already entered that blasphemous mode before the meeting in the wardroom was called. Tyrees no longer allowed decisions to wait upon concensus. Nor was there more speculation about immortality after Meta-sol's leaving. Tyrees pulled them back into the immediate.

"Hans. You've been playing with *Condor*'s MASTER-COM. Any probabilities?" A moment passed before Bolla focused on the question. When he answered, he was still gazing at the plasteel arch beyond which the Seer had disappeared.

"Huh? Oh . . . yes. No. MASTERCOM is an ingenious toy. Ingenious, but very specialized. She suits *Condor* like the human brain suits the human body—but in the same way, one is useless without the other.''

"She can't do probability runs? That doesn't seem—''

"Of course she can. But she's designed for data generated by physics, not social psychology. She's not Anavex.'' Bolla sighed like a father thinking of a long absent and favored son. "Besides, the data is degenerate—out of date and probably irrelevant now. Simply put, we just don't know enough about what's happening out in the spirals since we left.''

Tyrees nodded. "We will soon. We're headed out of the Hub now. I was hoping for some hints about what to expect back . . . home.''

Radis found this an odd choice of words, and smiled grimly. "Well, in that case *I* can do a probability run right here for you.'' He tapped his forehead with a thumb. "Expect . . . trouble. Headed where exactly?''

"Caanon. We got that message burst from them a while ago. We left Spel-sol there.''

"Oh. Yes. I seem to recall the place.''

Shaamlik looked at the three men quizzically, for she sensed a change here that impending danger did not explain. Her knowledge of the events preceding Kang-gor were sketchy, though she had heard stories among the crew. Bolla was staring at Radis, his heavy jowls quivering slightly. She could not know that he was looking once more upon the vision of Tyrees and the three Seers frozen into that tableau, under the pulse of their own light and linked by touch—and something else—to Radis's dying body. She saw Radis unconsciously move a hand off his knee to part a cape that was no longer there. The stories couldn't be true, of course.

Radis shrugged his approval. "I guess Caanon is the best choice. Spel-sol is . . . well, even more than Meta-sol, he has a special magnetism . . . and President Loriis is there.''

Shaamlik could stand it no longer. "Please gentlemen.'' The three men looked at her with mild surprise. "The restriction of my duties to the smooth functioning of *Condor* is a given.'' She looked boldly at each in turn and continued forcefully. "But I cannot make command decisions—

crisis decisions on the bridge—unless I'm fully informed. I must know what to expect."

Of the three, Radis was the only man who ever reacted to her in a way that recognized her gender, let alone her beauty—and she was well aware of it. The men among the crew were too intimidated by her to make approaches of any kind, and despite her natural sensuality and growing sense of isolation, she deliberately fostered the "cold bitch" label. She expected that Radis would be the one to respond— and he did, smiling apologetically.

"Sorry, Captain. You're right, of course. We forgot—"

"You forgot I was here."

"No," chuckled Bolla. "We forgot that we have a small history you weren't a part of. Let me fill you in."

Shaamlik listened as Bolla recounted the events immediately after their capture of *Condor*: the "seeding" of the Tercians, the hard evidence they had left behind of the Chairman's crimes, the secret ally Radis had suckled in Prisident Loriis of Caanon, a Regnum world that had long been festering under the Chairman's shadow.

Shaamlik listened carefully, but her eyes were moving probes, seemingly random and casual as they shifted from one man to another; nevertheless, they were hungry eyes, those of a hunter cat overlooking a herd's bucks from a distance. She saw Tyrees fall from the surface again as quickly and palpably as a bucket dropping down a well. In an instant he was a manikin. Radis leaned toward her, elbows on knees, hands clasped—a youngster keen to please the pretty lady. Looking at him, she wondered how such a man—a Cadre One at least fifteen years her senior, who had experienced things at firsthand that she could only imagine—could still exude such . . . *enthusiasm*. And the amiable Dr. Hans Bolla, happiest when he was talking, explaining the mysteries of a big, wide, wonderful galaxy to the uninitiated. He had that soft, self-indulgent jester's body, that ingratiating manner, and the mind of a post-doctorate crocodile.

". . . then, as Pol told me just a few hours ago, a coded message from Caanon arrived. President Loriis deems a quick visit safe enough. No Regnum Battlefleet vessels within two weeks' range—they're spread thinly, of course—

and the time is ripe in my opinion,'' he chuckled, ''even without Anavex to bolster it.''

For the first time, Shaamlik told herself, I am the object of their attention. Even Tyrees was drawing back up, out of his well.

''If there is a risk, why do we go at all?'' she asked.

Tyrees looked at her sharply—for a change without attention directed simultaneously elsewhere. Shaamlik saw the blue eyes come. She felt them hit and penetrate, sliding smoothly, but irresistibly inside her. She shivered. It was as if a tidal buildup had suddenly gushed through earth-anchored locks. It was . . . hotwet. It pushed deep and carried . . . carried . . . carried. She gasped silently— an intake of breath. Then it was gone.

''Because it is time,'' he said quietly. ''There is *no* time without risk, unless what you do has no significance.''

''Don't!'' she blurted, fighting to regain her composure. Both hands jumped between her knees and turned into fists. ''Don't . . . talk like Meta-sol. Please.''

Tyrees shrugged. ''We've done all we can in the Hub. There's momentum to ride, momentum that will die unless it has something to feed on. It's out in the spirals, thanks to the Seers. Yes, there is risk—high risk—but we are cresting. We ride it now . . . or we drown in it later.''

Tyrees didn't add, ''Are you all with me?'' He rose and strode from the wardroom without a backward glance.

Bolla muttered, ''Yes, well. Huh,'' and bulged out his ample cheeks to empty his lungs. Radis slowly, smugly, clapped his hands three times. Shaamlik felt her thighs begin to burn, and rose from her chair also.

Bolla looked at her strangely. ''Captain?''

He was ignored. She didn't know why, but she could still hear Tyrees's footsteps, and she was going to follow them.

Out in the corridor she just caught sight of him turning a corner. She hesitated, but her mounting confusion only translated into urgency, and she sped after him. By the time she made the turn herself, he had disappeared. She broke into a trot, muttering curses as she checked inter-secting corridors, seeing no one because this was officers' country and not a duty period. She was breathing heavily and flushed with an obscure anger, when she saw a light above an elevator portal wink off. Level Four . . . nothing there but storage and . . . the gym.

The gym was a large exercise room located where the gravity was highest on *Condor*. It was equipped with the standard training machinery and floor mats. It occurred to Shaamlik that it would be typical of Tyrees to take his exercise when the facility was least likely to be in use. She relaxed then, knowing he would be there. Straightening her severe tunic, touching her hair, she stood staring at the elevator doors for several minutes, until her pulse slackened, before punching for Level Four.

When she got there, the gym was empty, but half of it was alight. She slid into the darkness near the entrance and waited, still ignoring the part of her that was asking why.

Tyrees came from the change room naked. Shaamlik took one nervous, sidling step back toward the door, and stopped. The light in his half of the large room was brilliant; her half was deep in shadow. She leaned against the wall to watch.

At first he just stood, head and shoulders slightly bowed, his nakedness displaying a tightness, a strained tension she had never seen on his face. Then he locked his fingers behind his neck, heaved in a great breath, and threw his head back. His teeth bared and every muscle in his body leaped into sharp resolution. Shaamlik stared. She knew the bulging, knotted physique born of male vanity, but this was something different. In a relaxed state Tyrees's body was unremarkable—certainly when clothed. Trim, lithe, fluid of movement, but unremarkable. In this state, however, he was a Greek statue bursting with understated power. *Every single muscle* was sculpted into definition. Nothing protruded or bulged; everything was hard, flat curve. Under the harsh light she could see even the rounded bars running back along the tops of his toes.

Then Tyrees began to quiver—at first delicately, like the petal of a flower straining to open, then with increasing violence, as if an electric current were charging through him.

And he leaped.

He leaped like a gorilla going for a high branch, his feet

sailing to a point somewhere above his own height. It was a leap that released both physical and emotional tides, the cry that accompanied it almost a primal scream. The sound came from within and was beyond language; it was the call of a wild animal beaking for freedom.

"My God," whispered Shaamlik as Tyrees turned smoothly at the apex of his leap, descended at what seemed an incredible, insolent slowness, and landed with a soft thump on the spread fingers and thumbs of his two hands.

If the wall were not already supporting her, she would have reached for something else. Her knees were wobbly and she found her mouth full of saliva—she had to keep swallowing as she watched him execute a series of leaps and rolls and striking maneuvers that had to have their source in combat training. The blend of one movement into the next, however, had the precision and grace of a dancer rather than a warrior, and she was stung hotly by the sensual beauty of this primitive, forcefully thrusting choreography.

Excepting the first leap and the fluidity of movement that followed, Tyrees did nothing that a honed athlete could not do—if he were first filmed, and that film artificially accelerated for viewing. The speed defied human capability.

The exercise continued for several minutes, but at the end of it Tyrees was breathing only lightly, much more lightly than Shaamlik, though his skin was glistening, bouncing the brittle light off its higher planes. When he stopped, his back was toward her. He hesitated a moment before walking to a bench to pluck up a towel. He rubbed himself down as he headed for the change room, but turned at its entrance, the towel held casually over his loins.

"Did you wish to speak to me, Captain?"

Shaamlik felt the jolt of an exposed voyeur, and her blood began to burn, but she fought off the quick words that jumped to her tongue and said nothing. Instead, she walked into the lighted area as if he weren't there, reached for the tie at the back of her head that kept her hair pulled into a severe cap, and pulled. She shook her head and long, chestnut hair billowed down. Very slowly she lifted both hands to the top of the stiff uniform collar and one by one began to flip open the clasps of its blouse. All the while she gazed at Tyrees with a slight inclination of the head and an expression that a polite waitress would use as she awaited an order. The blouse was on the floor, then the belt, then the short boots were slipped loose and flipped casually away from the ends of bare toes. As the clothes fell away, the flat, military lines broke, melted into soft roundnesses. When she finally stood boldly naked—small, firm breasts thrust slightly upwards by her rib cage—she smiled coquettishly. Then she raised her arms like a ballet dancer, fingers touching to close a bow high above her head. The action pulled her breasts even higher.

"My turn," she whispered, and rose on her toes to turn a slow, graceful pirouette.

Tyrees's eyes flickered.

Shaamlik, still very slowly, finished her pirouette, approached him slowly and placed the fingertips of one hand on his upper chest. The wrist was held high in mock-formal seduction as she looked over one shoulder and began to trace the line of his collarbone as she moved around him. The touch was light, trailing a soft circle up to his shoulder, around the back of his neck, and down again to the vulnerable pit of his throat. His eyes flickered once more, but he remained motionless. Her fingertips fell, featherlight on his skin, down to his navel, then turned downwards, her palm caressing one thigh, then the other.

When her hand closed around his penis and it began to swell to her touch, he erupted.

"No!"

His hand, fingers widespread in panic, smacked into her face and pushed, as if thrusting away an insect-laden fruit. Shaamlik felt his revulsion—and his fear—as palpably as the blow, and in her shock failed to register pain when her buttocks hit the hard floor.

Tyrees stood over her, panting. He tried to speak. "You . . . you . . ."

His terrible blue eyes began to cast, taking in everything but her. Coughing sounds came from his throat. A tiny trickle of blood leaked from Shaamlik's nose. She stared up, eyes blasted wide with incredulity and—something new—humiliation. She blinked tears. Blinked tears that fell heavily upon her breasts. Her knees drew up protectively, and she hugged them. Nakedness had always meant power to her—and pleasure. Now it was a raw vulnerability, an open throat. Her nostrils filled quickly with phlegm, which she allowed to drip to her bare knees as she waited. Her hair formed a tent around her huddled figure, reaching almost to the floor. It was soft and the color of smoky fire, except where it touched her face; there it was gummed with tears and sweat and mucus.

Then, lightly, she felt a whisper of a touch from fingers that trembled, moving through her hair at the nape of her neck. It made her shiver, and she whimpered with the small sound of an injured bird. Huddling more, she waited.

Feet padded quickly away. She looked up and he was gone.

Here, on a starship, in a place in space where the notions conveyed by the words *far* and *nothingness* were ridiculously inadequate, she sat naked, like a primitive in a desert plain, and sobbed uncontrollably. When she stopped, she wiped her nose on the back of her hand like a child. The air felt cold. She staggered to her feet in the hard light and stood staring at the sordid pile of her clothes, then at his towel.

"I might kill you," she said.

CHAPTER FOURTEEN

President Loriis himself was there to greet them, openly. Caanon's leader was a small, quick man who fed on his own sporadic energy. His movements, his speech, his enthusiasms were a series of explosions. He pumped Radis's hand.

"Well, well, well. You're here at last. So much has happened, eh?"

Radis smiled. "And more to come. Good to see you again, Mr. President."

"And this . . ." Loriis gestured to take in *Condor*'s impressive hangar bay. "I knew these magnificent beasts existed, but I've never seen one before. What a prize!"

"I'm afraid she's one of many, Mr. President—all of which belong to the enemy. And *Condor*'s our most immediate concern. You greet us with such open fanfare."

"Not to worry, not to worry," Louis snorted with a wave of his hand. He tilted his chin up at Radis with the hard-won confidence of the little man whose real stature is no longer questioned. "No one off-planet knows you are here, and the Regnum treats us like a naughty boy going through a phase. Other than declaring we won't listen to Daddy anymore, we haven't caused any trouble. The Chairman and his minions are busy with the Hub rebels, and trying to chase you down."

"He thinks we're still in the Hub?"

"Of course. I believe he still refuses to accept your . . . magical mobility."

"Good, good. You are our first real penetration into the Regnum. We want to continue that process. We want to start a wave that will wash over and clean out the old order."

Loriis nodded and turned away. He looked through a porthole at the shuttle that had brought him up from Caanon minutes before. From behind he looked like a wiry adolescent, fidgeting with his own uncertainty, hands in and out of pockets, feet always shifting. Abruptly, now several meters away, he turned back to face Radis. A face designed by heredity to remain perpetually young was suddenly riven and gray with the anxiety only the old and scarred can know.

"Yes," he said. "The old order. But what follows?"

Radis was taken aback. "What?"

"What does your man—Tyrees—what does he want to replace it with? The Regnum is . . . moribund. Tyrees, I think, may just be the one to deliver its death blow. A merciful one, thank the Maker, because a generation or two would have paid dearly. Nevertheless, my—Caanon's—protest is only a simple demand for freedom. Just what are we caught up in now? What replaces the old order?"

Radis was about to answer glibly, "A new one," but suddenly realized how inadequate this would sound—and how absurd, how romantically visionary was the image, the hope/dream in his heart. Mankind was a single, knitted family gathered around the hearth fire of their galaxy, seeking challenge worthy of their collective strength. It was embodied by Pol-Nesol-Rast—Vitar. Life-Giver.

How could he speak of it? Loriis's old, boyish face waited impatiently.

"Aren't you rushing things, Mr. President? Right now we're mostly worried about saving our asses."

His attempt at light and disarming realism was ignored. "No, you're not. You're . . . you're bearding the lion, spitting in the Chairman's face. At first I thought it foolhardy, even dangerously impetuous. Now . . ."

"Now?"

"*Rast—Vitar*. What do they mean?"

Radis started. Those same words still echoed in his skull. Then he shrugged. "Tercian. Titles of respect. Why do you ask?"

Loriis looked hard at Radis for a moment before whirling away again. He slapped two hands on the bulkhead, bridging the porthole, and leaned on them. He spoke to the misted sphere glowing dully behind his shuttle craft.

"Caanon has been . . . I don't know what to call it. I don't suppose you realize fully. Your man—Spel-sol—has whipped up a fervor that frightens me. They call it 'Vitarus.' Tyrees is Vitar. I don't understand it. My advisors tell me it's just a form of meditation, but . . . What the hell is going on, Radis? I thought we were engaging in a *political* struggle here. What is going *on*?"

"It's just . . . a new mental discipline, Mr. President. I gather Spel-sol has done well."

Loriis snorted. "*Well?* It's beyond . . ." He shook his head like a stunned boxer. A heavy shock of richly disheveled, iron-gray hair made the motion oddly threatrical. "Forget it for now. You'll see shortly, and perhaps you'll understand my concern. Spel-sol is waiting for us—or rather, for Tyrees."

While *Condor* circled the planet, a grim and silent Shaamlik in command, Tyrees, Radis, and Bolla made landfall with the president some distance from the capital. They transferred to an air car for the short flight to Government House at the city's heart. They passed swiftly over modest, greening mountains, a pacific surrender to man's sporadic impulse toward orderly and productive beauty. Bolla, weary of a life in space that suited neither physique nor temperament, was ebullient.

"This is lovely, Mr. President. Lovely. I can see why you and yours have tried to keep Caanon out of the fray."

"Not exactly, Commissioner—oh . . . sorry. Habit. Old titles die hard. What do I call you now?"

"Hans will do nicely."

"Hans, then. We *need* a galactic order, sir. Need it, I say. But in its present form the Regnum is like . . . like a referee presiding over a cruel and bloody sport. It regulates how blood is to be let! My most profound anxiety is the fear that they might be right. Perhaps man's nature is such that the best he can hope for is controlled violence. Perhaps *our* efforts—yours and mine—will lead to something worse.''

Bolla's high spirits hissed to earth like a pinpricked balloon. He looked across at Tyrees, whose remoteness had been flint hard in recent days. There was a subtle cast of grimness, a patina of—of pain?—over the habitually composed features. The man is holding something inside, he thought. He always has, but there is something else now. He assumed Tyrees hadn't been listening, but as the silence drew out, the blue-hot ice of those eyes turned slowly to Loriis.

''Mr. President. Anyone overcome by fear of the future would be wise to accept the present—without complaint.''

Loriis bristled. He switched his head angrily, throwing his iron mane off his forehead. ''That's—that's blind foolishness, Mr. Tyrees. We may be coming to a time of apocalyptic upheaval. Caution . . . preparedness—''

''You are right. We *are* coming to that time. Accept it. Ride with it. That is the best you can do. *Prepare* for it, you cannot.''

The manner was that of an ancient potentate, deeply marbled with arrogant assurance. Tyrees turned away, dismissing the matter. Loriis's eyes widened.

He was about to respond in kind when Radis gasped. ''Holy . . . good God!''

The air car was designed for low altitudes only, and had just topped another of the gently rounded green mountains to begin its swoop over the capital. The city covered a large, flat plain, and its size and beauty startled the eyes; but that was not the cause of Radis's cry. Government House was a surprisingly delicate cluster of linked and spired structures which formed the hub of a vast, spoked circle of open pavement. The perfectly rounded area—forcing the city to pack densely at its circumference—was so huge that even at their height, the far edge was not visible.

It was full of people.

A low roar rose to greet them. The sound heightened, deepened, seemed to be erupting from the earth itself. Its

power grew until its intensity rubbed nubs of fear into
them all. Tyrees twisted forward in his seat, hands lifting
slowly to rest on the window beside him. He whispered
something.

Bolla shook his head. "Not this," he muttered. "I
couldn't have predicted this."

"You see?" said Loriis. "You see, Radis?"

The air car circled lower over the crowd. They could
see—on a platform jutting from the highest spire of Government House—the white figure of Spel-sol, face up-
turned to them. At ground level three gargantuan screens,
each at the foot of a spoke where it met the hub, displayed
that same tall figure from a lower perspective. Spel-sol
still wore the Tercian-style shawl, but this was dazzling
white, a material that bounced back the sunlight and
made the eyes blink, rendered his figure indistinct and
compelling.

As the air car began its descent to the platform, Spel-sol
lifted his arms to them. The host below followed suit—it
seemed spontaneously—in a spiral wave that billowed out
from the hub. Sunlight splashed off the sea of white hands.
The roar intensified still more, buffeting the air car as it
drew lower. Bolla had thrust his amazement aside and was
studying the spectacle below with avid objectivity. This is
not the roar of a sports crowd, he thought, though there is
jubilation in it. There is something more . . . something
. . . He let the sound wash over him, drifted with it, and
by the time the air car touched down, recognition sure and
potent hit him.

Ecstacy. It was ecstacy.

Bolla was afraid. For the first time he was seeing—and
hearing—the kind of flesh and bone surge of change that
he had been studying, quantifying, all his academic life;
but until now it had always been swathed beneath the
innocuous numbers and the blasé hum of his computers.

As the door opened and Tyrees stepped out, the roar
began to shiver. That opaque wall of sound began to stir to
something rhythmical that grew in counterpoint, crashing
ever more strongly against its granite containment. Soon
the pulse broke through, and the wall was obliterated.

"Vitar . . . *Vitar* . . . *VITAR* . . . *VITAR!*"

Bolla could see only Tyrees's back as the man in black walked slowly, like a man walks through his own dream, to the edge of the platform. He watched the head swivel, also slowly, through an arc that spanned the sea of faces, the sea of arms.

Spel-sol's ascetic face was radiant, beatific. The light exploded from his white shawl. Tall, splendid, he moved around to face Tyrees, between him and the rhythmical tumult below.

"VITAR . . . VITAR . . . VITAR . . ."
And he knelt.

CHAPTER FIFTEEN

No one harbored illusions now. On two points the members of the Council of the Regnum were forced to accept bitter realities: that the Regnum was fighting for its life, and that they had become the minions of the Chairman for good or ill. Those who had, through want of courage or an excess of diplomacy, opposed him without total zeal in the past, now regretted it; but they knew well that their fortunes—and those of the Regnum—were unalterably tied to his. The cost of compromise, of ambition, was being exacted.

What had hitherto always been the Chairman's veiled shadow was now ever present. The bull was unleashed. It would be ridiculous to say that he relished the recent flow of events, but for the first time in his political career he found himself able to be and do as he felt. His head lowered and the Council table fell silent.

"You're telling me he's become a god."

The Cadre Proctor shrugged. He was haggard, had the look of a man upon whom fatique and stress had finally stamped a mark that could never be erased.

"In effect, yes."

"Caanon's still a member planet—at least technically. How did that bastard get on and off the planet without our knowing?"

"Our people on Caanon knew, of course, Mr.Chairman. But the whole globe was shut down for several days before

120

and after the Gathering. Even the Cadre field-support office—"

"No communications? That's another blatant slap in the face of Regnum law!" Blood rose, purpling the Chairman's heavy face. He stabbed a finger at the Cadre Proctor. "Place Caanon under interdiction."

There were murmurs of protest from around the table. Interdiction was unalterably put to a Council vote. The Chairman ignored the sounds.

"Put out a general order. All Cadre personnel. Tyrees is to be killed—by whatever means, whatever the risk or cost—on sight. On *sight*."

The Cadre Proctor slumped back in his chair. He fingered the collar clasp of his cape. "I've never issued such an order, Mr. Chairman. It's not the Cadre way. Besides, a standing order of that nature would eventually find its way into the public sector."

The Chairman's chin was now so low that they could see the top of his head and the whites of his eyes under pupils that threatened to roll upwards into his head. Veins pulsed visibly at his temples.

"Listen to me," he said quietly. "All of you. Listen to me." No one breathed. "It may be that you don't recognize it. Only a few trickles of blood are being shed, and they are falling in rebel space in the Hub. Easy to ignore. The Pax Regnum has lasted a thousand years. Easy to assume it will last forever. But we are at war. You've just seen unequivocal evidence"—he gestured at a now inert holoviewer—"in the Gathering on Caanon. Do not deceive yourselves. *We are at war*."

CHAPTER SIXTEEN

Condor was once more shattering the airless order of the Greater Void. She was an alien—unafraid of and unchallenged by the terrors of nothingness in intergalactic space. But she did not belong here. Only the cold light pricks of distant galaxies, like stubborn but hopeless promises, belonged here. Nevertheless, cursed as she was with the relative ephemerality of all creatures of the wing, she reveled in their special freedom: the grace granted those of speed, willed direction, and a space to fly in.

As with her namesake, her flight to heights where none could follow—as heady as it was—was also a preparation for the screaming dive, the surrender of freedom for the power that survival demanded. She reached her zenith and drew breath. A creature of wing and of the heights, she poised for her stoop into the depths.

Tyrees. Bolla. Radis. Meta-sol. Four more different human beings would be difficult to imagine, but at this moment they shared an awareness that few of their species ever experience: that their decisions now—right or wrong, enlightened or perverse—would alter the shape of human destiny. That awareness sobered, chastened—frightened—them all.

So it was that their silences were long and not without welcome. None could put from his mind the memory of the spectacle on Caanon. Even if the saltings of the other Seers throughout the Regnum had less effect—and how could they not?—the magic given to them whispered tempt-ingly. It sprang unbidden, restlessly, from the well of their nighttime dreams and daytime fantasies. It came from a place of shadows that so harbored impossibility, it es-caped even repression, and for a time robbed them of measured thought and speech.

Radis smiled intermittently and shook his head at the floor. Bolla, a cup of coffee resting in two hands on his belly, kept expelling air through bulged lips. Meta-sol was still, a delicate statue exuding a sense of other place, other time. Tyrees, too, was a statue, but without set, line, or ridge of muscle that would identify thoughts beneath. But some kind of pain was etched into the stone itself.

He was the first to speak. "We must visit our seedlings."

Bolla squirmed. "But that will take months. In the mean-time the Chairman will—"

"Will do very little. *Can* do very little. He has no military targets to strike."

"That's right," said Radis, eyes suddenly agleam with excitement. "Our weapons are ideas. You can't fight ideas!"

Bolla closed his eyes and shook his head as if at the folly of a child. "Nonsense. Your romantic enthusiasm again, Radis."

"But really, what can he do? He can't catch *Condor*. He can't stamp out a . . ." Radis hesitated, unable or unwilling to put a name to it. ". . . a galactic movement, a forest fire, as if it were a flame in a wastebasket! Oh, he can swat at our friends in the Hub, but we're *inside* now. We're inside the Regnum's guts!" He shook a triumphant fist at the ceiling.

Bolla got to his feet with a grunt and walked over to Radis, who still sat holding his fist in the air, smiling his certainty. He stood over him a moment, jowls quivering, feet wide apart in his fat man's stance. Then he whipped his half cup of coffee full into Radis's face.

Radis was so taken by surprise that his exclamation was never voiced—he could only sputter and choke on the coffee. Bolla was swabbing him fastidiously with a napkin before he could speak.

"I apologize for the melodrama, Radis, but you get my point."

"What point, you old—"

"Relax, my young friend." Bolla's voice took on the familiar professorial tones. Delicately, he tilted Radis's chin to dab at his neck. "You didn't expect that drenching because it was irrational—especially coming from a fat old toddy whose bones you could rattle at will. Now . . ." He stepped back to inspect his work, and seemingly satisfied, waddled back to his chair. "Before, we were an irritant to the Chairman—and the system that sustains him. Now we are a lethal threat. Don't expect him to behave logically, to weigh costs and consequences or seek compromise when he is frustrated."

Radis had recovered, but remained miffed until he saw the shade of a smile on Tyrees's face. Radis snorted then, and rose, speaking as he walked to the automated pantry and filled another cup with coffee.

"So you're saying we can't expect the Chairman to go by the rules of any game we care to play. So what? As long as it's our game?"

He stood over Bolla's chair, and closing his eyes, sniffed the aroma of the coffee but did not taste it. "Ahh. I do have regrets, at times." Bolla, apprehensive now, glowered up at him as he held the steaming cup daintily between thumb and forefinger over the ample lap. "But I do take your point, Doctor." He let go of the cup.

Bolla started, his knees coming together convulsively and his hands flying to cover his groin.

There was a soft smack as the cup hit the palm of Radis's other hand just above Bolla's thighs. The coffee barely stirred. With a deep bow, Radis offered it.

"I apologize for the melodrama."

Bolla sighed and accepted the cup. "Thank you. I see you have made some progress." He raised the cup to the silent, motionless figure leaning on his cane. "Socrates. Abelard. Svengali, perhaps. Jesus? The rarest of men—teachers, alchemists who mine gold from lead. Your name will lead them all, Meta-sol." The figure remained as it was. Bolla sipped. "Yes. Games and rules, games and rules. Even the worst of us—the Chairman, too—follow *some* set of rules. It's part of the human psyche." He swirled the coffee gently, studied the motion on its surface. "This being so, one would assume that man's behavior is predictable. Alas, such is not the case."

"Hah!" exclaimed Radis. "Your whole career is based on precisely that exercise."

Bolla smiled and shook his head. "No, my friend. Numbers. I need very large numbers. So much so that I had to build Anavex to handle them in conjuction with psychological data. *Individual* behavior is as much a mystery now as it ever was. A man cannot even predict or understand fully his *own* actions." He lifted his eyes from the cup to look at Tyrees. "So don't form expectations concerning the Chairman's behavior—better yet, expect *anything*—except capitulation. Cornered rats, you know."

Radis nodded pensively. "Well, then, what's the worst he could do, Doctor? You don't really think . . . a bloodbath?"

"It's possible. Remember Tercet."

"But that was covert! And most people didn't even know of Tercet's existence!"

"Granted. Nevertheless it demonstrates the man's capabilities, and he was far from desperate then."

Tyrees was suddenly on his feet. The others said nothing as he walked to the observation bubble and stared out at the Void. It was some time before he spoke, his back still to them, the words coming softly.

"The Doctor's right. We're not a little . . . cadre of rebels anymore, are we? We were only asking for our freedom then . . . now a whole galaxy of people. . . ." The others watched him reach out a hand to touch the bubble's skin. "I wonder if he *knew* what his words really meant."

Silence. Radis and Bolla looked at each other.

Finally Tyrees turned. "Lucifer."

"The devil?" asked Bolla, mystified, and a little worried.

"The rebel angel. An ancient Christian epic—*Paradise Lost*. Lucifer said to God, 'I will not serve.' Not 'I will destroy you' or, 'I want your place.' Just, 'I will not serve!'

"I said it, too. So did you. It's not a flaming call to arms, is it? It just means leave me alone!"

Bolla's eyes narrowed. "And now you bewail the position you're in? You don't like the notion that a bat of your eyelash could plunge this galaxy into a river of blood?"

"Overstated, perhaps," said Tyrees, smiling grimly.

"Not a whit." Bolla stabbed an uncompromising finger at him. "And you, my friend, had better keep the record straight. You may have started out with a simple 'I will not serve,' but we all know that changed. You soon came to demand *more* than Lucifer."

"Doctor, you're—" Radis, shocked at Bolla's harsh words, had begun to object, but the doctor cut him off viciously.

"No! We can't afford any illusions here, Radis. This man made his decisions." He heaved himself out of his chair and shambled heavily—like a circus bear breaking out of his comic act and suddenly becoming dangerous—to Tyrees. "You didn't expect the water to become this deep, did you, Pol? Well, it is. For years you considered yourself a puppet, dancing to the string pullers. Now *you* pull the strings. You didn't know it could be so rough, huh? You wanted to be a hero and they made you a god."

Tyrees's eyes flared. With an audible smack his hand landed on Bolla's chest, fingers closing into a fistful of shirt. Bolla was heaved to tiptoe. The fat old man hung there ridiculously, bulbous nose rising into high crimson as the sound of overstrained fabric rippled. But he stared straight into the blue inferno of those eyes.

"There will be blood, Pol," he said. "You've already spilled it. You will spill *more*. Accept that."

A small, whinish growl escaped Tyrees's throat, and Bolla's toes left the floor.

"Vitar."

Meta-sol's word paralyzed him. It was several seconds before the fist at Bolla's chest began to quiver, then release. "Oh, God," he sighed. Bolla's heart was racing again. He gulped air and rubbed his chest, feeling faint. He looked at Tyrees then, who seemed doll slack, suddenly robbed of bone and sinew. Reaching up, he patted Tyrees's cheek. "Some god," he said. "I have an excuse because I'm only human. Poor excuse, I know."

Tyrees only stood there, a figure in black, eyes gone

blank, arms hanging lifelessly at his sides. Radis looked
from one to the other, a lost child. Meta-sol's cane struck
the floor—once, twice, three times. The black, blind eyes
glittered.

"Yes, Vitar. There will be blood. But as the Doctor
said, we have . . . already spilled it. You were less . . .
affected then. Why are you now?"

Tyrees shook his head. "This is different."

"Is it Doctor Bolla's numbers, Vitar? Many lives are
more . . . significant . . . than a few?"

Tyrees sighed and walked back to the bubble. "Perhaps," he said.

"Is it not also the thought that you can now cause
death at will—*and without* willing it?"

"Perhaps," whispered Tyrees to the Void.

"Is it not also the thought that you"—Meta-sol raised
his cane and pointed it at Tyrees's back—"*take joy in
it!*"

Tyrees whirled around. In a face that others, excepting
Meta-sol, rarely read emotion, they saw first anger, then
confusion, then resignation. He walked slowly to his old
mentor and put a hand on his shoulder.

"Perhaps."

Meta-sol smiled, closed his eyes and nodded. "That is
good." The sudden vitality that he took on when he first
called out to Tyrees drained away from him. He seemed
feeble again, skin a fine but pale and fragile porcelain.
"That is good. You fear your own . . . impulses, Vitar."
He reached to place his hand over Tyrees's where it rested
on his shoulder. Bolla and Radis remained silent. They
recognized a communion beyond their understanding.

"Is that enough, Meta-sol?"

"Yes. If you have belief also. Belief that goes . . .
beyond self. So says *The Teraac*."

Tyrees removed his hand, and once more returned to the
bubble. Once more he spoke to the Void.

"Yes. There it is. 'I will not serve' . . . I believe in
that. 'Beyond self?' I can only believe in the right of
others not to serve. What of those who choose not to serve
me?"

Meta-sol's head fell until his filament of a beard curved off his chest. Its strands were stirred by his breath. His face was a delicate parchment, an exquisite ephemerality, a thing of air and light that the slightest touch would destroy.

"I . . . cannot say. On Tercet one man might fight another. But we have no . . . war. That is a new and . . . despairing word for me. We made war only against death. Perhaps . . ." Now bitterness laced his soft words. "Perhaps that is a sign of our . . . savagery."

Radis was aghast. The two men in the universe who had come to mean everything to him, who had more to offer than all the rest—*all* the rest—were beaten low by what they saw as weakness in themselves. He snatched Bolla's now empty cup out of his hands and hurled it with gusto into the bubble. The cup impacted so powerfully that fragments ricocheted for seconds through the wardroom.

"Well *I* can say!" he exclaimed. *"You."* He pointed with conscious drama at Tyrees. "You also believe that billions of people are being shepherded through their lives by an increasingly visible tyranny. You believe that must stop! That's not enough? *You.*" His point swung to Meta-sol. "You bring a way to self-knowledge, a challenge that makes the idea of war an absurdity!"

The others were startled by his vehemence; only Bolla smiled. Radis took a deep breath.

"And now that I have your attention, I'll add this." Again the arm swung to Tyrees. *"You* said not long ago that those who don't ride the tide and make their decisions are condemned to follow! That sounds like another belief to me." His arm fell. "Do you stand by that?"

Tyrees looked at Radis for a long time—so long that Bolla said something he was reluctant to say.

"There has always been blood, Pol. Always."

Tyrees blinked once. Nodded. "Yes."

Radis said, "One more thing. You're like me—ex-Cadre—but I've never known what to call you. And no one alive knows better who you are." He gestured with his powerful chin at the bubble. "They were right back there on Caanon. Meta-sol is right. You are Vitar. Life-Giver. You gave life to *me*. So to me you *are* a chunk of . . .'' He looked at Bolla defiantly. ''. . . god.''

Bolla almost came back with a glib remark about divinity usually being accompanied by infallibility, but he realized on the instant that he shared Radis's sentiment to some extent. He refused, however, to voice it. He could still feel the invisible marks where his skin and his dignity had been abraided; besides, he could not see how his feelings about Pol Tyrees would do any of them any good. He said nothing.

Radis turned back to Tyrees. ''You have problems about what this kind of power means. Like Meta-sol, I *prefer* a man who worries about it . . . but you've got to keep going.''

''Thank you, Radis,'' said Tyrees softly. Then he shrugged, sighed. ''Thank you all. I . . . need you three. Without you . . .'' He shrugged again. ''Very well, then. We will try to keep the body count down. I see only one way to do that, but the risks are higher.''

''You've changed your mind, then. We don't visit our Seers?''

''No. We have Spel-sol and his acolytes do that, with the help of the president of Caanon. Their numbers will more than compensate for our speed.''

''And us?''

''We wait for their reports. Advise them. The same with Mace in the Hub. Stretch the Chairman's resources as thin as we can, but stay out of his way.''

''Excellent!'' said Bolla. ''And I don't see that the risks are higher.''

''They are.''

''How? If we—''

''Because as we coordinate those activities, we'll be making plans for a preemptive strike. On Regnum.''

''What?'' Bolla felt a flutter in his chest.

Tyrees continued in a tone as implacable as the wall of a tidal wave. ''As we grow in strength, the Chairman will pull out the knives. The pattern is already there. The conflict will escalate—perhaps gradually—into your river of blood. We will cut the process short in the only way possible: by destroying the center of galactic government—

and the Chairman—in one blow. We will attempt to kill several million, mostly innocent lives, in order to spare several hundred million.''

''Pol, *no!*'' whispered Bolla.

''That is the choice—or quit,'' said Tyrees. ''You see now?'' he added bitterly, ''And I am called Live-Giver.'' They listened to the crunch of the cup fragments under his boots as he returned to the bubble. ''But that is the way it must be.''

The silence that began the meeting returned, smothering them. The four men had long ceased to hear the almost subliminal hum that meant that *Condor* lived on. Meta-sol did not stir. He seemed like some filmy creature of the depths, nearly without substance, but bearing great pressures.

Again Radis was the first to fight off the oppression. ''Or the *Chairman* might quit. That's a possibility. You've already said that we can't predict his behavior, haven't you, Doctor?''

Bolla ignored him. ''*When*, Pol?''

Tyrees spoke to the Void. ''When the Chairman pulls out the first knife.''

CHAPTER SEVENTEEN

As *Condor*'s leaders planned their audacious attack on the most heavily guarded planet in the Regnum, reports began trickling in. The president of Caanon was acting as their communications middleman in both directions. He sent message bursts at prearranged times to pathways in intergalactic space that only *Condor* could reach. He and Spelsol had begun the process of renewing contact with the "seedlings"—the Seers who had been scattered thinly on likely planets throughout the Regnum. The public communications network had already brought some news of the progress of the New Covenant to the citizenry at large, but only in the form of small news items—the Chairman's unofficial hand at work.

Mace had been directed to step up initiatives against the Regnum, but to avoid pitched battles. A virtual library of data supplied by Tyrees and Radis about Cadre tactics and personnel added significantly to the effort. Old territories were consolidated, new ones claimed. Before, the Hub had always fought a tentative, rearguard action; now it was beginning to flex new muscle.

The reports emanating from the Seers made it evident that the growth of the New Covenant was virulent. Even now, if *Condor* and her passengers were to disappear forever, the wave would continue to build until it eventually washed over the galaxy. Few of the seeding spots were as spectacularly fecund as was Caanon, but fewer

still proved barren; from these the seedlings were ordered
unearthed and replanted.

On still other worlds—untended—the lightly publicized
movement had already sprouted hybrids of unknown varie-
ties. Whatever the nurturing soil, however, two constants
held: the practice of some form of the basic Tercian disciplines of self-control, and the worship of the Vitar.

Vitar. Divinity embodied in man. A *real* man, of flesh
and blood, who could give life. He moved through the
stars at will. The Seers had lived and learned and slept and
ate with Him, and they told their stories of His miracles.
He had at once the remoteness and omniscience of a god,
and the immediacy of blood kinship—because He was
what they were meant to be, and with dedication, what
they had the possibility of becoming. The proof of His
righteousness lay in *The Teraac* and in the simple, undeni-
able evidence of their new sight, since they were able to
do on this day what they could not do on the day before.
He lived in them. He *was them.* Others had seen Him and
given testimony. He would return. The Seers carried His
word. The New Covenant. Vitar.

The movement was as yet largely localized on a few
dozen planets, and its message beyond that limited to the
tongues of travelers—some carrying the word with messianic
fervor, some with the innocent prattle of gossip. The
public made no connection between this new phenomenon
and the Trade Wars in the Hub, nor did they make one
with any opposition to the system under which they lived.
This was in the Chairman's interest lest the New Covenant become a rallying cry for political enemies; it was in
Tyrees's interest because he feared a holocaust if that were
to come about.

Stalemate. Each awaited the other's moves, conserving
strength and fearing a vulnerable commitment. The pawns
in the game knew nothing of their peril—and dying pawns
they would be, regardless of the outcome, for that has
always been the lot reserved by history for those who
accept a modicum of personal comfort in exchange for a
skeptical and active vigilence of their leaders.

The debate over tactics for the strike on Regnum—were
the Chairman, as expected, to take more violent measures

against them—was hot and frustrating. The destructive
power of *Condor* was awesome, but concentrated. In any
situation numbers would be ridiculously against her. Even
the remote possibility that one of the few others of her
kind would be permanently stationed near Regnum could
not be ruled out.

In the end they decided that their fortunes had to bank
on the same advantages that had served them so well in the
Hub—speed and surprise. Tyrees would choose an intergalactic pathway that would catapult them into Regnum's
system with the sudden impact of a stone into a window.
In the few minutes when they were stooping through conventional space near the target, they would unleash the
same kind of devastating horror meant for Tercet two years
earlier. Regnum would be reduced to a cinder in the eye of
the Void—if those few minutes of time allowed.

So the reports from Loriis were studied, the galactic
communications net monitored, and refinements to the
strike plan attempted. The last proved impossible, since
the best course seemed never to rise above the sophistica-
tion of a bear turning to charge his hunters.

In the meantime the crew chafed. Many had been over
two years inside a protective shell, an artificial environment that sustained but did not comfort. Conceivably they
could survive indefinitely as outlaws, believing as they did
in their cause and having faith in their masters. But psy-
chologically two essential elements were lacking, and like
primitives with full bellies who suffered from malnutri-
tion, those needs went unrecognized: productive activity,
and the disorderly ease of a normal, domestic existence in
which movement and space were matters of arbitrary conve-
nience rather than survival. Morale was fading.

Shaamlik was part of the problem. Her demand for
precise efficiency had grown more ruthless, and in this
time of waiting, was a constant irritant to the crew. Drills that
had been performed to perfection weeks earlier now fell
below her standards; whether standards or performance
had changed was a moot point. "Captain Bitch," they had
come to call her. They had long ago come to the
conclusion—one born of both fear and respect—that "Black
Rast" was unknowable; but Captain Bitch, they felt they

knew: a sexless ball breaker who got her jollies by using rank to belittle and humiliate. Her competence was unquestioned, but eighty days swinging from an invisible anchor in the dead calm sea of intergalactic space, as nicely placed for safety as anything in the universe could be, rendered that competence temporarily redundant.

As only he could, Tyrees had frozen out the incident with Shaamlik in the gym. He had made it into a chunk of the past, to him as irrelevant as an undersea irregularity at the bottom of a massive iceberg. Dr. Bolla, had he known, would have considered it relevant indeed, given his training, his knowledge of Tyrees's history, and the fact that the iceberg was a classic analogy of the human psyche.

Condor's becalming in the doldrums of space came to an end; it was time for Tyrees to take her out to test the winds and chart the waters. The strike plan depended upon the most exquisite navigation of intergalactic pathways, as the use of a galactic pathway to bring them into Regnum's system would greatly diminish the surprise effect, and would require a prior entry into the Milky Way. Condor was to leave her roost among the cliffs and fly over the galactic valley, testing drafts and lines of sight, seeking out a strike path that would lend the most speed and terror to her stoop.

Tyrees was back in the command chair, Shaamlik standing behind him, beautiful and deadly, supervising the bridge crew. He was resting now, pacing himself, for the process of reading the pathways was still draining in spite of his ever-increasing mastery of it. In less than a day *Condor* had already folded her wings twice to streak part way down a strike line toward the target. There were others, how many he did not know, yet to be tested.

Three of the bridge crew, depending upon the shift time, functioned as NAVCOM. But when Tyrees was in the command chair, it was always the same one at the board. Her name was Earthe, but Tyrees didn't know that; he knew only that when he reached into the Void, when he was "seeing" and murmuring numbers like a psychiatric patient under hypnosis on a couch, she always understood. They had come to be symbiotic. The reassuring tap of her sure fingers on the comkeys was his only link to the universe his mind had perilously abandoned. She seemed to know when he was uncertain, and her patience over-matched his. She seemed to know when he was losing grasp before he did, warning him in ways the bridge crew could not recognize, that he needed to come back, needed to rest.

Earthe was old for space crew, almost matronly. She had that soft, placid beauty that comes to some women in middle life after conventional physical appeal had been denied in earlier years. Slightly overweight, slightly graying, she had the unobtrusive competence and empathy acquired only by those who have been able to dispense with per-sonal vanities enough to look outward for fulfillment. No one was aware—least of all, Tyrees—that the figure in black incumbent upon the command chair had become the ineffable chalice of her soul.

Tyrees stirred. "NAVCOM."

"Yes, sir."

"Extrapolate. Estimate of elapsed time in Regnum's solar system."

"Yessir . . . thirteen minutes, twelve seconds, sir."

"Huh. Still too long, I think. . . . FIRECOM."

"Sir?"

"I understand we don't need maneuvering time within the target system to assure a hit?"

"Well, uh, it depends, sir. If we assume the worst case scenario—a pathway dump at the greatest possible dis-tance from target, and in a bad attitude—hit percentage would be about ninety. But that's extreme broad beam."

"Ninety is an acceptable margin. Broad beam is a problem?"

FIRECOM shifted in his chair. "Again, sir, it depends. On the kind of, uh . . . damage we want."

He was obviously reluctant to continue. Tyrees emerged quickly from the lassitude that always enveloped him after a pathway search. The blue eyes flared, the jaw line hardened as he swung to face FIRECOM directly.

"Explain. Precisely."

"Yessir. Extreme broad beam cuts a very wide, low-energy swath, sir. At a parsec's distance, little or no structural damage to the planet itself, little or no concussion. Intense heat, flash fires, induced meteorological effects—tidal waves, hurricanes, ice-cap melt—destruction of surface buildings. . . . Like that.'' He shrugged. Earthe noticed Tyrees's shoulders slump a little.

''Survival rate?''

Another shrug. ''Eighty, eighty-five percent. Mostly from the secondary effects.''

Tyrees's face was a stone. Earthe almost reached out to him. She wanted to cradle his head at her breast.

'' 'Secondary.' that also means 'slow.' ''

A nod. ''Yessir. Slower on the other side.''

''What?''

''The unexposed side, sir. Maybe only *fifty* percent there.''

Tyrees sat still in the command chair, but his eyes lost focus. Earthe's heart cried out to him.

''Regnum. The city. Can we time it well enough to put her on the exposed side?''

''Uh . . . don't know sir.''

FIRECOM leaned uncertainly to his board. He watched his hands pushed with brusqueness to one side. Shaamlik was reaching over his shoulder and punching keys angrily. After a moment she paused to stare at a figure on the screen. She punched again, stared again, then lifted her head, almost triumphantly.

''No,'' she said. ''Can't be guaranteed. Not unless we pop out almost in orbit. Regnum's rotation is too fast.''

''So,'' he sighed, ''we might decimate the population and leave the Chairman and his Council totally untouched.''

''Chances are, we'd get them,'' said Shaamlik grimly.

Tyrees muttered without looking at her. '' 'Chances are' . . . my river of blood. No, that's not war, that's terrorism. We'll keep looking for a better pathway. Close enough for a narrow beam. NAVCOM.'' Shaamlik turned away.

''Yes, sir.''

''Record those last coordinates. Prepare for another session.''

Earthe hesitated. She looked over her shoulder at Tyrees splayed in the command chair five paces away and slightly above her. He was wan with fatigue. Her eyes brimmed with concern.

''Uh, please, sir. You shouldn't . . . you need rest.''

Now Tyrees hesitated, more out of surprise than because he was considering her suggestion. Before he responded, Shaamlik was screaming.

"NAVCOM! You're relieved. You are here to *follow* orders, not question them. Leave your station!"

Even for "Captain Bitch" this was strong, and the bridge crew's faces showed it. Face flushing, Earthe was rising from her chair when Tyrees stopped her with a motion of his hand.

"No. Stay there, NAVCOM. She's right, Captain. I do need a rest. Stand down, bridge."

Through the bridge ran a staccato of clicks as toggles were flipped. The ever-present hum took on a lower, softer key. The light changed its source from a semicircle of bright islands to a generalized glow as most of the instruments went dark.

Shaamlik took one step toward the command chair. Her lips pulled back from her teeth like a carnivore. Tyrees turned to her, saw the look and frowned.

"Captain?"

Shaamlik hissed like a cat and exploded from the bridge. Tyrees remained as he was for a moment, then nodded slowly to himself. The bridge crew paid careful attention to their instruments. Tyrees rose, pointed wordlessly at Shaamlik's exec at the FIRECOM station, received a "yessir," and followed her off the bridge.

The captain's cabin was closest to the bridge, so he found her there just as she was turning to close the door. She stared at him, nostrils flaring. Her hair was the helmet of an ancient warrior, and her expression matched it.

"Yes?"

"Captain. I'm sorry. I shouldn't have countermanded your order in front of the crew."

"No, you shouldn't have."

"But NAVCOM was right. Two sessions is enough. I wouldn't have been functioning properly. All I can do is apologize for not handling it differently."

"Very well," said Shaamlik coldly.

Tyrees nodded and was about to leave, but he stopped with his hand on the jamb to look at her closely. He saw bluish veins standing out under her upper neck, the muscles there taut, stretching the skin tightly around her jaw line, giving the beautiful face an ugly, skeletal look. She had lost weight. She looked back at him with hollow eyes.

"Sit down," he said. She frowned. "Please."

Shaamlik took the two steps to her desk chair, swiveled it to her and sat. Her knees came together and with both hands she made a single fist in her lap. Tyrees moved to her and gently turned the chair back around again until she faced away from him. When she felt his hands on her neck, she started violently.

"Please," he said again, and his fingers began to probe. They touched lightly, surely, along the cords of muscle and tendrils of nerve from the base of her skull to the bottoms of her shoulder blades. Almost immediately Shaamlik felt her body let go, as if one by one knots were being untied. As she came loose, the fingers grew more insistent, though still gentle. They probed deeper, massaging away tightness she hadn't known was there. Neither spoke. Soon she was drunk under the tender power of his hands, the soft drunkenness that comes somewhere between sensual pleasure and sleep. She was dreamily aware that she had never felt so intimately touched before without some sense of violation as well. She was sorry when Tyrees spoke, because she wanted nothing else but to feel the hands.

"We are all under pressure," he said, "but I think it will all be over before very long—one way or the other." A soft chuckle. The sound brought her up, out of her reverie, because she had never heard him laugh before. "You know, in the Cadre you get a lot of training in muscles, bones, and nerves—but not for this sort of thing. This is more Tercian." The hands stopped, and she felt abandoned. "You're better now."

"Yes . . . thank you." Her voice was no longer knife-edged, only glum.

Tyrees moved to the door, but turned back before opening it. "The crew is doing their best, Captain. Why are you so hard on them?"

He watched the back of her head snap up. She rose slowly from her chair before turning to him. She took a deep breath.

"Why did you do that in the gym?"

His face froze. "What?"

"I have to know. I have a *right* to know. Why did you do that to me?"

Fear rose into his eyes. "I-I . . . meant no offense," he stammered.

Shaamlik's face broke into an expression of pleading; her cry was that of a child unjustly punished. "But why? *Why!*"

"Please . . . I . . . don't know. I'm sorry." Tyrees leaned against the door. A hand came up to rub his eyes. "It had . . . nothing to do with you. Nothing."

"Nothing?"

"You are a very attractive woman and I . . . wanted you. But . . ." His other hand joined the first, though he had stopped rubbing. His hands covered his face from his forehead down. "But I can't . . . I can't . . ."

Shaamlik realized with a shock that the strongest, most contained man she had ever met was breaking down rapidly before her eyes. She moved to him without thinking and grasped both his wrists.

"Let me help you," she whispered, pulling gently. It was like pulling on the hands of a marble statue. "Please." The hands trembled, but stayed. "Please . . . I love you."

The hands convulsed, fingers turning them into fists. Then, finally responding to her pressure, they came away from his face. It was the face of a very distraught, very young boy, crushed by something terrible which was beyond his understanding. The blue eyes swam in tears and pain and the cheeks glistened. His nose was running.

"Oh . . . Pol, oh Pol," she murmured. Gone was the confident seductress of the gym. It was hurt recognizing, reaching out to other hurt; it was strength buttressed too long by will, reaching out to greater strength, and greater will finally giving way. Neither understood anything else except an awareness of that rare communion. Neither had ever permitted such vulnerable exposure.

She took him to her bed and rocked with his head cradled in her arms, rocked and sobbed until her stroking hands were wet with both their tears.

After a time they slept.

Shaamlik awoke many hours later, and he was gone again.

CHAPTER EIGHTEEN

At some cost to Pol Tyrees, the optimum pathway was found. It exposed *Condor* at the bottom of her attack stoop for nine minutes within Regnum's system. Two of those minutes, if she survived them, would be enough to claw the heart out of Regnum's galactic civilization. Each of the seven thereafter only served to increase the chances of *Condor*'s extinction.

Condor once more flew back to that appointed place in the Void where she received messages from Caanon. She had been so long separate from her kind that isolation was becoming her natural state. She was grim and somber now, and perhaps accepting. It had been so long, so long . . . that loneliness had taken on a softer touch, an embrace that was strangely comforting. Certainly she did not despair. She was flying as the last winged hunters flew— proud but knowing.

She had come to know *what* she was, though the actual process of her metamorphosis remained a mystery to her. She had become a thing of the Void. It was not she, nor she it—but each defined the other as alien defines alien, as white defines black—*Condor* was what It was not. This seemed enough.

So she waited. She waited and accepted words from the spinning fuzz of weak light below, from a place so far away and so long ago, that only tugs of involuntary memory kept her course constant. She had to resist the lure of truths the Void kept whispering, hints of thought that tantalized with a knowing more profound than the words flickering up from the baubles of timorous light under her wings. Everyone aboard *Condor* heard the fearful whisperings, but few acknowledged them; only Meta-sol welcomed them.

Shaamlik had taken care to salve the marks of her whip on the crew. She did not lose the title of Captain Bitch, but it was increasingly used in that time-honored, grudgingly possessive, almost affectionate tone of foot soldier grunts when referring to their commanding officer; they might call him ''iron balls'' and then go out to die for him.

All—with only two exceptions—favored the theory that Shaamlik and Tyrees had become lovers; hence the fortuitous mellowing effect. They had noted how she looked at him of late, had seen her hand once or twice rest lightly on his shoulder as he sat in the command chair. They remarked that sometimes, after emerging from his semicomatose communion with the pathways, his eyes seemed lost or frightened until they found her nearby on the bridge.

The exceptions were Bolla and Meta-sol: Bolla reserved judgment because he was both wise and a psychologist, and because he knew a great deal of Tyrees's past; Meta-sol never voiced judgments in such matters.

The first message after they reached their nest in the Void was massive, since they had been out of communication with Caanon for several months. There were detailed reports of the continued growth of the New Covenant as Spel-sol's minions gradually made contact with and lent aid to the scattered Seers. These highly trained, highly motivated converts also carried with them shining stories of Vitar's visit to Caanon. They told of the bold, black figure standing calmly, high above the multitude as they called His name. They told of the stillness He held, of the long silence He kept, until throats were sore, dry rasps from calling His name, and their roars had died to whispers. They told of how His arms were slowly raised then, how He looked to the horizon of the sea of faces and shouted a simple message. They told of how the sound of His voice rolled like thunder over the sea. They told the message.

"I . . . AM . . . YOU. YOU . . . ARE . . . ME. WE
. . ARE , , , *GOD*."

A few of the most adept of Spel-sol's people went to
follow lonely ministries in other worlds where the New
Covenant was only a rumor. A few more had already
begun to spread out from the worlds of the other Seers.

In the Hub, Mace was ruling the roost. There, also, the
name of Vitar was still only a rumor; but the name of Pol
Tyrees, ex-Cadre One and leader of the rebel cause, was
on everyone's lips. Commander of the invincible *Condor*,
he fought on, unscathed in the very heartland of the tyran-
nous Regnum.

All but Meta-sol were on the bridge a week later, awaiting the second message burst. They were mellow with the
sense of rich ripening the last news had brought, and had
long since contented themselves with the self-imposed determination to wait.

"How much more, TELCOM?" Radis was at ease on
the bridge. Cadre Ones were bred for leadership. When he
was present, Shaamlik automatically fell one link in the
command chain. This was not so for Bolla—much to the
doctor's satisfaction.

"Just over six minutes, sir, but we're already on receive."

"Good. I just love news from home."

Bolla chuckled. "Home? You were only on Caanon for
a day!"

"Ahh, but our anchor rests there, Doctor, though the
line is long. Besides, ask *any* Cadre man where his home
is. I doubt that many would give the name of their birth-
place after thirty or forty years. I would probably have said
'Sector HQ,' and then thought a minute for the name of the
planet."

Bolla nodded. "Well, this is *my* home now." He stamped
once heavily on the deck. "Be she ever so humble. Three
quarters of a gravity becomes the old and fat—and fading.
Aside from that, it's rather nice to sit up here snuggly,
watching the universe go by. Right, Pol?"

Tyrees smiled. He turned but did not lift his hands from
where they rested on the back of the command chair.
Shaamlik sat there, as was his preference when he wasn't
reading the pathways.

"Are you goading me again, Hans?"

"Oh, by no means, my boy. If this 'rendering up' is as impressive as the last, I shall be genuflecting soon." Tyrees's smile faded somewhat, but he said nothing. Bolla, afraid he had overstepped, changed tracks. "That Spel-sol is a wonder. All the Seers have that . . . that special quality, but not like him. He's a pied piper . . . on a galactic scale."

"Yes," said Radis, "that's true. He has the . . . well, a prophet's appeal. He inspires on a grand scale, as you say. But to me . . . there's something he's *missing*."

"Oh?" said the doctor, hiking his waistband to a more comfortable position around his girth. "Pray tell, what is that?"

"Humanity."

Bolla laughed. "And just what is *that*?"

"Among the Seers," said Radis, deadly serious, "it's generally strong—especially in Meta-sol. It's the . . . call it a background matrix—an unstated first principle. You've read *The Teraac*, Doctor. It breathes out of every line."

Bolla was mildly surprised. "Hummph. Radis, you are exhibiting some interesting philosophical tendencies of late. Hitherto quite latent. But answer my question: What is 'humanity'? What is this 'first principle'? Do enlighten me! Talk to the old professor!"

Radis's powerful shoulders bunched involuntarily. His eyes fell to the floor and he hesitated, then spoke without looking at Bolla.

"Don't patronize me, Doctor. Even you have things to learn."

Bolla looked at him sharply. A sardonic retort was loaded and aimed, until he saw that Tyrees was listening attentively, watching them both with a strange intensity. His favorite technique with bright students had always been a glib and mocking irony. It tended to separate those who played for the audience—by throwing out clever, ad hoc notions—from those with more disciplined minds, who had probed deeply into something that mattered to them.

"I'm sorry," he said to Radis. "I didn't mean to make light. Old defense mechanism. "Please explain your first principle." He noted that Tyrees's hands had left the back of the command chair so that he could turn. They hung at his sides like those of a weary fighter. His features were hard to make out, now that he faced away from the bridge consols.

Radis raised his eyes. "No profound revelations, Doctor. 'First principle' is my own term for it . . . but it pervades *The Teraac*, and everything Meta-sol says. Nothing supercedes the sanctity of human life. Nothing. No idea, no belief—certainly no political system. And humanity has a . . . a destiny. That, too, has sanctity."

Bolla thought for a moment. "Those two things—the sanctity of human life, and the destiny of human life—you don't see the potential for contradiction in that?"

"No."

Bolla nodded sadly. "You do. You do. Otherwise, you would not have condemned Spel-sol for having a holy vision of our destiny at the expense of human life."

Radis frowned. Tyrees stepped toward them. Before either could speak, a soft ping interrupted the even, electronic hum of the bridge.

"It's time," said Shaamlik.

Tyrees turned back and they all stared at TELCOM's station.

Nothing.

Shaamlik leaned forward. "TELCOM?"

"There's . . . nothing, Captain. No signal."

"Double check your settings, TELCOM."

"Yes, Captain." TELCOM knew there had been no mistake, but went dutifully through the motions. "Everything checks. Just no signal." Shaamlik turned to Tyrees.

"Trouble?"

Tyrees shook his head. Caanon had never missed a transmission time by more than a few seconds. "How long are they overdue?"

TELCOM consulted a timer. "Over four minutes, now, sir."

"We'll wait."

Thirty minutes passed. Each one of them added to the level of tension on the bridge. When she could do so unobtrusively from her NAVCOM station, Earthe kept a close watch on Tyrees, seeing things that only Meta-sol— and perhaps Bolla—could see. To her, his every word, every motion, was reluctant. If it were possible to age ten years in a few months without changing physically in any obvious way, then he had done so, she thought. At the same time she was certain she could also detect a new calm in him that was different from his habitual, rigid control; but there was . . . sadness in it. Resignation?

Earthe had been waiting to hear the order for most of the half hour, but still winced when it came. Her empathy for Tyrees was such that his plunges through the Void told on her almost as much as they did on him.

"NAVCOM."

"Yes, sir."

"Set the pathway coordinates for Caanon. Captain?" Shaamlik vacated the command chair and Tyrees settled in. "You'd better get some rest, Captain. We may need you when we hit normal space. God . . ." He smiled at her in mid-sentence, as if he had just come across a private joke. ". . . knows what we'll find there."

Shaamlik nodded, but hesitated. The brittle eyes she always carried on the bridge softened. "Please . . . be careful," she whispered, and walked quickly away.

As Tyrees had taken Shaamlik's place, so Radis took his behind the command chair.

"Vitar?"

Tyrees turned to him with a look of exasperation on his face. "Radis, why do you insist on calling me that?"

"Because you are a man with many names," said Radis smugly. "Tyrees. Nesol-Rast. The doctor calls you Pol. You even had the same Cadre title as mine not so long ago. So, what the hell?" He lifted one shoulder in a shrug of mock confusion. "I decided to use the most common one, even if no one else on *Condor* does."

Tyrees sighed and turned back to the screen. He shook his head, but more to himself than Radis. "We're an odd lot," he muttered. "An odd lot of fallen angels." He snorted softly.

"Beg pardon?"

"Nothing. You were going to say something earlier?"

"Oh. Yeah. When we get there—Caanon—we're not going to find anything we like, are we?"

Tyrees stared into the black screen for a time before answering. "Hope for a transmitter malfunction," he said, but there was no hope in his voice.

As Tyrees and Earthe went through the ritual in preparation for entry onto the intergalactic pathway, Radis, too, thought about the changes in the man he had chosen to serve. He looked at the back of his head and shoulders and listened to the quiet, assured voice. Still dressed always in black. He had taken lately to a simple tunic with a round collar. Radis decided that it was not so much a misplaced or nostalgic loyalty to the Cadre that inspired this Cadrelike, one-man uniform; it was the man's basic personality: Spartan, committed, starkly uncompromising. That *hadn't* changed. What had? Perhaps . . . yes. The *passion*. The burning pursuit. It was gone. Why?

Destiny. He had always considered that word melodramatic pap when applied to a single man—but no longer. Yet Tyrees now seemed as one who did not shape events, but rode with the tug of their current. Perhaps that *was* destiny. Perhaps that was what he had discovered: that once a man *had* the consummate pride to choose his destiny, he found that there were no more real choices. Paradox. The defiant demand for freedom resulted in a kind of slavery to one's own destiny, because such a thing once set in motion . . . And there were all those people, all those lives that current had taken up. . . . Radis shook his head like a fascinated child who had looked at the night sky too long and became dizzy with it. Feeling vaguely embarrassed, he looked sidelong at Bolla, who was folded wearily into his seat, chunks of bulk molded softly into the nooks where gravity felt best to cradle them. The bald pate caught a gleam of light as the old man returned his look. He smiled, and strangely, nodded.

Condor broke into Caanon's system at full battle alert, but there was nothing in local space—nothing at all. Shaamlik was back in the command chair, with Tyrees behind her again. After SCANCOM had done a full search and reported that simple fact, Tyrees's eyes closed, cutting off their magnetic blue for a moment. When they opened, something vital had left them. He spoke very softly.

"Not a single vessel, SCANCOM?"

"No, sir."

"Set for Caanon orbit, NAVCOM. Full speed."

"Yessir." Earthe made the inputs with smooth precision, but she was aching inside.

A half hour later *Condor* was in orbit. The face Caanon habitually showed to visitors was reminiscent of ancient Terra's: a cheery turquoise beneath capricious swatches of white cotton. Now, the overhead screen displayed an irregular ball of brackish, black-bitten gray. A shroud.

Tyrees's voice became even softer. "Do a read, SCANCOM."

The man at the SCANCOM station was the youngest of the bridge crew. Mouth agape, he was staring at the screen.

"SCANCOM!" shouted Shaamlik. "A read!"

SCANCOM started violently, but his hands leaped to his board. Seconds passed in a silence that was broken only by the soft thump of his fingers on the keys. He reported his readings at short intervals, and his words came with the restrained cadence of a doctor recording his findings as he performed an autopsy.

"Nothing on the communications channels . . . no radio activity . . . intense energy sources . . . diffused in spots. Fire—must be fire. Storm readings . . . all over the place . . . concentrations of dust—or ash—in the atmosphere . . . high in the atmosphere . . ."

"That's enough," said Tyrees. He leaned over Shaamlik and brushed a small square of light on the command chair's arm. The screen went dark. Everyone continued to stare at it.

"Should we . . . go down?" said Shaamlik. Her voice was a croak.

"To do what?" said Tyrees harshly. "Count bodies?" He looked at Earthe with such deadly hatred that she shivered.

"We go to Regnum."

CHAPTER NINETEEN

The Chairman dominated the room. In the past that domi-
nance had usually been penned, kept in check but blood-
ready and visible in the near background. Now it was in
the center of the ring. The lowered head, the small, darting
eyes, the bullish shoulders hunched aggressively forward,
his whole bearing bellowed a ruthless challenge. He pulled
the members of the Council close, where he was most
lethal.

"Yes," he was saying, "your hearing is quite unim-
paired, I'm sure. Caanon is dead. Survivors—if there are
any—are now reliving the Stone Age."

The Cadre Proctor, the only Council member with fore-
knowledge, nodded sagely. Shock and fear hummed a
harrowing cycle around the rest of the table.

"No."

"Chairman, you have . . ."

"This can't be . . ."

"A member planet . . ."

"No!"

"Oh, my . . ."

"Shit shit shit shit!"

The Chairman's eyes flicked back and forth around the
table, but his expression did not change. He was calmly
taking note of how each of the Council members reacted as
he waited for the babble to subside.

"Yes, a strong measure, I grant you. That is exactly

what has been lacking in this affair. The same goes for the Hub—but we'll deal with that later. I have used the emergency measures granted to me by the Council of the Regnum to take the first decisive step in this mess. If I had waited any longer, *no* action, no matter how drastic, would have reversed the process. Up to now our caution, our indecision, has allowed a parasite to continue unchecked, to eat away at our bowels. Caanon was a house infested with pestulent vermin, ladies and gentlemen. I could not hesitate to put such a house to the torch when the plague had begun to spread.''

Most of the Council members were still too shocked to respond. Political and personal ambitions notwithstanding, they had been the caretakers of the Pax Regnum—a thousand years of peace. That concept had been shaken in the past generation, but it had always been the ideal, the principle that overrode all weaknesses. With the exception of the Chairman, even the most corrupt of the Regnum's guardians regarded it as sacrosanc—not necessarily because they were at bottom altruistic believers, but because it formed the foundation of the house in which they were the masters.

But some were true believers.

A man near the bottom of the table stood up. He was visibly shaking. The others were surprised because he rarely spoke in Council sessions at all.

''Th-the granting of e-emergency powers does not en-en-compass insanity,'' he said. ''I move . . . I move for the impeachment of the Ch-Chairman.''

So the double row of Council members had to absorb a second shock, and it numbed most of them. They didn't know what to feel, what to think, even where to look. Only the Chairman's eyes were in motion as the silence continued to draw out like a metal filament toward its breaking point.

''I *said*,'' prodded the speaker, in a voice that was now a screech, ''I said that I move impeachment—of the Chairman!''

Slowly, a long-standing member, one whose sins as a public guardian had come long ago to be countless, stood as well. In words formed from a tired sigh, he said, "Yes. Enough . . . enough, I second the motion."

Then a third stood. "Aye," he said.

A forth. "Aye."

There may have been a fifth, and perhaps more, but no one ever found out. A Cadre One entered the chambers and swiftly directed with hand signals the half-dozen armed Fours with him. The standing men were stiff-marched away. There were no protests, because no one was particularly surprised. They recognized its inevitability on the instant the Cadre One appeared. One Councilman even managed to keep his sense of humor.

"I don't suppose there is any need to discuss the motion," he said.

The Chairman offered no justification for the unprecedented arrests. He resumed as if nothing had happened.

"I want the Council to be aware of the policies the Cadre Proctor and I have laid out, then the strategy. Agreed?" A perfunctory pause. "Our first priority is to *reconsolidate*. Swiftly, and expediently, we will reclaim lost ground. The first step in that process is to eliminate Tyrees; then we must . . . *fumigate*, get rid of this disease called the New Covenant. The second priority is to crush the Hub rebels. In both cases the Regnum—sadly, for the first time in her history—must remove her velvet gloves." Now the pause was not token. The Chairman's round black eyes hit every single member of the Council in his turn. None took advantage of the opportunity to speak.

"We have already set in motion the mechanisms to beef up the Regnum's military arm. Proctor?"

The Cadre Proctor launched into a litany of measures taken to increase military strength rapidly—manpower, weaponry, vessels of war—all of which had hitherto required formal Orders in Council. When he finished, a hand was raised. The others held their breath, but the speaker was not foolhardy.

"Mr. Chairman. These measures will take time. No doubt we have enough so they'll help in the Hub. What about Tyrees?"

The Chairman smiled one of his rare smiles. It did

something grotesque to his face, like the addition of a vending machine to a barren planet.

"We have fourteen Battlefleet vessels of the CX class— *Condor*'s class. *All* of them were recalled before Caanon was . . . fumigated. By tomorrow, they will all be in this system."

"But I don't see how—"

"Tyrees will be coming *here*," hissed the Chairman, black eyes agleam. "Caanon was his invitation!"

CHAPTER TWENTY

Condor was in her stoop.

She dove down an intergalactic pathway ensheathed in her own womb of time and space. It was a place of being, alien to and secure from the tides of painful time and constricted space that wrapped the galaxy into which she dove. It was a birthing she had known before, but each falling heightened her awareness of the transition from water to sand. Each tunneled entry scraped deeper. Tender senses screamed louder.

So it had to be with all things that fall into life, and so it was with her. Repetition only made that lesson more poignant. As the cost of life mounted, so did her demand for significance.

"Entry in five minutes," announced Earthe from her NAVCOM station.

Tyrees rose from the command chair. Since the pathway coordinates had been carefully established before their return to Caanon, he had only to monitor this plunge into the Regnum system, and the drain on him had been minimal. Shaamlik took his place.

"Battle alert, all stations," she said calmly. "Full shields, FIRECOM."

The crew was a smooth, integrated team of veterans now, but their disciplined skills could not erase their fear. Response time was still fast—perhaps faster; voices still maintained the articulated monotone; hands were still steady and confident. Nevertheless, the subtle vibrations of fear born in their minds hummed through the air, resonated with those of their fellows, and created the jangling atmosphere known even by the bravest when they anticipated battle.

Some soldiers, ancient and modern, buttressed resolve by taking drugs; some simply called upon whatever inner strength they possessed. Some fled. *Condor*'s crew, however, did have another resource. They had the training of Meta-sol. They were the lowest of acolytes compared even with such as Radis, but it gave them a measure of self-control. It was a gift more vital than any drug, because it did not distort reality.

"One minute," said Earthe.

Shaamlik flipped open some keys. "Ready all systems, FIRECOM. Maximum range."

"Yes, Captain . . . systems readied."

Shaamlik turned in the command chair. "SCANCOM, I want your readings *fast*, understand? All sensors at max range, and you start spouting the instant we hit normal space."

"Yes, Captain." SCANCOM hunched closer to his console, fingers flexing over his board.

Shaamlik felt a touch at her shoulder and started to turn, but arrested the movement when the pressure increased. Tyrees let his hand rest there only a moment, but the tension in her neck cords softened, and she nodded minutely.

Earthe began the countdown. "Ten . . . nine . . . eight . . ."

"I love you, Pol," whispered Shaamlik at the blank screen above them.

"Three . . . two . . . one . . . now!"

Condor shuddered slightly as she fell off the pathway into conventional space. A second later the screen was still a swarm of fireflies seeking form, but Shaamlik was barking orders.

"Full power! Regnum coordinates, NAVCOM! Report, SCANCOM!"

"Sorry, Captain, it's still too . . . now it's coming. . . ."

The swarm on the screen was struggling into resolution. "Bandit! One bandit, Close! Point one five parsec—"

"FIRECOM! Lasgun. Arm and fire!" Shaamlik opened a key.

FIRECOM stabbed rapidly at squares of light on his board. "Targeted . . . fired!"

"We should be in time," muttered Shaamlik. "Surprise should make the—"

"It's a class CX, Captain! It's size . . . It's returned fire!"

Shaamlik thumped the arm of the command chair. "Impossible! How could they react so quickly?" They were still building speed, and evasive maneuvers at that close range would have been futile in any case. She leaned forward. "We'll have to take the shot."

They watched as a dot of light on the screen flared, was swallowed by the surrounding blackness, then reemerged again, an innocent firefly.

"Their screens were up," said Shaamlik softly. She had time to turn to Tyrees before they were hit. *Condor* shuddered.

"Power drain fifty percent, Captain." The bridge was silent, waiting.

Tyrees looked down at her. Something in the blue eyes died. "They knew," he said.

From SCANCOM: "Another bandit! No . . . two! Point four parsecs and coming fast out of the sun!"

Again the bridge waited.

Tyrees seemed frozen. Nothing about him spoke of panic—he simply had the look of a man who had just watched the dice fall, roll, and settle indifferently into place. Black dots on a white surface telling him he had risked more than he had a right to bet, that he had bet more than he realized. Finally, he spoke quietly.

"It doesn't matter, does it?"

Shaamlik shrugged. "Half power. Speed, armament, or shields. Which?"

"It doesn't *matter*, does it?"

"No."

Suddenly Radis was behind them. "Shields." Shaamlik hesitated. "Shields! Hurry!"

She shrugged again, but turned to give the order. "Full
shields, FIRECOM." As the shields built again, *Condor*'s
speed leveled.

"At least they'll know this way," said Radis. "After
we take another shot or two, we'll be defenseless—but
they'll *know* it. Anything else is suicide."

Tyrees shook his head. "It's *all* suicide. Why shouldn't
they finish us?" Vitality had been washed out of his
expression and his words. His head swiveled oddly to take
in the bridge crew, then stopped when his eyes met
Shaamlik's. What he saw there made him turn away and
walk to the observation bubble. Had he a cane, the walk
would have been Meta-sol's.

"Might as well give them the choice," muttered Radis
to his back.

"Lasgun shot! No—two!" called Earthe.

Shaamlik, too, watched Tyrees, but she responded.
Calmly, almost with disinterest. "Can we take them,
FIRECOM?"

"I—I don't know, Captain. Shield still building . . .
just hitting eighty-fi—"

Every consol exploded. They flared—without concussion, but with heat and flame, as ship systems overloaded
then erupted in the time it takes for one electron to jar
against another. In an instant the bridge was an inferno, a
closed fist of angry fire—and screams.

Most of the crew manning consol stations died before
their screams died. Those farthest from them felt intense
heat for a moment as their arms flew up instinctively to
cover their eyes, but shock was the only real blow. The
fire, having in a single heartbeat already devoured all there
was to feed upon, was gone as quickly as it came—the
wing of a terrible bird.

Even Tyrees did not have the time for any action more
positive than turning to register the horror.

FIRECOM and SCANCOM were slumped over their
dead boards, hair gone, clothes smoldering. Others who
served monitoring functions near the instruments lay on
the deck. Only one or two stirred. Radis had no eyebrows,
and there were red blisters on his face, but he was still on
his feet, swaying. Tyrees could see only the top of

Shaamlik's head above the command chair. It gleamed.
Little skin and no hair remained. An acrid stench lifted off
the command chair, carried by lazy black smoke.

He ran to her. Her face! Her face! It was a mask of
blood just beginning to flow. He reached out, but was
afraid to touch her. His senses were screaming with the
minutiae of obscenity drawn upon her face. With a moan,
he fell to his knees. His head swam. An image, like a
picture mounted on a carousel, flashed, flashed, flashed
under his closed eylids. The Purging. The Tercian ritual
that marked the birth of a Seer. He had seen it once, and
now he saw it again. A young boy in agony blinking away
his sight, skin peeling off his face as he stared for three
days up at the indifferent burning of Tercet's three suns.

For the first time in his very unnormal life, he wanted
oblivion, wanted it with a craving more deep-seated than
the most enslaved addict ever craved his drug.

Fingernails scratched feebly on the back of his hand. He
looked down and saw another hand, fingers moving convulsively over his on the deck. Earthe's bulky figure was
stretched in lines of pain toward him. He could not see her
face. It was only a charred form, reaching.

A shuddered whisper. "Vitar," it said.

CHAPTER TWENTY-ONE

Condor was a lifeless shell. Two umbilicals—one carrying life support systems and the other the only means of exit—connected her to a class CX. Even to space crew they made a strange sight: two very imposing identical sisters, hand in hand, made a stately promenade around their neighborhood solar system. None of the neighbors could tell that one of the sisters was incapable of motion without the other—or that she was now mindless.

She was also a prison. Her captors found her admirably suited for the purpose—secure, isolated, and anonymous. Except for the bridge, which was useless in any case, Tyrees and his followers had the run of the ship. Even on-board guards were unnecessary, and this pleased the captors, too, because they were nervous about the "mind tricks" devotees of the New Covenant were said to be capable of.

So the Chairman was able to exercise with some confidence the option of keeping the human cargo of *Condor* alive for two reasons: the perils of martyrdom, and the secret of the intergalactic graviton pathways. The latter, his experts assured him, was more likely the result of an advance in science than the freakish ability of a single man.

The New Covenant was another matter. The Chairman had excised the tumor of Caanon. The heart of the contagion had been neatly sliced out. But he knew that the cancer was widespread, though diffused. More Caanons

would either destroy the body itself—or worse, the surgeon. The best solution would be to have Tyrees recant—
declare publicly his apostasies, repudiate the New Covenant.
For the time being the Chairman would keep to the optimum path, since conditions had made that possible. Should
Tyrees prove totally recalcitrant, he and his band of here-
tics could be dumped into space and other means employed.

As it was now, he was in charge, and the capture of
Condor had tightened his grip on the reins. The Council
was his plaything. He might even decide to retain that
institution for tradition's sake when everything was straightened out to his satisfaction.

This was the train of thought that went through the
Chairman's mind as he sat in his office almost a parsec
away from the hand-holding sisters. It gave him immense
satisfaction to stab the buttons that called up the images
aboard *Condor*.

There . . . There he was. Tyrees. Renegade Cadre One.
The great *Vitar*. Sitting on his—what do they call it?
Pallet? Cot? Surely not bed?—bent over like a prisoner in
the dock, staring at the floor. Now *there*, ladies and
gentlemen, is a beaten man! A few kilograms of powerless
meat! Vitar indeed.

And . . . there. The famous Dr. Hans Bolla. That must
be the sick bay. He looks more like a basset hound than
ever—old fool. Mace's bit of spawning beside him. They
tell me she was a looker—now she's a vegetable with a
plastic mask for a face. Hasn't moved, hasn't spoken a
word since we took *Condor*. I wonder if I can get this bit
of film to Mace somehow. Serve notice, as it were?

Now . . . there. The traitor Radis . . . and that old
Tercian. Both staring at nothing. Are they meditating?
Don't look as beaten as Tyrees . . . but the old bugger
doesn't look like anything at all. Hard to believe that that
fifty kilos of shawl and beard started all this. Dangerous,
though. How in hell do those . . . *Seers* inspire such
devotion? The New Covenant is too popular, and still
spreading. Can I tell them I have their *god* canned like a
sardine and floating in space? Can I chance a quick exter-
mination of *all* of those Tercian priests scattered through
the Regnum? . . . No. Not yet. Officially, the members

bought the story of a raid from the Hub on Caanon—but only officially. They're waiting, watching me. Well, let them watch.

The Chairman reached out and pushed a pad that erased the still unmoving images of Radis and Meta-sol from the screen. He settled back and mused for a moment, fingers of one hand playing with the wiry hairs on the back of the other. Then, abruptly, he swiveled his chair and tapped another pad. A muted beep sounded.

"Priority One transmission. Council Eyes Only. From the Chairman to the Cadre Proctor aboard CX Vulture." He waited impatiently for another beep. "Procedural Directive: begin interrogation of prisoners. Maintain established objectives. Record and transmit entire. Highest security. Acknowledge . . . End transmission."

CHAPTER TWENTY-TWO

"You intended to destroy a planet, Tyrees. What can justify that?"

Tyrees hunched in a wardroom chair, elbows on knees, manner and voice anesthetized with indifference. He sighed. "Nothing."

The Cadre Proctor's eyes narrowed as he looked at Tyrees's back from above. He stood, a tall, austere figure caped in black. The uniform lent an oddly religious ambience to his presence that jarred with his function. In some ways he resembled Tyrees's grandfather, his predecessor. They shared the same ramrod, ageless body, the implacable presence, the rigid will that habitually subjugated an imposing intellect. Like his prisoner, he had been Cadre since the age of fifteen—and he was thirty years older. His loyalties were therefore magma deep, and all men know—without conscious thought—that to disturb such a foundation was like embracing the devil.

The Proctor was frustrated, had been through several sessions. As the silence stretched out, measuring the length of that frustration, he fingered the lasgun under his cape. The man didn't *care*. Nothing moved him. Threats and promises alike broke like slender levers when pressure was applied. Ultimately he would have to resort to drugs, but the rumors he had heard about this man made him even more leery of that avenue than he usually was. He walked around to stand in front of the prisoner.

"You *can* save some lives, you know. Your Seers, for example." Tyrees lifted his head slowly and fixed the Cadre Proctor with a long, blank stare. Unnerved, his interrogator turned away, covering his unease by parting his cape to sit. "You know now that no escape is possible—no revenge. Your refusal to cooperate—"

"No *revenge*?" These were the first of Tyrees's words that had any inflection in them, so the Proctor was encouraged—but only for an instant. "I can kill you now, Proctor."

"What? . . . What?"

"I could have killed you at any moment since you entered this room. The gun in your cape is irrelevant—so are your combat skills. Don't speak of what I can and cannot do."

The Proctor recovered quickly, and smiled. "I am well aware that you have acquired certain . . . disciplines, Tyrees. But I am not one of your acolytes. My brains are not misted over by a . . . a self-induced religious fervor. The finest human physique has certain limitations, and the slightest aggressive motion on your part would result in . . . eeaahhh!"

On the backs of his eyeballs the Proctor registered the attack—but only after it was over. In one splinter of time Tyrees was still hunched on his elbows in the chair; in the next the heel of one hand was under the Proctor's jaw and jamming his head back painfully. The other hand gripped his throat as if it were a stalk of corn about to be ripped away and thrown into a basket. A knee and shin pinned his arms and upper body to the chair back. The vertebrae going up the back of his neck pinched together with an audble "snick"; the cords of muscle up the front stretched—stretched like the strings of a violin—to a screeching tightness. In a time whose shortness he could not measure, he was a helpless infant in the cruel hands of a madman.

He was held there. Held there a few ounces of pressure from death. A little push would send him over the edge of the cliff, and he was forced into a tortured stillness, forced to feel his teeth jamming against each other and his eyes bulging from their sockets, forced to look at the cold, merciless blue of the other eyes a short lifespan away.

"You see? You see what an easy thing it is to die?"

Tyrees released him almost as abruptly as he had attacked. He was seated again before the Cadre One burst in, lasgun raised to fire.

"No!" The Proctor held up a hand. With the other he was massaging the back of his neck. "Leave us . . . leave us!" After the man had backed out—with obvious reluctance—the Proctor looked at his prisoner with new eyes. "Could . . . could you have gotten to him before he fired?"

Tyrees shrugged. Indifference had fallen back over him like a cloak. The Proctor had recovered from the shock, but his manner changed. When he spoke now, it was not in the tones of an interrogator.

"I suppose you knew there wouldn't be any point to it. *Condor* is completely sealed off—and a floating coffin without our umbilicals. Thank you for not killing me in any case."

Tyrees smiled. "As you say, there wouldn't be any point to it—except revenge."

"Touché."

The smile faded. "And I'm not a killer."

"You will forgive me if I find your . . . your generosity just now difficult to explain. You were going to *fire gut* Regnum! Your presence here has no other explanation!"

Tyrees nodded. "Just as the Chairman did—to Caanon."

"So you *were* acting out of revenge."

"No."

"Then *why*? How could you—"

"How could *you* serve such a man as the Chairman?" Tyrees was again animated, though mildly. He cocked his head to one side, as if awaiting with interest the excuses of a schoolboy truant.

"I have served *under* several Chairmen," he said with some dignity. "I have always served one master—the Regnum."

"Yes . . . yes," sighed Tyrees, the words carried on a long exhalation of breath. He rose and walked slowly to the observation bubble. The stars were cold and distant. "You also served under many Cadre Proctors—one of whom was my grandfather."

He looked out on the Void oddly, thought the Proctor, like a traveler might look upon his home valley from the mountains.

"Until the Chairman murdered him." Slowly, Tyrees turned back to face the still seated Proctor. "Do you believe that?"

The Proctor hesitasted. "Perhaps you believe it," he said. "It doesn't matter whether I believe it or not."

Tyrees walked back to his chair. He looked at the Proctor a long time before dropping into it. This man was no Radis. Too many compromises had been made for too many years. Turning back now would be a denial of a lifetime.

"Yes, I know, Proctor. You serve the Regnum."

The Proctor's chin went up a fraction, but he said nothing.

Tyrees folded his arms across his chest and leaned back. "So. Let's not waste any more of each other's time. You want to know how we traveled the intergalactic pathways. I told you—I can *see* them." The Proctor winced. "You also want me to publicly repudiate the New Covenant. I will not. You might as well get on with the chore of killing me."

"I have no intention of doing that."

"You will when so ordered," said Tyrees sharply.

"I don't believe such an order would ever come, Tyrees. I'm sure the Chairman knows the extent of the powers of . . . of a dead god."

Tyrees sniffed in scorn. "Perhaps. He may keep me alive if it's expedient—but only for a time. So I have nothing to gain by becoming his puppet. That was my condition for most of my life." His voice became as soft as the hiss of a snake. "Never again."

"You *want* to die!" The Proctor's words were piped high with his discovery.

"Not really." Tyrees looked wistfully toward the bubble. Then he turned and grinned sardonically at the Proctor. "Not really . . . but it couldn't hurt."

The Cadre Proctor was nonplussed. He stared at Tyrees, his mouth open to form words that didn't come. The grin mocked him. Finally he licked his lips and tried the last gambit.

"You don't care about your Seers, then. You can let them die. Not to mention their followers. How about Radis . . . Bolla . . . Meta-sol . . . Shaamlik . . . Mace? You've lived . . . intimately with them for almost three years. They mean *nothing* to you?"

Tyrees said nothing. The inhuman smile, like that chiseled upon a stone image of some savage deity, remained.

The Proctor waited, though he knew it was useless. Tyrees is a madman, he thought. A strange, gifted, frighteningly proud madman. He rose and fled the wardroom.

As the door hissed closed behind the Proctor, Tyrees's smile trembled and melted away. He looked again to the bubble, and closed his eyes.

CHAPTER TWENTY-THREE

Silence in the sick bay was a third presence defining that of two others, because it was what they were not. It formed a dark backdrop that outlined the sounds of their breathing. After a time the two sounds merged, becoming one. Lights were muted, there being no need for more, so the dark walls were like the silence, serving to display dimly the two softly illuminated figures.

Tyrees stood at the side of the surgical bed, as he had now for hours, with a stillness whose perfection matched that of Shaamlik, who was stretched upon it. His eyes never left her face.

Her face.

Burn damage below the neck had been treated successfully and was already virtually healed. Above it most of the skin, tissue, muscle, and cartilage had been seared away. No miracle of grafting could replace the loss in time to keep her alive. Instead, she now wore—a medically inaccurate term—a polymer mask that served as a permanent artificial skin. She now had a smooth, stylized visage, an inflexible, expressionless mask like those ancient cultures placed over the faces of their dead. It curved almost without visible demarcation into the skin of her lower neck. She had no hair, no ears, no eyes. In theory, though she would never see again, she was capable of hearing; but since the time of the inferno on *Condor*'s bridge, she had been totally catatonic in spite of the doctors' claim that there had been no brain damage.

Tyrees had unconsciously matched the rhythm of his breathing to hers. His nature and the circumstances that shaped his life had cast for him a lonely destiny, and long ago he had become aware of it, even accustomed to it. But the last few years, the last few hours, had heightened that awareness into the pain of driven spikes. *He was alone.*

Finally, in the shallow silence, in the moribund light, he lifted a hand and slowly reached to touch and trace the hardened planes that had become Shaamlik's face. His fingers moved over the insensitive convexities that had once been her eyes. They lingered there, and his own eyes closed. After a time they moved slowly, delicately, along her jaw line, then down to the point where mask and skin merged, then around her neck in an upward curve until he felt the bedsheet pressing against the back of her head. Suddenly his other hand moved to find the spot on the opposite side, and he raised her head gently. The fingers of both hands now moved toward each other along the edge of the mask until they met in the valley of an inverted V at the base of her skull.

He breathed deeply, hesitating only a moment before he willed his awareness down his arms . . . down his fingers . . . down into the darkness of the life beyond them.

Once he was committed, it was like being carried on a raft captured by a current and propelled into unknown waters. As the current strengthened, the rafter's control was rendered less and less possible—until he was simply clinging to the wildly tossing and splintered mesh of wood. Then all was a gamble. The bet was desperately crude: that the indifferent and violent chaos that bulled its destructive way through the cosmos would take no notice of a fleck of absurd consciousness that had the temerity to claim another fleck of time and space for its own.

So Tyrees clung to his raft with a tenacity even he didn't know he could muster; but even he could not have predicted how perilously close to oblivion the random storms of entropy could take him. The journey was so terrifying that his destination, his lodestar, quickly became—ignominiously—secondary. What good was *any* goal that exacted being as its tithe? The only choice left him now was elemental: let go and be consumed, or assume the ridiculous and claim the right to be. He chose. A man who was fully capable of choosing not to be, had even courted that whore of choices, decided to fight, to rage against the darkness precisely because he fought for *another's* right to be.

Then he crashed against the wall. It was not a wall in any ordinary sense because it had the substance of a thick, heavy sheet of driven rain—but he could not penetrate it. The wild torrent behind kept flinging him forward; the demented crush of watery wall kept flinging him back. It was madness. Her madness. He was caught.

The rag doll of his consciousness had been taken up by horribly cruel hands, and was shaken, shaken, shaken— until, after an infinity of time, he felt himself coming apart.

But simultaneous with the sense of dreadful loosing, came another sensation—pain. It came quickly, ruthlessly, a powerful scream shouldering aside everything else. The scream went on and on in the blackness, louder and louder, until he craved, begged for the oblivion he had only courted earlier. Then the scream was joined by another of a different pitch.

"POL! POL-NESOL-RAST! Pol . . . NESOL . . . RAST!"

When Tyrees opened his eyes, he looked into those of Meta-sol. He was lying on the sick bay deck, his head cradled in the old Tercian's lap. His mind still sung with pain for the moment it took Meta-sol to withdraw his thumbs from the back of his neck.

"Ahh." Meta-sol slumped. "You are . . . returned. Good."

Tyrees said nothing. He felt only emptiness. He felt no desire to speak or move—did not know, or care, if he was capable of either. Meta-sol sighed again and began to rock him gently, like a baby.

"I am sorry, Pol of the hidden stars. I have never brought such pain to another. But you were . . . lost." He continued to rock, his filmy beard grazing Tyrees's cheek.

Tyrees moistened his lips. His voice was a croak. "She's insane, Meta-sol. Shaamlik is insane."

"I know, my son."

"You should have left me there."

"No."

With some difficulty Tyrees rolled to one elbow and pulled himself to his feet by hanging on to Shaamlik's bed. She remained the same—a still figure, sheeted and masked it seemed, for burial. Knowing what was behind that mask, he shuddered inside. Meta-sol rose to stand beside him.

"Come. You must rest."

Tyrees stared at the figure on the bed. "Rest for what?" he muttered.

"If not for yourself, for me."

"I can't do you any good, Meta-sol. I wish I could. I can't do anything for Shaamlik, either. I'm all out of miracles."

Meta-sol said nothing, but he waited. Something in the silence gradually made itself known to Tyrees, for it was not the silence usually embraced by his old mentor. It demanded recognition. Tyrees finally turned to him and saw in the old, washed eyes something he had never seen there before—burning anger. In spite of his present state of mind, Tyrees was vaguely alarmed.

"Meta-sol, I'm sorry, but I just don't—"

With a resounding smack, Meta-sol's palm struck him full on the cheek. Not since Tyrees was sixteen had anyone been able to strike him with an unexpected blow. He was shocked by both the blow and its source. With a speed that defied time, Meta-sol had also gripped him by the arms and held him—gnarled, fragile-looking fingers clamping down like hard metal.

"You must listen," hissed the old man. "You cannot succumb to the . . . temptations of self-pity. Only men who are alone, men who have nothing to give, have the right. You have not the *right*!"

Tyrees was still shaken by Meta-sol's passion, but he hung his head like a small boy and shook it back and forth.

"No, Meta-sol. It was all for nothing."

The fingers gripped tighter. Meta-sol was a head shorter,

a wizened acorn of an old man, and he almost literally
held Tyrees upright.

"Nothing? I have lost my Tercet . . . forever. Bolla and
Radis have lost their places, too. And Shaamlik, she has
lost even more!" Meta-sol shook him. Tyrees felt his
universe jar and jolt just as he did earlier in the mad place
of rain and river with Shaamlik. Finally Meta-sol released
him and turned away. "Now you say it was all for nothing."

Tyrees slumped against the bed. He held his head in his
hands. "Please . . . please, Meta-sol." His voice came
from far away, its sound crushed flat with the fatigue of
despair. "I tried. What can I do now?"

Meta-sol had gathered up his cane from the floor. He
looked like a very old, very blind man as he tapped his
way toward the light from the outside corridor. He turned
at the entrance. The light touched his white beard gently.

"I do not know what you can do," he said. "I only
know that if you can do . . . nothing, then no man can.
And that you no longer . . . try."

He turned away again, and Tyrees listened to the taps
until they faded completely. He looked down on Shaamlik.
The mask glowed softly, its expression horribly indifferent. He began to sway, and half fell, half slid against the
bed to his knees. His forehead bent to touch clasped and
shaking hands. His sob was half cry, half prayer.

CHAPTER TWENTY-FOUR

The lifeless shell that had once been *Condor* swung on her invisible tether around Regnum's sun and most of its system, as she had for many weeks. Few had come to know that her swings, like those of all of history's pendulums, measured the pace, long or short, taken between those events that determined the course of human destiny. It mattered not that most vessels capable of holding awareness in this tiny bit of space had no sense of her swinging.

The Cadre Proctor took his time, because his last meeting with Tyrees had taught him caution, and because the man he saw before him now was not the man he had—metaphorically—fled from earlier. The latter was uncaring, even morose, but he exuded latent signs: power, confidence, vitality. This one was a beaten dog! Emaciated, weary to the point of slurring his words, he had gone beyond indifference into some pit of self-neglect! Bones jutted from under his sallow skin and from under his clothes; all intensity had retreated from the blueness of his eyes; timbre had abandoned his voice. Everything about him announced defeat, surrender. Still, the Proctor had seen what he had seen. He had to be sure.

"You will forgive me if I find your sudden change of heart rather hard to accept, Tyrees."

"What do you want from me, then?" said the flat voice. Tyrees looked at him as a condemned man might look at a priest on his mandatory visit. The eyes peered from deep sockets. "Isn't this what you asked for?"

"Why did you change your mind?"

"Because you were right. Lives will be saved." The voice was still toneless, but the Proctor could detect no deception in it.

"You no longer wish to be a martyr, then."

Tyrees stared at him for a moment. He was sitting in a corner of a couch, hunched. Now he drew his knees up and hugged them to his chest, diminishing himself.

"No," he said, almost in a whisper. "No."

"You will recant—publicly?"

A touch of defiance—perhaps it was petulance—renewed the volume in the voice. "I have nothing to recant, do I? I will preach nonviolence . . . peace."

"Not enough," said the Proctor firmly. "Three things. One"—he tapped three raised fingers in succession—"you will admit to your treason. Two—you will proclaim your conversion to the Regnum's principles. And three . . ." He paused for emphasis. "You will renounce the so called New Covenant and any . . . any 'deification' it may have conferred upon you!"

Tyrees scrunched up even farther into himself. His head touched his knees, but the flat voice was clear.

"Yes," he said. Then he looked up. "I would do the last in any case."

This, more than anything, convinced the Proctor.

"Very well. I will make arrangements for your removal to Regnum. Then we will begin—"

"One moment. I want it clear." Tyrees uncoiled. For the first time his attitude was aggressive. "You buy my cooperation with guarantees. No one connected with me or the Movement—is harmed. No one is arrested. Is that agreed?"

The Proctor hesitated. He knew that the conditions beyond *Condor*'s shell were deteriorating. The skirmishes in the Hub were escalating, but that bothered the Chairman less than the burgeoning growth of the New Covenant. And the prison orbiting Regnum's system could be kept secret only so long.

"Obviously, *you* may not be allowed to go free."

Tyrees nodded. "I accept that."

"*Condor*'s crew—yes. But they will be removed and isolated on Tercet."

"Agreed."

"Your . . . *lieutenants*. The old Tercian, Radis, Bolla—they will be imprisoned."

Tyrees shook his head violently, like a dog nipped in the ear. "No, no, no. Then I will not cooperate. They must be allowed to go free!"

The Proctor was exasperated. So close, and yet so far. "You must be reasonable!" he shouted. "How could we be expected to do that? How could we allow the core of a rebel leadership the freedom to subvert us again! . . . Come, come, come, Tyrees."

Tyrees actually pouted. He shook his head again and pulled himself to his feet. "No. Never. Forget the whole thing."

With rising apprehension, the Proctor watched him shamble to the bubble. Again, the stars were cold and impossibly distant. Again, he looked out with the longing of a lifetime refugee gazing at last upon his homeland.

Desperate, the Proctor seized upon a thought. "All right, all right . . . Listen. I think the Chairman will agree to this: no hard incarceration, no harm, all the amenities, in fact. But no freedom . . ." The Proctor waited until Tyrees turned before adding his last phrase. "And they stay with you."

Tyrees's mouth started to form words, stopped. His head twisted back to the bubble, and for an instant the Proctor thought he had lost him. But Tyrees spoke with a cracking voice, aimed at the Void, as if he were ashamed of his words.

"Shaamlik, too?"

"Of course."

CHAPTER TWENTY-FIVE

After almost four years in limitless space the leaders of the
New Covenant were brought to earth and confined to one
small building—perhaps the most closely guarded in the
galaxy. Few were permitted to see them. Fewer still were
empowered to talk to them: the Cadre Proctor, a single
Cadre One, a personal aide of the Chairman. The Chairman was withholding that privilege from himself for the
time being, but anticipating it with exquisite savor.

Preparations were under way for a live, galaxy-wide
holovision production to consist of a prepared statement
from Pol Tyrees followed by a press conference conducted
by the Chairman himself. As yet no announcement had
been made, because the Chairman wanted to have every
fine detail orchestrated beforehand. The general public,
now preoccupied with the Trade Wars and the rebels in the
Hub, had only two contradictory bits of information about
Tyrees: that he was the leader of an astonishingly virulent
movement called the New Covenant; and that he was a
former Cadre One pursued by the authorities for reasons
unknown. Their curiosity had been growing long before
his capture, itself still a secret, and since they were members of an ostensibly open society, their clamor for more
information had become increasingly insistent.

Another factor forced the Chairman to proceed cautiously. Leaders of the New Covenant were becoming

vocal about Caanon. Since that operation, they had received no communication from their Vitar.

So the five prisoners lived in solitude—almost as much from each other as from the outside world. The three men had agreed reluctantly to Tyrees's deal with the Proctor, because it seemed pointless to do otherwise. Shaamlik remained as she was. For hours at a time, when he wasn't involved in the endless negotiations connected to the holovision production, Tyrees sat with her, staring at her perfect, unhuman face. He allowed no one else to replenish the liquid pumped into her body to keep her alive.

No one ever came upon him asleep. He ate only after outrageous intervals, and then reluctantly. He took on the appearance of an ancient desert ascetic. In his late forties, now, Tyrees had begun to take on an aspect that ressembled Meta-sol's. About the time he had turned thirty, time seemed to have stopped for him, and he had remained there. In the last months it had caught him up, thrusting him ruthlessly into the future.

He never sought the company of his few companions—except that of Shaamlik—and soon, partly because they had the evidence of their eyes, they were willing to avoid him also.

Dr. Hans Bolla, wearing always now an expression of bemused perplexity, had taken up once again the commitment that had absorbed his life until Pol Tyrees entered it: the academician held in thrall by abstractions, consumed by the desire to add a strand or two to the spellcasting web of conjecture. He had since come to know that such devotion was blind, since it did not countenance the true object of all study—man. Indeed, it was ironic that his field—sociological psychology—focused as it was on mass human behavior, ignored the efficacy, the passion, perhaps, of the individual human spirit. He smiled rarely now, but when he did, it was in recognition of this simple fact and the irony, the *havoc*, it could bring to bear on the glib theories he had promulgated in the past. In short, there was an intangible, an x-factor that had to be added to his equations. A Pol Tyrees, for example. How would that influence prediction? Could it be that the x-factor would reduce such prediction to folly? Could it be that the emer-

gence of a Tyrees was an Aladdin's lamp syndrome which
only temporarily altered human destiny? Or was the effect,
though rare, so powerful that the dominoes fell forever?

So the good doctor resumed his calling, oblivious to the
bitter realities around him, just as he was in happier days.
The Proctor was wise enough to provide Bolla with limited
access to the little understood Anavex, the computer-
programming infrastructure that the doctor himself had
developed.

Radis was a horse of a different color. At first he was
simply bitter, though the target of his animosity kept shifting. Even Tyrees took his turn. In time the bitterness
became confusion, then despondency. He could accept
neither what he had been nor what he had come to be.
Then, inevitability, he and Meta-sol were drawn together
once more. In Tyrees Meta-sol had lost a son; in Tyrees
Radis had lost a father. In each other they found a reason
to keep going—like Bolla—in this limbo of places.

Radis was not as gifted a student as Tyrees, but he was
just as dedicated. There were times when twenty-four
hours, the ancient measure of the human day, passed for
Radis as quickly and smoothly as the drawing of a breath.
Sleep during these times was as unwanted and unneeded as
food, because it was a time of discovery—and part of the
discovery was the ability to control those things.

He became as Tyrees was during those early days on
Tercet, when the universe began to turn inward into a
Black Hole of the *self*. Man had squandered too much of
his history pulling with screeching fingernails after the
knowledge he'd captured of the external, physical universe. He had ignored—perhaps because of his fear—the
lode of knowing and power *within*.

"Can you see, Radis?"

"I . . . no . . . no, Meta-sol."

"Make your mind a black slate, my son. I will wait.
Take whatever time you need. Do not be . . . impatient."

They were in a darkened room, and Radis had to struggle with it. Meta-sol was always in a darkened room. An
hour passed, slippery, silent, swift.

"*Listen*, now. *Listen*. Can you *hear* it?"

"I . . . I . . . Yes! Yes, I can!" Radis's voice was a

bare whisper, but the note of discovery was a blare of trumpets.

"Good . . . good," came the answering whisper with infinite calm. "But stay with its rhythm. Do not allow your excitement to shield it. Stay with the sound . . . stay with it . . . stay with it. Listen . . . listen . . . listen. You have it?"

"Yesss. Yesss. I have it."

"Now . . . follow the path of the sound . . . follow it . . . follow it. Ride its rhythm. . . ."

"Yes . . . yes, I think I . . . Eeaahh! Oh! Ohmygod. Oh . . . my . . . *god*!"

Radis swooned. He had been sitting cross-legged on the floor, facing Meta-sol, and a heavy nausea washed over him like a tide of ether. An image had brought it on. A frighteningly clear, naked image of a heart expanding and contracting, an impossibly delicate and tremulous mound of uncertain muscle pulling in and pumping out the stuff of life. His life.

Leaning over, Meta-sol took an edge of his shawl and wiped the clammy sweat from Radis's brow.

"Yes, yes," he sighed. "It is . . . a thing of fear at first. I do not know why we respond so. We can look upon a star swallower—a Black Hole—in the night sky with less fear. . . . Breathe now, breathe slowly. Let the air wash your lungs. . . . Yes, it is a mystery. Of all of the frightful things in the universe, we are most afraid of ourselves."

Radis shuddered, shook his head as if ridding it of repellent thoughts. "I *saw* it, Meta-sol. I did. I saw it beating there. . . . It was awful. Awful!"

"Yes, I know." Meta-sol's tone was very sad. "I know. Perhaps it is because we know ourselves so . . . slightly. Perhaps it is because we sense the power there. We are accustomed to . . . wielding power only upon the outside. Power forces change, you know. To use it *inside* . . . Perhaps we cannot accept such changes."

Radis had recovered somewhat. "Do you . . . do you think this is what happened to Pol Tyrees?"

Meta-sol shook his head. "I do not know. He went far beyond us." The blind eyes lifted to the ceiling. "I do know that he had begun the outward turning."

"I don't understand," said Radis.

Suddenly the old Tercian's head dropped and he closed his eyes. In spite of the darkness, Radis could see him tremble.

"What's wrong, Meta-sol? Please."

Meta-sol raised his head once more, but did not open his eyes. "I am sorry. Your words—'I do not understand'—I heard them often from Pol-Nesol-Rast. In the beginning. On Tercet. After a time I heard those words no more. Now it is *I* who does not understand." His old, veined hands slowly lifted to his temples and fluttered there like dying birds.

Radis was touched. He wanted to take the old man in his arms. But he knew that Meta-sol would not suffer that.

"Please," he said again. "Tell me. What is the outward turning?"

"You have read it," said Meta-sol, nodding gently. "It is in *The Teraac*. Some of our Seers—in the past, and some now—some of us have . . . flirted with the outside." He smiled. "Is that suitable. *Flirted?* Sometimes I . . ."

"Yes, I think so." Radis, in his hunger for revelation, had already put aside the personal miracle he had undergone a few minutes earlier. "Go on."

"I have told you before. We seek control. Inner control." Meta-sol began to blink. Radis saw tears fall, running down furrowed cheeks. "You see? I make water. I cry." He huffed out a short, dry laugh. "More often I use this control *not* to cry." He swabbed himself as he had Radis earlier. "But when a man is able to . . . progress to a certain point, as I have, as some others have, he gets . . . glimpses? Intimations? He gets startling . . . hints of the beginnings of control over the *outside*. They, too, are fearful."

"You mean . . . like the Vitar and the pathways?"

"Yes, but the beginnings are much more . . . modest. I remember Pol of the hidden stars. . . . Did you know that was his name on Tercet? The first name we gave him?" Meta-sol didn't wait for a response. He spoke with deep nostalgia, a sense of lost innocence; he spoke for himself more than his listener. "He watched me do the dance of

the dust motes. I could make tiny flecks of dust spin—
dance—in a beam of light. The Vitar was . . . amazed.''
He tilted his head, a sad smile growing on his thin lips.

His voice softened with memory. ''He was like a child.
He clapped his hands like a child. He . . . smothered me
with questions. He wanted so much to learn. In a few
weeks he could do the dance of the dust motes. And much,
much more.'' The smile faded then. Meta-sol reached for
his cane, which lay near him on the floor. The first
movement was absentminded, but when his fingers failed
to touch the gnarled wood, they groped angrily for a
moment before finding it. He pulled the rub-polished knob
up under his chin, gripping it tightly with both hands.

''Are you listening to me, my boy?'' he said, his voice
no longer soft. ''I was one . . . hundred . . . and thirty of
your years before I could make those motes of dust dance.
They spun like Tercet herself spun. Like this . . . Regnum
spins. I can no longer do that. I . . . can . . . no . . .
longer . . . even . . . find . . . my cane.'' He rested his
forehead on its knob.

Radis felt tears, tears he had not summoned, as Meta-sol
had, brimming to the surface. ''Meta-sol, I—''

''But Pol-Nesol-Rast gave me hope. Gave us all hope.
For a time . . . a time.'' He stabbed the cane once, a
single, sharp rap on the floor. ''I do not know who is the
greater enemy—time, or our *selves*. Time defeated *me*.
But the Vitar? . . . . Aaahhhh.''

The sigh was long, slow, welling up from the deepest of
pits. Radis came to his knees, reaching to the old man.

''No,'' whispered Meta-sol. ''I am sorry. Please. Leave
me now.''

CHAPTER TWENTY-SIX

"Vitar?"

The room was dark—so dark that no one would expect it to contain an unsleeping occupant.

"Vitar?"

Radis stood at the entrance, not sure that the vague, still shadow was more than a trick of the darkness—until the answer finally came in the form of a quiet, ghostly voice. It was akin to the darkness.

"Don't call me that, Radis."

Radis hesitated. He had the feeling that he stood at the threshold of a place of dangerous revelation, a place guarding a knowledge of things better left unknown.

"May I come in?"

The voice carried a shrug. "If you wish."

Radis moved inside a few steps, but stopped for a while to let his eyes adjust. He was still capable of surprise, of a thrill of pride at what his newly trained senses could now do. The shadow grew solid out of the darkness.

"You could use a little light."

"Could I?"

Without answering, Radis lowered himself into a chair. He studied the figure opposite him for a long moment, and slowly there arose out of his bowels a keening ache of despond. Its rising threatened to drown the new sense of well-being he had carried into the room. Why he had carried it there, he did not know. He was still struggling against the tide when Tyrees spoke again.

"Your training with Meta-sol. It goes well."

He nodded. "Yes. I . . . I never realized before. I think I understand now . . . what happened to you."

"Do you?"

"Well, to some degree, perhaps. It's a wonderful feeling. Like doors opening. Doors you didn't even know were there. They open slowly, sometimes painfully, one at a time, but they open."

There was a nod from the gray shadow.

"But it's . . . scary, too."

Radis caught a flash of blue, as if Tyrees's eyes had trapped a single spear of light. His voice was still quiet, but it took on a timbre of interest.

"Yes. That happens, too. The fear will grow, too, Radis."

Radis frowned. "Why? Why should that be? We are only . . . discovering ourselves, after all."

Tyrees snorted softly. "Perhaps I shouldn't speak of it."

"Why not?"

"Perhaps you're only on lesson forty-two. Meta-sol might be saving it for sixty-two."

"Don't be ridiculous, Vitar. Can't you answer an honest question?"

Tyrees sighed. "Very well, Radis. If you will drop the *ridiculous* title."

"All right, then. Tell me. Why am I afraid? Why is Meta-sol *not* afraid?"

Radis saw teeth gleam in the darkness. "Meta-sol is more afraid than you are. He knows more. He is also afraid of dying. He is almost as afraid as I am."

"Of dying?"

"Of living."

Radis shuddered inside, but he scoffed. "Please, no riddles, uh, Mr. Tyrees. Just a straight answer."

"That *was* a straight answer."

Radis felt his anger rise. He shifted his big frame in the armchair. "All right . . . Look, I don't know you well. I guess no one does. But to me you were special, worth fighting for. I've done my best for you, and in spite of the way we ended up, I have no regrets. All I ask now is . . . treat me as if you . . . *care*."

For a moment the dim figure opposite Radis remained perfectly still, perfectly silent. Radis felt a tingle in his scalp, as if the very nature of the air in the room had changed. Then the shadowed head inclined, and the voice returned.

"Yes. You are right." A dark hand rose to the head and lingered there, though Radis could not make out the fingers. "I owe you what I can tell you of the truth. For what it's worth . . . for what it's worth. But you may be better off not hearing it."

"Have *you* ever believed that?"

"No."

"Well, then?"

"Radis . . . you are probably older than I—but you seem so young."

"Please."

Another sigh. "Very well. Meta-sol teaches you control— as he taught me. You begin to realize the naked, raw *power* that you've been hiding from yourself. It's been locked down there under your skin. Why? Why didn't you, why didn't others tap it before? For the same reason that Prometheus was so ruthlessly punished by the gods."

Radis felt the tingling again. He squirmed. "You are saying man isn't ready?"

"Yes. Perhaps he never will be."

"I don't believe that. It's *there*. It . . . it shouldn't be denied."

"Should it not? Then why are we afraid of it? Why is it that every incursion into our *selves* imposes a greater fear, a stronger resistence? The reason is so simple!"

"Oh, no. Oh, no," said Radis. He gripped the arms of his chair. "I don't accept that. We are what we are. It is in our nature to reach for more." He saw the outline of the skull opposite him moving from side to side as he spoke.

"There is also a voice of warning in our nature. It calls out when we reach too far. We call it *fear*."

"Hah!" exclaimed Radis, with too much gusto. "All you're really saying is that we are afraid of ourselves!"

The voice was relentless. "Yes, that is so. And there is nothing in this universe more fearful. You talked of doors. Each one opens upon another lode of power. Each one demands more control. There comes a point . . ." The voice faltered. Radis could hear lips being moistened. "There comes a point where . . . where you find yourself trying to hold a *nova* in your fist! Don't you see! Don't you understand!"

The shadow melted farther back into the darkness. Radis could hear labored breathing. They had talked of fear. He had never known more than he did now. When he could speak, he did so more out of desperation than conviction.

"Then . . . then fear is the enemy, not ourselves. We face it, we push it back . . . as far as we can go." He pulled in a long breath, and all his courage into himself. "Is that not all we can do?"

An insidious laugh came out of the darkness, as did the shadow when Tyrees leaned forward again.

"A truly noble sentiment," he said. "But remember what happened to Prometheus."

Radis felt his gorge rise. Nausea swept over him. He shoved himself to his feet. "I don't care what the myth says!"

Tyrees stood as well, more slowly. "So it doesn't matter what *I* say, does it?"

"Yes . . . yes, it does, damn you! Because if *you* can't fight it, none of us can!"

"Ah," said Tyrees. "Thank you for the compliment. Thank you, Radis. But here am I—a prisoner. And here are *you*. What difference does it make?"

Radis retreated like a boy from a drunken father. When he reached the hall outside the room, he stopped. He wanted to do something, to say something. It was all so unreal and so unjust! He whirled and plunged back into the darkness.

"Give up, then!" he shouted. "Just stop haunting us!" Taken up by a fury that he didn't know he possessed, he slammed his fist once, twice, three times at the spot near the entrance on the wall where there was always a light tab. Suddenly light hit the room like a cruel blow. Radis caught his breath.

Tyrees stood there, a stick of a man. The only thing of substance was the blue of his eyes. He was shrunken, diminished to bone and pale skin. He was completely bald.

Radis ran away.

CHAPTER TWENTY-SEVEN

An announcement was read on the galaxy-wide public service network by its prime-time newsman. "We have a very strange and interesting release from the office of the Chairman of the Regnum which was handed to us less than an hour ago. This is it, verbatim: 'Former Cadre One officer Pol Tyrees has been detained and held for questioning by the Security Cadre. He has requested, and will be allowed to make, a voluntary statement in twenty-four hours time. The Chairman of the Regnum will hold a press conference immediately thereafter.' " The newsman raised his head to the camera.

"That's it. We have been unable to gain further information. A blanket of secrecy seems to have been thrown over the story. The man, Pol Tyrees, has come to be better known—thoughout the whole galaxy—as *Vitar*, the demagogue of the incredibly fast-growing movement known as the New Covenant.

"He has remained a very mysterious figure in an age when mystery is a fleeting thing. . . ."

Since the newsman's voice and three-dimensional image were carried by means of permanent relays parked on the graviton pathways, the farthest planet from Regnum was less than a standard day away from the broadcast. For the first time in many months the Trade Wars took a second seat in public concern. The release had been so carefully phrased that, though the clamor for information was high,

especially among followers of the New Covenant, the
dominant reaction was confusion. As well, given the short
notice, they were compelled to take on a wait and see
attitude.

But the simple fact that the Chairman himself would be
conducting the press conference—an almost unprecedented
sally into the public forum—guaranteed that a record number of the viewing public would be seated in front of their
holovision sets the next day.

Two hours before broadcast time, an armored and heavily
escorted ground car arrived at the comfortable prison to
pick up Pol Tyrees and his fellow inmates. Meta-sol, Bolla,
and Radis gathered near the main entrance to await their
leader. They had been allowed to attend the proceedings—
indeed, were encouraged to do so—but only cameras would
be permitted access to them as they looked on.

Armed Cadre Fours, impressive with their disciplined
silence and proud, black capes, lined the walls of the
foyer. Their thoughts were unreadable, but each was surprised by the lack of threat in the appearance of three of
the men they were charged to guard: an absurdly fat old
man with a distracted air; another ancient relic, frail beyond
belief, leaning on a theatrical cane, wearing a poor woman's shawl and staring at nothing with blank eyes; a large,
physically impressive man who might be considered dangerous were he not so obviously introspective and trou-
bled. They did not speak; they did not even *look* at each
other. Each seemed locked into a baffling world of his
own.

The sound of feet from a hallway shifted their attention.
The Cadre One in charge emerged first, inspected the
group in the foyer quickly, and turned to let Pol Tyrees
precede him.

Bolla's sharp intake of breath made the guards start.
Only Radis had seen Tyrees recently, and he had not
spoken of their meeting. Bolla actually rubbed his eyes.
He saw a child's drawing of a man, a grotesque figure of
stick limbs and bulbed joints and hairless, chalky skin. It
was dressed absurdly in a black tunic that swung and
wagged and flapped as it moved. Bolla could only think of
a holofilm image from the distant past of a victim of a

space ship explosion—first blasted, then starved for many days before rescue. But the eyes were the most striking thing of all—luminous, with such an intensity of blue that they were difficult to look upon.

"Pol," he whispered. "Ohmygod . . . Pol."

Radis simply looked at the floor. Meta-sol remained exactly as he was. Tyrees stopped among his fellow prisoners for a moment, seemingly puzzled at first by Bolla's reaction. Then he smiled, thin lips stretching over perfect, white teeth, and reached out a hand to touch Bolla's cheek.

"It's all right, Hans."

He turned to the Cadre One. "Let's go."

Silently they filed out of their prison to the awaiting ground cars.

The entourage of vehicles was impressive, causing curious passersby to stop and stare, though they had no way of knowing the identity of the passengers and were unable to see them through the opaqued windows.

The ride to the building housing the Chairman's offices was short. The prisoners were ushered into a facility obviously designed for press conferences: a backdrop of rich curtains; a podium upon which stood a lectern with a symbol of the Regnum imprinted on its front; all the paraphernalia of holovision transmission, including suspended cameras; several rows of plush seats for representatives of the media, none of whom had been allowed, as yet, to enter.

The Cadre One directed Tyrees and his people to seats on the podium behind the lectern. His men melted into discreet nooks here and there about the large room before it fell silent. The eerie lighting, the esoteric equipment, the bleak and insular attitude of the disparate men facing the darkness beyond the cameras—all added to the tense atmosphere of the place. It was not just a waiting of the expected; it was a waiting of the inevitable, of an ending. Each of the four seated men awaited it differently; each awaited it alone. Time stretched on its own, screamless wrack in the quiet.

Like a brooding animal suddenly astir, the dark half of the room contracted with the opening of a door. Outlined in its rectangle of light was the Chairman. He took a single step into the room and stood there, staring at the men on the podium. He formed a sharp shadow. Low, hunched, powerful. Slivers of light showed between his low hanging arms and his body. No bloodcurdling scream of victory could be heard—nevertheless, one was there. He stared at them for a long time. Only Meta-sol reacted.

"Ah," he said in his gentle voice. "So he comes. This is the man."

Then the Chairman was joined by the tall, caped figure of the Cadre Proctor. Together they walked into the light, toward the podium. The Proctor took care of the amenities.

"Gentlemen, the Chairman of the Regnum. Mr. Chairman, this is Pol Tyrees—"

"He doesn't need introductions," interrupted Tyrees.

The Proctor looked at him sharply. He wanted things to go smoothly and was determined to conduct the proceedings according to the smallest shadings and nuances agreed upon. But he could still hear with painful clarity the sound of bones mincing in the back of his neck. Tyrees, he knew, was a man of infinite surprise, of rare gift, of dubious sanity. Looking at him now, however, was reassuring. He suspected that some nervous disease was now sculpting a new, more ephemeral body out of the old.

"Very well." He opened his cape deftly to retrieve a few sheets of old-fashioned paper, folded along their length. High level government press conferences still held to the tradition of paper because of its suggestion of a close, personal working. "This is your statement. It's exactly as agreed upon." He held it out.

"That won't be necessary. I've memorized it."

The Proctor hesitated. Before he could say more, the Chairman finally spoke. He looked at Tyrees with passionate intensity, bull head lowered, eyes rolled so that he was glaring up the slope of his formidable brow.

"You are to add nothing, delete nothing. You are to *deliver* the release and sit down. Is that understood?"

Tyrees, still seated, smiled. The Proctor remembered that smile. Something just beneath his skin tingled uncomfortably. But Tyrees answered mildly.

"Yes, I understand. Your technicians would cut me off in any case."

The Chairman returned the smile. On both faces the expression was so alien that the Proctor thought of gargoyles facing each other on the facade of an antique church. The Chairman's massive shoulders swayed to one side; his short legs almost comically scurried to catch up with the heavy momentum building above them. He flicked his head at a gloomy corner.

"Let them in."

The Cadre One emerged and moved to an entrance, signaling as he went. Dim lights came on over the seats, again making the dark animal convulse backward. It settled, crouching, against the wall. The Chairman retreated quickly behind the curtain at the prisoner's backs. As he did so, his aide, the man who had acted as his personal liaison during the negotiations, came out of nowhere and stepped to the lectern. A spotlight washed over him, making him blink. He squinted at the main aisle, down which were already pouring, members of the Regnum's media elite. He waved an impatient hand just over his head until the spotlight was reduced in intensity.

He waited with bureaucratic expressionlessness until the shuffling of the audience abated. A nod brought tiny winks of light to life on each of the unmanned cameras. By this time not a single Cadre man was visible. The outer lights dimmed, and the beast returned to skulk behind the cameras again. The Chairman's aide cleared his throat lightly, and began.

"Ladies and gentlemen. Thank you for coming." He licked his lips somewhat nervously, but continued in an even voice. "The Chairman considered this press conference necessary in order to present to the public the undressed facts regarding the activities of the former Cadre One officer, Pol Tyrees. He did not wish, in a time of temporary upheaval, to add to the growing rumor and speculation surrounding this man. Pol Tyrees has been a fugitive from Regnum law—a condition that is automatic from the moment an officer of the Security Cadre quits his duties—for several years, but he is now in our custody. He has been granted permission to make a voluntary state-

ment. Thereafter, the Chairman will have a fews words to
say and will answer any questions you care to put.'' The
aide turned to deliver a stiff nod to Tyrees before he left
the podium. ''Mr. Tyrees.''

The small audience watched Tyrees rise and move to the
front of the podium, ignoring the lectern. They watched
him with a hungry curiosity that belied the comfortable
cynicism of their profession. Men like the Chairman were
remote, but not mysterious; the mechanics of his powers
were political, not spiritual. Their expeience compared
with the common run of men and women was so vast that
they had sensed the uniqueness of the one called *Vitar* long
before this moment. As well, they had few illusions about
the scruples of the Chairman, though they spoke of their
suspicions only to each other. Had Tyrees become a victim
of the Chairman's machinations? The simple fact that followers of the New Covenant were notoriously oblivious to
chauvinistic cries—or even patriotic ones—would be reason enough to raise his ire.

They watched the others, too. A strange, mismatched
trio. The only thing they seemed to have in common was
the look of defeated longing that surfaced on their faces—
like islands in a lowering tide—when their leader stood
silently at the front of the podium. It was a look that
bespoke of dying dreams, of diminished significance, of
scanted sizes, of the simple, sad knowledge of being mortal.

Tyrees gazed out, but not at the audience. He looked at
the darkness above and beyond them. A few could not
resist the temptation to follow his eyes into it, twisting
their necks self-consciously, looking for what he saw. But
their eyes were always drawn back to his. They were
voracious. Their blue was the pure blue of perfect burning.
All substance—his own body—was consumed by the intensity of their fire. They began to be afraid.

From the moment when he sat at the back of the podium, Meta-sol had not moved. The time and the silence
had stretched out so far since Tyrees had risen and moved
to the front, that Radis and Bolla were finally pulled from
their solitude. They looked at each other in puzzlement. A
small, irregular tapping noise in the silence gradually broke
into their awareness. Meta-sol's cane was rattling softly on

the floor. The gnarled hand at its top was quivering. The rattling became louder, almost exposive in the dead quiet of the room. Meta-sol's whole arm now jumped spasmodically. His expression did not change, but the gray parchment of his face suddenly whitened. He stood so quickly, like a magician's illusion, that there was no sense of transition. The cane fell to the floor. He reached out one hand to Tyrees, and his mouth opened.

Then Pol Tyrees, *Vitar*—vanished.

CHAPTER TWENTY-EIGHT

When Pol Tyrees—Cadre traitor, failed rebel, and erst-while god—rose and moved out on the podium, he still did not know what he would do. During the weeks of forced confinement on Regnum, when there was nothing to absorb his anxious mind but the hours of negotiations, he had begun to delve inward again.

These journeys were never more daring than during his vigils beside the figure of Shaamlik and her inscrutable mask. Since he cared deeply only for her, since all else of importance to him was lost, then he could gamble for ultimate stakes without fear of the cost of losing. He could bet his life and shrug carelessly, should the cast die go against him. It was the optimum stance of the gambler: there was nothing of significance that he could lose. He could play the game just to see how it would turn out. He could not be frightened, he could not be bluffed.

On his other journeys he had sought control—of himself, primarily, and little by little, cautiously, of the other-than-self. This was different. There was *no* control possible on this frontier. This was not a question of seeking a lever with which to nudge physical reality into a direction of his choosing; it was the opposite: a letting go, a giving in to the wash of invisible tides whose potency was irresistible in any case. They ignored things of substance, things like the horrendous bellying of a bursting star, as blithely as a whale ignores waving seaweed. It was so because in the ultimate accounting of such things, the explosion of a star was irrelevant.

Tyrees made the most simple, the most obvious of discoveries: only *time* was significant in the ledger of the universe. Nothing that was subject to birth, nothing that died, could claim supremacy. Time was the true god, ignoring all of substance but its essence—energy. Time was matter purified, matter purged, matter made holy. Indeed, time was not the enemy of life; it was life itself— sanctified. Time, once realized by life, was sainthood.

This came to Pol Tyrees when he was able, for the first time, to leave behind with his ultimate gamble, the detritus of substance, such paltry things as dying stars. He could not control the miasma of time, but he could join it. He could not fight it, but he could become a part of it. He could tip his awareness downwards into the darkness as a diver would, searching for pearls. He could take the ultimate risk, leaving all that was of the substance of himself somewhere above in shallower waters, nearer to the light of a familiar star. He could *deny* what he hitherto had supposed was his being.

Soon he could step with assurance into the stream: past, present, time to be. He could look, but only with awe, at what reality was. All that really left him was awareness, and that was all that was allowed. At first he perceived it only as the wild current that had tossed him willy-nilly when he had tried to help Shaamlik. That was because he had fought it, a drowning swimmer whose mad thrashing for life only shortened it. He found that when he did not fight, when he did not try to breath air that did not exist, he could ride the flow, almost become a part of it. Although the currents were too strong, too alien to move downstream, he could surge ahead with ease. Indeed, he had done so before, but so full of panic and dread that his jaded awareness had only been one of harrowing motion, not time.

Time.

So in the darkness and solitude of his prison, he had stepped into the stream many times. He "went" nowhere in terms of place, but he traveled almost forever in time, and saw many stars bloat and die.

Indeed, he almost saw *himself* die. In the beginning he came to see his own substance as an insulting tether anchoring him to the dross of life. It was an unholy, degrading thing, the feces of mortality. So he ignored it, denied it, stretched the tether longer and longer—until it was near breaking. When he came to a point where he began to lose all sense of self, where he and the currents were becoming a mindless unity, there was one, last, desperate tug on the line that was his self—and he answered it. He responded to his own demand to be. The body he had left behind was ravaged, but not lost.

Yes, in the darkness and solitude of his prison, he had learned to share one of the secrets of time, but there came with that secret a lesson: that pride is a fond joke; that vanity is an obscenity. In time, a star leaves nothing to mark its passing. What, then, leaves a man? Yet pride is the fuel of a reaching awareness . . . so says *The Teraac*. Pol Tyrces pondered this paradox, accepting its mystery, and vowed never again to fall victim to the greater folly of vanity.

Returning again to the nutshell world of men, the closet-boxed confines of the spit of a galaxy over which they fought, was not an easy thing. A second birthing is no easier than the first. As he sat there on the podium, looking over the heads of the audience into the crouching darkness, he had almost come to the decision to spout the carefully manufactured words of his ''release'' and let things go as they would. Then he would be free again to chart the currents of time, to watch stars grow and fade. But the sense of Bolla, and Radis, and Meta-sol beside him, and the image of Shaamlik trapped in an even smaller, madder world than this, reminded him again of vanity.

He resolved to try . . . something.

When he stepped to the front of the podium, looking over their heads into the darkness, he was already in the process of leaving them behind—in time.

Their seconds became meaninglessly long stretches of time. In much less than one of them, he could witness the evolution of a galaxy. In one of his own, he saw them freeze into motionless, three-dimensional frames. He turned to walk to the curtains behind the seated statues of his friends, feeling his body protest, his joints ache as if with the natural strain of great age. Stepping over Meta-sol's cane, he whipped the curtain aside. There was the Chairman, one stubby finger raised with incongruous delicacy to part a curtain that was no longer there. He was leaning forward to peek.

Tyrees looked at him for a moment, feeling his loathing rise. Everything about the man frozen before him proclaimed a lifetime's exercise of brutal power; now as well, like a petty voyeur caught in a photograph, he showed his venality. Tyrees, believing that there was only one course of action open to him, knew he could carry it through joyfully. A modicum of guilt would come from that feeling, perhaps, but not the action itself.

The Proctor stood nearby, head turned to face the Chairman. The nuances of his expression were subtle, difficult to read, but they said one thing clearly: he did not like what he saw. His tall, dignified bearing rose more clearly to the surface as a statue, and it became him. He reminded Tyrees of his grandfather.

"You," muttered Tyrees, "you can live."

He parted the Proctor's cape and removed his lasgun. He checked the charge and released the safety. He raised the weapon to the Chairman's forehead, and took a breath.

"Pol."

So immersed was Tyrees in his role of executioner, so isolated into his nub of time an infinitesimal fraction ahead of the others', that he wasn't aware of Meta-sol's own transition into it. But he was not particularly surprised. Lowering the gun, he turned his head to smile at his old mentor.

"Meta-sol. You've come."

"Yes." He smiled, too. "I've *followed*. I have always hoped that you would bring me . . . here. Before I died."

Tyrees shook his head, letting his eyes fall to the floor. "I would have come to you earlier, Meta-sol. But . . . it's not . . . what you think. It's not . . ."

"Immortality, Pol-Nesol-Rast? Is it not?"

"No. It's the opposite. Just look at me."

Meta-sol chuckled softly. "You mean, if I could see you as others do, I would see an old man."

"Older than you."

Meta-sol nodded slowly. "So. Time exacts a . . . toll. For opening its gate, no?"

"Yes."

"Yet you have paid the toll many times, like . . . like a man consuming a drug?"

At this Tyrees hesitated. "Yes," he said finally.

"You have found something of . . . unspeakable worth, and you would willingly destroy it by destroying yourself?"

Tyrees turned away. He looked at the Chairman again, still peering absurdly over his upraised finger.

"Why not?" he said. "What difference does it make?"

Meta-sol's voice took on a hard edge. "It makes a difference. You take yourself away from us. We need you. Shaamlik needs you."

"Huh," snorted Tyrees. "You need me. All I've brought you is false hope. And pain, and death . . . and madness. This is all I can do for you now." He raised the gun again.

"No!" Meta-sol shouted. Tyrees froze as rigidly as his intended victim. He didn't know if it was his own will or Meta-sol's that stayed his fingers on the gun.

"Listen to me, my son. Listen to me." Meta-sol moved to him. Tyrees could see the still, white, plaster faces of the media people over Meta-sol's shoulder as he reached for the gun, removing it from unprotesting fingers. They seemed to be a particularly attentive audience, rapt by a poignantly staged drama.

"You have come so far, and you know so little. Listen to me."

Tyrees sighed. "I'll listen, Meta-sol, but somewhere along the line, you'll have to tell me what—"

"Look at those people, my son. *Look* at them. Remember *The Teraac*. The New Covenant. *They are you*. Destroy yourself and you destroy the . . . deepest part of *them*. You destroy their *eyes*."

Something inside Tyrees squirmed. "But what can I do? I am not a bloody, damn god!"

Meta-sol's sightless eyes closed. His hands took Tyrees by the shoulders, rocking him gently.

"Yes, you *are*. And you abandon us!"

"Stop talking nonsense!" Tyrees shook him off angrily.

"Gods don't die. I will—with no good reason for having lived."

Meta-sol had to speak to his back. "You will not die, because you live in us," he said with fervor. "If the last man dies, *then* God dies. Then *chaos* is God." His voice sank to a whisper. "Then *all* is meaningless. Then time itself has no meaning. *The Teraac* has no meaning." He sagged, breathing deeply. His eyelids began to flutter, and one hand went to his face. Suddenly he sank to the floor without a sound.

"Meta-sol!" Tyrees went to his knees and pulled the old Tercian to a sitting position. Meta-sol elbowed him back feebly and turned onto hands and knees. He started to crawl.

"My cane," he said. "I am weak. I need my cane. Help me find my cane. I cannot see. . . ." Tyrees scrambled to pick up the ancient piece of wood, returning to place it in the old man's hands. When he had it again, nestled under his chin as he sat on the floor, Meta-sol recovered somewhat.

"Ahhh. This is . . . this place in time is hard to keep, Pol-Nesol-Rast. Where have you brought me?"

Tyrees felt a tiredness that threatened to melt his bones. "I guess . . . nowhere, Meta-sol. Nowhere." They lapsed into silence for a time—a time during which the many living statues looked on, and remained as they were. Tyrees on one knee, Meta-sol on two and leaning on his cane, looked back at them.

"Pol?"

"Yes?"

"You have opened one gate in time. One. May there not be more?"

Tyrees shrugged. "Who knows? Perhaps."

"Who will open them for us?"

Tyrees laughed He laughed until tears flowed. Meta-sol joined him. Their audience looked on.

CHAPTER TWENTY-NINE

On the instant that Tyrees disappeared from the podium—before his image in the fabric of their eyes could fade—Meta-sol was gone as well. There was no reaction to either of these miracles beyond their register in the brain. *Because there was no time.* It was like trying to separate framed pictures passing at high speed on a film. There may have been time for a blink before a third, macabre frame dropped into place.

Tyrees was there again, and so was Meta-sol, both smiling. Between them, with a single finger raised strangely below his wide nose, was the Chairman. He was starkly, grotesquely, outrageously—naked. His body was so heavily hairy that it gouted in gnarled bunches on the tops of his shoulders and all but hid his genitals. He appeared to have been posing for a pornographic caricature, for after a moment he lowered his finger and blinked rapidly, his neckless head swiveling.

"Whaaa? Whaaaaa?" he whined.

By this time there were odd noises coming from the audience, too. When the first snicker came, the Chairman looked down upon his inglorious nakedness.

"Whaaaaaaa?"

His hands flew to cover his groin; his natural crouch deepened; his eyes strobed panic-humiliation-rage-bewilderment. Some of the media people, making noises of incredulity, were getting to their feet and moving down the short aisles for a better view. The Chairman looked from them to his two smiling companions to the winking cameras. He had awakened from everyman's nightmare only to find it was the living reality. His slightly bowed, skinny shanks began to tremble, and he bobbed up and down like an agitated chimp. Then he bolted.

"Whaaaaaaaaa!" He headed for the half-opened curtain, past the now onrushing Cadre Proctor, whose hand was searching frantically under his cape for a lasgun that was no longer there. From one side the number One was coming, too, but his gun was already raised. The room was exploding with human voices in every register.

Bolla and Radis were on their feet, the latter heading for the armed Cadre man when—with no sense of transition—another frame fell into place. The audience was again comfortably seated, but some in the front row were gagging. Each of these spat from his mouth a recording crystal.

"Holy shit!"

"What the hell . . . ?"

"Hey! This is no joke!"

"Somebody had better start . . ."

At the back of the podium where the prisoners had been, all of the Cadre men were gathered like dark flowers. A dozen or more sat on the floor in a tight circle. They were facing out and propped up so that their backs supported them against each other. Radis stood over them, eyes wide, a lasgun in his hand.

Tyrees stood behind the lectern, facing the audience and the still winking cameras. He was ghostly pale and no longer smiling. Bolla also found himself seated again, but now to one side of the podium, with Meta-sol beside him. The old Tercian had assumed his classic pose: utterly still, eyes closed, body leaning slightly forward, two hands resting atop his cane. Radis was the only one able to summon up enough composure for deliberate action. Perhaps by now he had guessed. He waved the gun gently at the stunned Cadre men.

"Stay quiet," he said solemnly.

Tyrees looked out at the audience and the cameras with eyes sunk deep into their sockets, but they blazed with a

hot blue fire. When he drew breath to speak, the silence
was total, but it was not his voice that broke it.

A thin wail came from above. It was a few seconds
before one of the media people saw its source.

"Look! Up there!" He pointed to a spot high on the
back wall behind them, where the shadows were deep.

"Where?"

"I can't see anything!"

"There! It's the Chairman!"

"On that strut!"

"I don't believe this! What the hell . . ."

As the media people, one by one, turned and squinted
into the high shadows to make out the huddled figure of
the Chairman, the wail grew more plaintive and arhythmic,
though no words were distinguishable. A series of narrow
structural members joined wall to ceiling, forming a row
of high triangles. In the center triangle, buttocks wedged
between the wall and the strut, arms and legs locked
around it like a frightened gorilla on a tree branch, was the
Chairman. Before long the wailing faded into whimpers,
then into soft, pitiful mews, then into silence. A woman in
the audience who had retained some presence of mind,
finally tore her eyes from the Chairman and addressed
Tyrees in a loud, determined voice.

"Mr. Tyrees! Whatever your name is! Please, tell us
what is going on!"

Another shouted, "Will you answer our questions?"

Tyrees raised his hands for quiet, and shook his head
wearily. He gripped the lectern in a way that suggested he
was having difficulty staying on his feet.

"No. No questions now. But I do have something to
say." Their attention was complete. He glanced at the
winking cameras before continuing. "That man up there—
the Chairman of the Regnum—is guilty of crimes on an
inhuman scale. One of the latest is the destruction of one
of your member worlds, Caanon." From the audience
came exclamations of shock—and a few knowing nods.
"Some of you now have recording crystals. When you
play them, you will hear the Chairman ordering the deaths
of several million Caanonites. When the time comes, you

will have all the evidence you wish concerning the Chairman's activities. It's only a few floors above us.''

Several excited questions from the seats interrupted him, but he shook his head again. Light reflected off his hairless skull.

"Listen!" His voice welded their tongues, riveted them in place. "You have witnessed no tricks here . . . and no miracles. We practice a discipline that develops natural human capabilities. We are called the New Covenant. Our teachings are open to all. We have been forced to defend our freedom. We now find ourselves in a position to dismantle the machinery that has brought the Regnum to the brink of self-destruction. . . ."

And in this moment he was almost happy.

Tyrees stood alone in the Chairman's inner office staring at the splendidly cushioned chair behind the oversized, gleaming desk. His eyes were vacant as he reached with his fingertips to feel the rich fabric on its high back. With a small push, he sent it moving slowly around on its swivel through a half circle to face him. He was sitting in it when Bolla came through the door with a heavily loaded printout carrier. He smiled as he dumped it unceremoniously on the desk.

"Well, well, well. . . . Settled in, I see. Does it fit? It certainly becomes you better than. . . ."

"No. It doesn't fit."

Bolla's smile died as Tyrees stood, calmly placed a foot on one arm of the chair, and catapulted it across the floor. It took a small table with it along the way, and crashed resoundingly into the wall.

"What's the matter, Pol? We've won, man! You're a savior, a *god* even! You've got it all now!"

Tyrees smiled wearily and sat on the edge of the desk. "No, Hans, there's a gret deal I haven't got—and never will." He rubbed at his eyes with the back of a hand. "But what *we've* got now is a whole galaxy about to fall down around our ears. We'd better start cleaning up the mess."

EPILOGUE

More than twenty-four hours later, Pol Tyrees returned to the isolated building that had served as his prison. Radis and Bolla were still hard at work in the Chairman's offices. They had already released the dissenting members of the Council who were helping them to hold things together. Mace had been contacted and a cease fire had been declared in the Hub. When it seemed assured that at least a hiatus had been reached, Tyrees had finally been prevailed upon to rest.

His exhaustion was such that he felt no particular elation over their shaky victory; he felt only a deep emptiness, and a haunting desire for sleep. Like a wraith, he moved slowly through the darkness of his room to his bed.

But he could not sleep. When he closed his eyes, the profoundness of his fatigue could not fill the emptiness. It continued to grow, a Black Hole that swallowed everything else. He fought it, turning his head back and forth on the bed. Still, it grew.

Suddenly he sat up. His eyes flew open, staring. He stumbled for the door and ran down the corridor, his body obeying ever more keenly as he went, until his speed was as deft and swift as a thrown knife.

He burst into Shaamlik's room, already knowing what he would find there, but willing it not to be. She was as she had been—a lovely woman's form stretched upon a surgical bed, lines of moving fluid attached to her body, a perfect mask for a face. Along her side was a wooden cane. On the floor was the crumpled body of Meta-sol.

Tyrees fell to his knees. "Ooooohhhh."

He gathered the old man to him. The filmy beard grazed his cheek. The lined face had the milk-white translucence of fine china. Parchment light, Meta-sol's body felt like that of a doll's—impossibly delicate for the rigors ruthlessly demanded by life.

"Oooooohhhhhh."

Tyrees rocked him as he had been rocked. A wave of cold swept over him, so he held Meta-sol closer.

"Oh, God," he sobbed. "This is not right. This is not right."

He rocked for a long time before he felt the fingers on the back of his neck.

"Pol?"

It was only the barest of whispers from above.